SALVACIÓN

SALVACIÓN

SANDRA PROUDMAN

WEDNESDAY BOOKS
NEW YORK

This is a work of fiction. All of the characters, organizations, and events portrayed in this novel are either products of the author's imagination or are used fictitiously.

First published in the United States by Wednesday Books, an imprint of St. Martin's Publishing Group

SALVACIÓN. Copyright © 2025 by Sandra Proudman. All rights reserved. Printed in the United States of America. For information, address St. Martin's Publishing Group, 120 Broadway, New York, NY 10271.

Book design by Michelle McMillian
Title page art by Shutterstock

www.wednesdaybooks.com

Library of Congress Cataloging-in-Publication Data

Names: Proudman, Sandra, author.
Title: Salvación / Sandra Proudman.
Description: First edition. | New York : Wednesday Books, 2025. | Audience term: Teenagers | Audience: Ages 13–18.
Identifiers: LCCN 2024052249 | ISBN 9781250895080 (hardcover) | ISBN 9781250895097 (ebook)
Subjects: CYAC: Vigilantes—Fiction. | Magic—Fiction. | United States—History— 19th century—Fiction. | Interpersonal relations—Fiction. | Fantasy. | LCGFT: Historical fiction. | Fantasy fiction. | Novels.
Classification: LCC PZ7.1.P7835 Sal 2025 | DDC [Fic]—dc23
LC record available at https://lccn.loc.gov/2024052249

Our books may be purchased in bulk for promotional, educational, or business use. Please contact your local bookseller or the Macmillan Corporate and Premium Sales Department at 1-800-221-7945, extension 5442, or by email at MacmillanSpecialMarkets@macmillan.com.

First Edition: 2025

10 9 8 7 6 5 4 3 2 1

For Joe, who has always made me believe in magia,
and for my mami, who has always taught me
to fight for what is right

SALVACIÓN

CHAPTER 1

The line of people waiting for un milagro stretched into the endless rolling green hills of the midsummer Alta California horizon. I watched from where Mamá and I sat outdoors on a couple of plain wooden chairs facing the newly empty stool at the front of la fila.

At midday, the sun shone directly on the spot Mamá had chosen for us upon our arrival in Coloma, a glade surrounded by tall pine trees, with a view of a calm river. We had set up halfway between our claim, where my brother and father mined sal negra, and the outskirts of town. Despite the sun shining on this spot for hours, it felt like bad luck to abandon it now.

In this place, Mamá had used sal negra on herself to reveal its magic to us, and it was here that Mamá and I—two women in flowing dresses, a barrel for sal behind us, a pail of it between us, our house visible off in the distance—had been healing the sick ever since.

"Loli, más sal," Mamá said, patting me roughly on the

forearm, diverting my attention from the others. Her tone was firm but tired as always as she wiped beads of sweat from her wrinkled brow and underneath her straw bonnet.

I grunted, a bit tired myself after a late night out. Then I set my cross-stitch down on the rim of my chair, acting as if the heat of the day made it hard to breathe instead of how tight Mamá had made the bodice of my dress this morning. I hurried toward a barrel to the right of Mamá that had once contained liquor and now held magia. The more people who lined up, the shorter the rope of Mamá's temper. And she always hated when I paid them too much attention.

It was my parents' wish that I feign a lack of interest in sal—or in Mamá as a curandera generally. I was just a girl minding my needlework, no real threat to someone who might want to take the sal from us. My job was to survive. I was here with Mamá only because my parents didn't want me home alone. And they didn't want me helping at the mines either.

Of course, I paid close attention to every miracle Mamá performed, and in the darkness of night, in my own way, I did help.

When I returned to Mamá, old man Álvaro was next in line. I'd been following his story for three days as he advanced to the front. His journey here became all anyone seemed to talk about. Blind, el viejito had traveled 150 miles on foot, accompanied by two of his eight children, the ones now leading him forward to the vacant chair.

Voluminous clothing hung from their bodies in tatters, ruined materials of fine linen and cotton now the only evidence of noble blood. Faces covered in dirt and grime bore the same dark circles around the eyes. The siblings dragged their feet as if hurting with every blistered step. Don Álvaro could barely walk *with* their aid. But they'd made it, survived the trek and endured the wait. Don Álvaro y familia had earned the right to the sal negra from our claim and to the miracle we shared with everyone who came to us.

Mamá welcomed the three travelers with her usual worn-out smile. She hadn't stopped working since we arrived in Coloma three months back, not even for a day. And she didn't eye the long line as I did or see how endless it was when every day brought more people. Three months ago, despite our own grueling trek, Mamá had been full of energy.

The line moved forward, and people in it continued to chatter away. There was a lull now—almost comforting, like the sound of grillos at night.

Before Mamá, the sal negra was going to be sold as black table salt, a minor commodity. Before Mamá, nobody had realized what it was they were really sent to find, what Abuelo had invested in because Mamá told him to. Despite the war, he dispatched dozens of men out here on his daughter's whim; he financed our entire voyage—and the venture had paid off. We were able to send word back to Abuelo that la magia was real. Mamá had been right.

Magia—for the very first time, evidence of real magic in our world.

And now . . . the plan was to mine as much sal negra as possible before the white man came to claim it for himself, the same way he had done with our lands. We'd lost the war. The Treaty of Guadalupe Hidalgo was signed. Abuelo urged us to hurry home before Alta California got too dangerous.

The dark circles around Mamá's eyes never disappeared, and

she was starting to develop a hunch from leaning over the sick and the injured all day. The sal negra she herself took never seemed to heal it. If she would only let me help, outside of bringing her more sal. But no.

Stay out of the way. That was all she wanted me to do—her and Papá, and sometimes I thought even my brother, Víctor. I had to pretend that I was weak and worthless and uninterested in anything besides elaborately designed vestidos like the one I wore today, expensive makeup, and trends: a true lady of Mexican nobleness who had been dragged into the wilderness.

At first, I didn't mind playing the part, because it had been true. I *was* brought to Coloma against my will. But every miracle I witnessed chipped away that side of me. In Sonora, I was a porcelain doll, but along the road, the glaze had cracked, and underneath it was something finer altogether—someone who actually cared about others, about everyone.

The siblings set el viejito on the stool in front of Mamá. She reached for don Álvaro's hand. The top of it was covered in lines and sunspots, while Mamá's fingertips were stained black from handling so much sal negra. The black salt might have healed any effects of overwork on her fingers, but the color never washed away no matter how many times she bathed in the river, no matter how often I caught her scrubbing them roughly with soap.

Despite the changes in her, Mamá was still the most beautiful woman in the world. Her pine-brown hair was tied back in a tight bun she smoothed with bandoline. Her features were still perfectly balanced, from the roundness of her cheeks to the curve of her nose. Her eyes wide, eyelashes long and glorious, she turned to me now, talking without speaking the way mamás do. She wasn't tall, was in fact shorter than me by more than a foot, but her presence was godly and could not be ignored.

I picked up the pace, breathless—wishing I could shuck off my dress right here, and the high-heeled lace-up botas—and managed to lug another pail filled with sal negra, the fourth one since Mamá got started at sunrise. It was the last we'd have until Papá and Víctor returned with more. Back in Sonora, I would never have been expected to do physical labor like this. I'd been so different then. I *had* been a girl who was interested only in dresses and boys and makeup. That was all I ever knew.

Now I knew magia.

I set the pail down, careful not to spill a single grain of sal, then stood to one side, eager to get a closer look before Mamá waved me back to my chair. Mamá nodded to me, grunted an acknowledgment. A *gracias* never escaped her lips casually.

She scooped up some of the sal negra with a tiny spoon made of plata fina that was etched with lavish designs on its handle. She cupped her hand under the bowl of the spoon. Small blue flowers sprouted from the few grains that made it through her fingers and dropped to the soil at her feet. However careful she was, a small bed of flowers always grew around her from the day's work, making Mamá look like una reina hada, a fairy queen—a miracle in itself that never ceased to amaze me.

I wondered what magia would feel like at my own fingertips. But so far I hadn't needed to be healed, and Mamá conserved the sal—always said it was to be used only on those who truly needed it.

And because Mamá's father was financing the construction

of this whole town, because her father owned the mines and had gifted Mamá our claim, our family controlled the supply of sal negra. What the workers here mined outside of our personal claim was sent back to Abuelo, who was planning to make a fortune selling it to his closest friends. The only problem had been the outcome of the war and the new dangers we faced after losing it. Abuelo had given us two more months, then expected us back home. But I was not sure Mamá would be willing to leave this place.

Mamá focused fully on her work, added the spoonful of sal to a sterling silver cup that sat on her lap and held a single ounce of water. Over the last three months, I'd seen la magia work every single time, but the injuries it healed had been newer—a broken leg or brazo or a gash that had gotten infected and was covered in pus, sicknesses that had made grown-ups suddenly cough up sangre or nauseated them so much they couldn't even keep water in their bellies—nothing that wasn't a recent injury or sickness yet.

"Open your mouth," Mamá said like a priest giving sacrament, and scooped one spoonful of the salted agua. Again, she cupped her hand underneath the spoon, kept the cup balanced on her lap. She held her breath as she moved it forward.

A single drop of water fell, una flor sprouting in the soil under Mamá in a blink as if it had always been there. Mamá eyed it, growled to herself, but kept going.

Don Alvaro opened his mouth wide and tilted his head up to the sky, as if the light of the sun could pierce the darkness he'd been living in for so long.

Every time someone received the sal, everyone else in line quieted, like they were dreading the possibility that la magia would not work this time—or ever again. I myself didn't doubt la magia; I just wasn't completely sure of its strength. Restoring don Álvaro's eyesight wasn't healing so much as building something anew, two different things in my mind.

I focused on don Álvaro, even forgetting the pain of my cinched corset. Who could breathe at a time like this anyway?

I knew the following: A simple wound like an infected gash or a broken bone seemed to heal within ten seconds. A sickness affecting the entire body could take whole minutes. But I wasn't sure how long it might take for sal negra to heal someone injured so long ago.

For the sake of Mamá's good temperament, this *had* to work.

I waited next to them for several minutes. Under the relentless sun, sweat collected at my nape and I wiped it with the back of my hand.

"Nothing's happening," don Álvaro's daughter said, anxiety straining her voice. Her lips were chapped and cracked and bleeding. Her once surely beautiful dress barely held together— dirt caked along its bottom fringe; the fabric was ripped in places. It fit her too big across the shoulders, and I wasn't sure if that was because her frame had shrunk so much on the trek or the dress had originally belonged to someone else.

Her nervous face fell and she turned in the direction that they had come from—through the grassy fields, across the river, and over the mountain behind it, giant and ethereal. Then she pivoted to her brother, who had the same worn look and who was too slight to have helped much when carrying their father. He must have been only a few years older than me. In all this time, he hadn't said a word.

"It usually works faster than this, ¿no?"

"Paciencia, hermana," he said now, asking her to be patient.

I wondered how much the pair must love their father to have made such a dangerous journey. They'd traveled the hardest route of all, up and then down the mountain, where one slip, one fall, one broken leg was too easy to come by; water was almost impossible to find; and bears roamed by the score, hungry.

At least it was midsummer; if it had been winter, they would surely have frozen to death. Yet even in the warmer season, many viajeros perished in the mountain passes. According to stories circulating in Coloma, pilgrims got sick from the water or too injured to continue; they got robbed by bad folks they'd met on the road and shot for good measure.

I'd been witness to all those things on the way from Sonora. We had started that journey with 160 in our group. Only fifty of us made it to Coloma. I couldn't imagine making the return trip with nothing to show for having come all this way. They probably wouldn't even try to go back home. And then what would happen to them?

Would Papá take them on as workers as he'd done with so many others?

As much as Coloma was a place of healing because of sal negra, with many new buildings going up in town as if the Treaty of Guadalupe Hidalgo hadn't just been signed, it would never feel like a permanent home to me. There were hardly any other kids here, hardly any women. It was a working town. People came and went—very few managed to endure Coloma for long.

Living where magia was born would always have its risks.

"Calma," Mamá whispered, closely eyeing don Álvaro, who remained seated, rubbing at his hands, lips quivering as if he was afraid nothing would happen. Mamá took in a harrowing breath, frowning, seeming to will la magia to come forth with the power of her thoughts. Usually, a spoonful of agua de sal negra was enough to cure even the worst ailments. But don Álvaro's daughter was right. La magia should have taken effect by now.

Mamá was never one to yield, though. She'd felt a call to Coloma and followed it to find magic. Now she added another spoonful of sal negra to the silver cup. "Una más," she said to don Álvaro, who consented without a single word.

Just as I was about to sit back down, one of don Álvaro's eyes cleared, his irises becoming a wondrous shade of dark amber. The other cleared almost as rapidly, like a marble washed of dust.

Don Álvaro let out a cry. "¡Puedo ver! Te veo," he said not to his daughter or son or to Mamá but to me. He was staring straight at me, weeping with joy. The viejito came over, took my hands in his, and warmth fluttered through my chest.

"Gracias—oh, muchísimas gracias."

I wondered if he could also see the secrets I was keeping and the person I'd become behind the frivolous disguise.

"Hija, hijo," don Álvaro said, placing a hand on each of their faces next. "You are beautiful, my children. Just the way I remember you from when you were small, running around in huaraches, chasing pollos on our rancho."

All three of them hugged, laughed, and cried together. The people waiting clapped; some cheered or whistled. All had smiles on their faces, even those I knew to be in pain. It was on days like these that I didn't mind that Mamá spent more time on this all-consuming duty than she did caring about me. What we were doing meant something to everybody who came to us for the miracle of sal negra.

Mamá watched the family, her hands clutching each other at her heart, that worn but honest grin on her face. Every time she healed someone, something came alive in her expression that I hadn't yet found the right word for. *Happiness* wasn't strong enough. *Pride* didn't fit. It made me happy that Mamá's life had some meaning here that it didn't in Sonora, where she'd been an outcast, a strange woman with a daughter and a son, who tried her hardest not to be perceived as such.

But I also feared that when the time came to leave Coloma, Mamá would refuse—for the miracle of sal negra was something wondrous. Abuelo had gifted her the town. Would three months turn into forever, or just until the Yankees came to tear la magia away from her—from *us*?

I wanted more than anything to bask in the moment together. Maybe that was why I did what I did—hoping to achieve with sal negra something I believed only Mamá and maybe a few others had realized so far. Mamá never cared what others thought of her. There was true freedom in that, something that I myself had started gaining along the way here from Sonora. And seeing don Álvaro with his children made me even freer.

"Thank you," don Álvaro's daughter said.

"Muchísimas gracias," the son added, tears streaming down his cheeks.

"Mamá," I said, signaling with my chin to the rest of the agua de sal negra.

She caught the hint in my voice, returned the spoon to the water, and gave don Álvaro's daughter a taste, then the son. The blemishes and scratches and bruises on their hard-traveled bodies vanished in a few blinks. Before they took off and we moved on to the next person in line, I filled a tiny water sack with the rest of the agua, a present we never announced but secretly gave to everyone for the rough journey home.

"Gracias otra vez y bendiciones." The daughter hugged Mamá, giving her a few coins as she let go. Sometimes travelers paid us, but not always. When it did happen, Mamá never counted the money, but quickly tucked it into the pocket of her dress. We didn't sell the sal outright, because that would feel like taking advantage of a miracle meant for everyone, so the little money we got went toward bonuses for the miners.

Don Álvaro's daughter embraced me. I hugged her tightly back, smiling and still feeling a warmth inside that wasn't due to the heat of the day. There was bliss in the work we did, true humanity that made you feel whole.

Don Álvaro couldn't stop beholding everything in sight, his lips quirked upward, soaking in the beauty of a world that no matter how harsh its wilderness, was still a marvel. "Tantos colores. So many colors that I'd forgotten about. And look at those mountains. They're so green and tall."

"You climbed up and down through them," the son said.

"Two miracles in a week, then," don Álvaro responded, eyes still wide with amazement.

I turned from the line as don Álvaro and his kids went on their way. Something tightened at my center, and I didn't want anyone to see me cry. Helping people with sal negra meant just as much to me as it did to Mamá. There was something divine about what was happening in Coloma, and we were in the middle of it all. We had the calling—we were the ones making miracles happen in real life.

Sal was a bendición y salvación—a salvation for so many. I hoped it always would be, but threats loomed on the horizon.

"Get out of my way," a gruff voice said suddenly in English.

I wiped my tears, not liking the tone, and glared in the direction the words had come from.

The voice belonged to a tall blond man. He had a full mustache and couldn't have been older than Mamá. He wore a revolver at his hip and had lost his hat at some point, his hair half-flat and half-disheveled as if he'd recently been in a fight. He was riding a white horse with blood smeared across its belly and legs. There was blood on the white cotton shirt he wore, too, on the gray vest, and on his brown scarf.

When he got to don Álvaro and his family, the blond man brought the horse to a stop. "Move aside," the man commanded when he was practically on top of them.

Don Álvaro stilled. As rumor had it, a horse had blinded him, and that was why he'd traveled to Coloma on foot. Now, face-to-face with another, he could not move.

The standoff made my mind fizz with an indescribable emotion akin to anger interwoven with sadness.

"Papá, vamos," his daughter urged, pulling him away.

"I said move out of my way, old man."

"Déjalos," a woman from the line broke in.

My body tensed.

The rider didn't skip a beat. His lips pursed and his eyebrows

SALVACIÓN · 13

rose as he went for his revolver, unclipping it faster than I'd anticipated. He pointed it at the woman who had spoken up.

I'd been awed by magia just a moment ago, but now my mouth was flooded by a sourness that wouldn't go away until this man left. I started toward them, but Mamá caught my arm. I hadn't been this bold in Sonora. The road had done that to me, too, made me into someone who couldn't stand to see injustice and suffering.

"What do you want?" Mamá said in perfect English, her serious tone showing just how strong and in charge she was. She stepped in front of me.

The man smirked, scrunching his features. He lifted up his shirt. He'd been shot. I couldn't see his back, but I ventured that the only reason he was still alive was that the bullet had gone right through him. Still, the entrance wound was set in deep dark red stains, blood everywhere.

The people in line gasped. I'd seen so many injuries the past three months that more blood was just another part of the day. The man's presence, though, made the hair on my neck prickle. White men acted as if Alta California hadn't been part of México only a few weeks ago.

I exchanged a knowing look with Mamá. A dangerous situation such as this one hadn't happened all that many times, but there were a few encounters, more in recent weeks. We were ready.

Underneath my dress, strapped to my thigh, I had a pistol. So did Mamá, underneath the layers of *her* dress. I could shoot a squirrel through the eye from fifty yards out, Mamá farther yet. If the man tried anything to hurt us or the people in line, we were prepared to stop him.

At least I was.

The man leapt off his horse, made a fist with his free hand, and pressed it to the bleeding. "You the healer I heard so much about?"

Mamá moved slightly to her left so the skirt of her dress hid the pail of sal negra from view. He'd obviously heard rumors of magical healing salt and was here to find out if they were true. Someone had told him about us, and here he was.

Still, I didn't blame Mamá for trying to conceal la magia. The sal negra was the last of our supply until Papá and Víctor arrived from the mine. If we lost it, we might not be able to help anyone else in line. This was one of the rare afternoons when murmurs of someone having passed away as they waited hadn't reached us. I, for one, wanted to keep it that way.

"Hey, there is a line," the woman called out again, this time in English.

The Yankee turned to her, still holding his revolver, and said, "You don't want to test me today, lady."

She backed away, knocking into a young man who yelled in pain as she fell on him. I moved toward the man with the gun, but once more Mamá took my arm.

A few others in line acted quickly to help. One gave the woman a hand up. Another checked on the young man. Everyone glowered.

I didn't know what to do. Mamá obviously didn't want me to get involved, and bloodshed was neither enticing nor a good omen for what we were trying to achieve here: a safe place for everyone who needed help, the sick and injured alike. Then again, Papá and Víctor weren't due back till sunset. It was up to Mamá and me to protect the people who came to be healed, who trusted us.

I reached for my pistol but stopped when Mamá spoke calmly to the interloper. "Señor," she said, beckoning him forward and indicating the chair in front of her. "Let me see your wounds."

My mouth was agape and my eyes burned in her direction, but Mamá ignored me.

The man beamed smugly to those in line, many of whom were in no position to take him on in a gunfight. All the people could do as he cut in front of them was look on with weariness and a type of rage that boils the blood.

The Yankee didn't sit, instead lifted the blood-soaked shirt with one trembling hand. Even from this angle, the gunshot wound was visible as a crimson circle. I was surprised he could stand. He would likely die if he had to wait in line to reach us, but that was the way we did things: whoever arrived first was seen first, no matter their wealth or status. We were fair.

"I need you to fix me fast, and then I'll mosey on out of here and you can continue your work in peace, do you reckon now?"

Mamá's face remained stern. She nodded, smoothed out her dress. "Loli," she called more softly this time, her voice soothing.

I gritted my teeth, feeling my pistol against my leg as I motioned the man over to the stool occupied moments before by don Álvaro, a kind soul. It was a silly thing to focus on, but it was what I thought about: How could this man and don Álvaro take up the same space in our world when only one of them was worthy of living in it? I understood his urgent need for care, I did. But everyone else had waited. None had thought their own lives more valuable than the lives of others. This man, he was throwing his weight around only because he looked down on us. He was doing this only because he felt entitled.

But sal negra did not choose who to heal and who not to heal.

At least I didn't think so.

"Sit," I said sharply.

"I'm fine standing, little lady," he responded.

I didn't force him into the chair, but I did keep my eyes on the man. He was a cowboy, I supposed, a Yankee who had traveled here, maybe even to fight us in the war, who now thought that because his armies were victorious, he had the right to anything under the sun. I took notice of his gun belt, counted the twelve bullet loops that still held cartridges, marked how many bullets were missing. Had he shot them recently—all in a battle he'd just fought?

Wars and battles were so absurd. People were strange to think they could take and own land. People were likewise strange to think they could own and take lives so easily.

"I don't have all day," he said dryly, uncaring. Despite his wound, he stood like a mighty figure, as if he *should* tower over others, dominating them.

Mamá moved to prepare a salve of sal negra, unavoidably revealing the pail at her side. It had taken Víctor and Papá almost a week to fill a barrel. The man stared at the pail, unblinking, and licked his lips greedily. I tightened my hands into fists, set my jaw. I wanted to act . . . yet I knew it was better not to provoke the man into hurting someone—especially if that someone was Mamá.

The bullet to the abdomen would surely kill him if left untreated. Mamá added some sal negra to a silver bowl and stirred in a spoonful of bandoline. "Keep still now," she said, and spread her ointment on the man's torso, front and back. At least she didn't do him the kindness of cleaning his wound beforehand.

It was hard to believe there was an entire sea of red inside every one of us.

The Yankee winced. "It's cold," he said, and then gave a sigh of relief. "God, I thought I was going to die." His voice softened, and it was the first time the man sounded human—instead of like a monster that presumed itself immortal.

I didn't expect a thank-you from this one, unlike others we had aided. I didn't look for gratitude necessarily. But . . . I was losing so much through all of this: My mamá was wasting away. I wasn't going to school anymore. I wasn't doing anything except sitting in this chair most days and minding whatever Mamá told me. I was giving up everything, so, yes, I thought people should at least be thankful to Mamá.

I glanced beyond the Yankee to those who were watching us. I saw silent anger in the people who waited, a hostility that didn't leave their narrowed eyes. There were things besides a miracle that could quiet people—danger could too. He had just bypassed at least six dozen men, women, and even children, all because he was willing to take things by force and because people wouldn't stand up to him when he did.

I didn't like the Yankee. I didn't want to help him. And it irritated me that Mamá wouldn't give me the go-ahead and let me show this stranger the way out of Coloma. I'd seen her call on Papá to deal with an outsider once. If Papá or even Víctor were here, she would have signaled them to action.

She knew perfectly well that I could take care of myself, yet I was expected to fake helplessness, risking exposure only as a last resort. Even though I wanted nothing more than to be someone who would protect others, someone people would realize they couldn't take advantage of. If I hadn't been so constrained, this man wouldn't even have attempted to approach us. If he really was to shoot Mamá, he would likely shoot me next and then target however many others before anyone got a chance to use the sal negra. Was *that* the last resort?

When la magia stitched the man's skin back together, several of those at the head of the line gasped as usual. Even I let out a small hum, seeing the sal negra at work—though I didn't think this man deserved to be healed. El milagro never ceased to amaze me.

"Now, please let us continue to help the others." After dressing his exit wound, Mamá invited the man to leave by gesturing to his horse.

Instead of departing, the man pointed the revolver in Mamá's direction.

Terror of losing Mamá quickly became fury, and I couldn't hold myself back any longer. As I was raising the skirts of my dress to pull my weapon, my shoulder felt a reassuring squeeze.

"Loli," whispered my brother, appearing at my side, "let Papá handle it."

They were early. I wasn't sure if I was thankful for the assistance or disappointed that I wouldn't be the one to put a stop to the madness. I wanted to release all my anger. I wanted to protect Mamá the way I protected so many others. Since arriving here, all I had ever wanted was to keep Mamá safe.

Still, maybe Víctor was right. I licked at my lips, the taste of sal spreading over my tongue. The air here always tasted of sal, which made me wonder whether we were healed just by breathing it in. Maybe that was why I'd felt so strong since arriving in Coloma.

I hadn't realized I was tensing my shoulders, gritting my teeth so hard that my mouth felt numb, until my brother arrived and I instantly relaxed.

"Give me the salt," the man said. Víctor, who was always so quiet, went unnoticed. We stood directly behind the man as he faced Mamá. "As much as I can carry—quickly!"

Otra mano landed on my shoulder, large and rough, as Papá walked past us to confront the Yankee. I smirked. The man was about to learn what kind of family he'd messed with.

He backed away a bit when Papá came into view. Papá, well-muscled and with a thick black beard, a black sombrero still on his head, was almost a foot taller than the stranger, after all. His face was covered in grime, too, which only made him look fiercer, intimidating to all those unacquainted with his kindness. Papá stood shielding Mamá, always her protector—always mine too. He'd saved me often enough during our journey from Sonora that I was fully aware I owed him my life twenty times over.

It was always like that: men stood their ground when up against the injured and infirm or against women whom they presumed weren't a threat. When a man as big and burly as Papá entered the picture, the bravado quickly changed.

"You—you stop right there or I will shoot you," said the Yankee, his tone serious, his expression calculated. He stood straighter now that his wounds had healed. "Stay right where you are. I have no qualms about shooting you. Not a one."

Papá studied the smaller man, gave a heavy sigh. Then, without a word, he pulled a pouch the size of a fist from his jacket and filled it with sal. He used his bare hands to do it, something that always rankled Mamá. This time, she didn't say a word, only nodded Papá on.

"Take this and be on your way," Papá said, tossing the purse over to the man, who caught it with one hand and brought it to his nose. I'd never thought sal negra smelled like anything other than salt, but perhaps it smelled like magia to some— like vanilla and pine needles and the hot summer breeze when night fell, mixed with the scent of the ocean.

The man had asked for all the sal he could carry. Would one small pouch satisfy him?

Apparently so. He put the purse in a vest pocket, eyeing Papá. "I didn't think I'd make it here. Thanks to you fine folks, now I plan to make myself right at home in Coloma. I'll be seeing you all, I'm sure."

The man reached to tip a hat, smirked when he realized it was missing. He backed off, slipped onto his horse in a fluid motion, and started away. The people in line cheered.

"We'll be with you all shortly," Mamá told them.

There was another cheer and sighs of relief.

"Are you all right?" Papá asked me. He searched my face and hugged me tight.

I couldn't help but grin widely. "You know I can take care of myself," I mumbled into him.

"I don't doubt that you could have, mi hija," he replied, softly nudging my cheek with his knuckles as he let go.

"Looks like we have a new devil in town, though," Víctor whispered. I flicked at Víctor's hat, which he took off to check for any damage before molding it back into shape. His curls could barely be contained, much less flattened. He grinned and showed off his dimples, as if what had just happened were no big deal. "He won't bother us," Papá promised, hugging Mamá, who held him tight. "Let's just keep an eye open for him."

"If he plans to stay," Mamá began, "brandishing his gun every time he runs out of sal—or if he spreads news of a magical healing salt to his people—things might get complicated for us."

"Oh, I doubt he'll be in town for as long as he thinks," I replied, exchanging a quick and knowing glance with Víctor, who had taken my needlework from my chair and now handed it to me. I clutched the fabric, furious, watching the blond man ride off with sal negra I was certain Víctor and I would be getting back by morning.

CHAPTER 2

L a noche spread across the horizon—the Alta California mountains painted negras against it, the air drier than it had been along the coast of México in Sonora.

I gazed at the stars while I waited in an alley between the saloon and an inn, two of ten new buildings that would be opening soon. We already had a bathhouse and a cantina, which I watched now. I wasn't sure why Abuelo was still funding the construction of this town, as if he thought we could maintain control of it somehow. To me, he was just bracing for a battle I wanted my family to have no part in. Perhaps he only feared, as I did, that Mamá was planning never to leave. Our return day approached, with only a few weeks left if we were to travel before winter.

I'd left my dress at home, and I was no longer Lola de La Peña, but Salvación. I wore riding pants I'd borrowed from Víctor—black and tight, made of a rough material I relished

SALVACIÓN · 23

against my skin—and a long-sleeved black linen blouse that I'd taken from Mamá's closet back at our rancho in Sonora. Boots that were meant to get dirty. A black poblano hat I fell in love with that one of Papá's men had left behind before he returned to Sonora to send word to Abuelo we'd arrived in Coloma, which together with my makeshift mask covered half of my face.

This is what freedom felt like: no constraints, no one asking me to hold back, no expectations about my becoming a woman.

In my disguise I watched as a group of fifteen or so men laughed as they rode out into the night, taking the newest haul of sal negra to Abuelo, back in Sonora. Other than that, the night was quieter than usual, most men tired from either toiling in the mines or doing construction work.

My attention was drawn to someone exiting the cantina, itself also quieter than usual, the doors swinging on their creaky hinges. I double-checked that my thick black mask was tied securely, fully concealing Lady Lola de La Peña.

I'd been waiting on the Yankee since the time it took the moon to move the width of two of my fingers. Way past when I was supposed to be home and in bed, safe, the way Mamá and Papá preferred. But whereas my window had been on the second story of our hacienda back in Sonora, my window in Coloma was easy to climb out of whenever I went out at night as Salvación, the masked hero of Coloma.

Finally, my target showed. The man whose bullet wound Mamá had healed stumbled out of the cantina, swaying along with the warm summer breeze. He fell over into the dirt before slowly picking himself up. He was obviously very, very drunk.

Luckily, he was also alone. I'd anticipated that much. Not many white men arrived in Coloma and then decided it was wise to stay in town. After I had a nice chat with him, he'd leave it solito too.

Good riddance y adiós.

If he'd been a smarter man, maybe he would have thought to use some of the sal negra to sober up, the way Papá did when he felt like he'd had too many drinks to think straight. But then again anyone who had been on the brink of death was bound to have dark memories, so I wasn't quite sure sobering up was what he wanted at all. Sal negra couldn't take away memorias oscuras.

I wondered about him. Who was he, and how was he so vile?

He hummed as if celebrating his own cumpleaños and proceeded to relieve himself against the wall of the cantina. *Disgusting.* Then he started toward his horse, hitched just within the edge of the darkness of the inn that was under construction, less than fifty yards from me.

The pouch was tied to his belt at the hip. El fuego in my belly rose to my throat, and I couldn't help gritting my teeth. Sal negra was a miracle; this scoundrel wasn't worthy of it. I wanted to recover the sal negra as much as I wanted the man gone. He didn't deserve Mamá's help or Papá's mercy, not after threatening our family, our neighbors.

The man whistled a folk tune going around Coloma lately. I hated it as much as I hated him. The lyrics glorified warriors and the West and things far too dark for such a happy melody. I could accept that the history of civilization was murky and always had been. I'd learned as much from my tutors back in

Sonora: of land taken, diseases spread, death and endless death. Naturally, I feared our world might only get bleaker as reports of la magia continued to spread. If only I could keep some of the goodness alive. But Abuelo already had plans to sell the sal negra to his friends, to anyone with enough money.

I counted the days till Sonora, when danger would be a thing of the past. I hesitated. I wasn't convinced everyone deserved a second chance. Papá seemed always to be suggesting it to Mamá, who was as hard as a diamond. Papá was more like stone—strong and sure, but after enough water had run over it, a pile of sand.

Papá's chivalry angered me sometimes. He could have used his fists and his strength to force the man to leave Coloma. But instead, he had stood down.

For all the love that I had for Papá, compassion was his weakness—but it wouldn't be his downfall, or our family's, or the town of Coloma's.

I—Salvación—would not stand for it.

Once the man moved to untie his horse from the hitching post, I crept out of the shadows and brought my sword to the side of his face, careful not to injure his horse or frighten it away. I couldn't risk leaving the man stranded in town.

He moved for his revolver, and perhaps to mi buena suerte, he'd drunk enough to be slow on the draw.

"Drop your weapon," I said, smirking as I slid my blade along his cheek.

He hesitated. I couldn't see it in the dark, but I knew the cut was deep enough to draw blood.

The subtle thump of a weapon hitting the ground was a relief.

"Ahh, aaaah, okay, just take what you want from my pockets and leave me be." His tone was mocking and let me know this man didn't deserve to walk away. He was a cruel person, and I couldn't let him stay. Not when I remembered him pointing his revolver at Mamá, how she'd stood there, willing to die for sal negra. Not when my one calling was also my way to finding the freedom Mamá enjoyed.

"Oh no, señor, you are the one who will leave today. May this serve as your only warning: untie the sal negra from your belt and leave Coloma right this moment, or on all that is holy, I will end your life."

The warning had always worked. I watched men ride off on their horses, Víctor waiting for them on high ground with a rifle, hiding in the mountainside that faced the way out of town, to make sure they left without even a glance back.

They always stayed away. They always rode on.

Víctor had never used the rifle. And as much as I despised the blond man, I still hoped Víctor wouldn't have to open fire.

"Oh, I see now." The man sniffed, rubbed at his nose, and snorted. "You're that vigilante everyone is mumbling about. What's the name? Salvación? Haven't stopped hearing the name since I arrived. People around these parts think you're some kind of angel."

I struggled to keep a grin from reaching my lips. I had to admit, the fact of my reputation was something I was proud of. Still, I managed to keep my focus, because the man didn't seem afraid but rather determined that Salvación wasn't going to ruin his day.

I made my voice deeper to sound older than my seventeen years, which wasn't so difficult; Víctor and other kids had always teased me for being so tall and curvy, but ever since I became Salvación, my height had worked in my favor.

"That's right."

"I don't believe the stories. You're made of flesh and blood, like me. You're not an angel. And either way, I don't think you'd actually kill a man. Aren't you a lady? Lady Salvación? A woman who hunts the wicked, the rumors have said. But nobody believes a woman could really be behind all of this."

The man seemed to know how his taunts were landing. Was he being this insulting just because he was drunk? Or was talking recklessly a natural trait of his? Everything he said was making me angry.

I'd been called "a lady" all my life outside my home: señorita Lola this and señorita Lola that. Back in Sonora, las monjas at school demanded that I talk, act, walk, eat, sew, cook, like a señorita. My tutors were just as adamant. But out here in Alta California, at least at night, at least while I was Salvación, I'd become the type of girl I wanted to be: free as the wind to be whomever I pleased, no rules holding me back. My whole body felt better when I was dressed as Salvación; even the knot at the back of my neck, always so painful in Sonora, was gone. The first time I realized this, I also understood I deserved to feel this way: completely unburdened.

Only Víctor and Papá would accept the real me now. I wasn't anything like what people expected of a girl who had grown up in a wealthy family. I was Loli. Me. I wore pants even when I wasn't outside, didn't brush my hair, wore boots, and was good with a sword. I didn't like the dresses I wore every day; I detested the heels that made my feet sore. Mamá made me keep them anyway, because she said that one day I'd go back to the world of rules. I had to be ready for that or the world would eat me alive. She never said *we'd go back.*

This new world wasn't much different.

The man didn't flinch, didn't make a move to go, and still had the sal negra on him. It suddenly occurred to me that maybe he wouldn't comply. Maybe he'd be the first to stand up to Salvación, and then I'd have to see if I was so willing to rid Coloma of a dangerous character that I'd kill for it.

"Cállate and do as I say." In my panic, I pressed the blade deeper into his skin until he finally whimpered.

"Okay," he said, voice hurried. "I'll leave." The man gestured toward his revolver, asking permission to pick it up.

"Leave it behind." I took a step forward to kick the weapon away. "And you can drop the sal negra you're carrying right next to it."

"My revolver is an heirloom, given to me by my pop the last time I saw him. I don't reckon I want to leave it behind."

"I'm not giving you a choice," I said, emphatic. "You lost the right to your possessions when you stole those of others."

My heart raced as he moved toward the ground. I kept my eyes wide, so I wouldn't blink and miss a moment. He might attack me, perhaps be quicker than me, perhaps shoot me square in the chest. I'd seen men sober up swiftly when facing death. Víctor wouldn't come down from his hiding spot in the hillside fast enough to save me—he was more than a mile away.

No one would save me. I'd be stone-cold gone from el mundo and maybe on my way to becoming a real angel.

Was I ready for that? I'd thought I was prepared to die to keep Coloma safe. I'd thought as much when I first encountered the man. I'd thought it when I created Salvación. But standing here with my heart beating so loudly I could hear it in my ears . . .

My pulse slowed down when he straightened. The Yankee took a last lingering look at his heirloom revolver as though carving it into memory. Or was he merely fuming over having to abandon it? He unknotted the small sack of sal negra from his belt and tossed it next to the revolver.

He mounted his horse, and I touched the middle of his back with the tip of my sword to stop him from suddenly attacking me. He shivered, straightened his back, and moved an inch forward to avoid my blade. His shoulders were tense, and I was glad. It meant he was afraid.

"Don't look back as you ride off," I whispered. Moments like these were a miracle. My hands were sweaty, my heartbeat fluttered nervously again, but my focus sharpened.

I slapped the horse on its side and watched the animal take off out of town.

The man peeked back against my warning, trying his best to see me, perhaps considering doubling back to fight me bare-handed. I'd already retreated into the darkness, heirloom revolver pointed in his direction and sal negra back in my possession, where it belonged. I watched him go, the town eerily quiet around him. I'd been so busy confronting the Yankee that I never checked to see if anyone else had come outside or spotted us.

I alone heard him say, "You're going to regret this! I will be back for my heirloom, Lady Salvación. You sure better be watching your back."

Others had given me the same warning. None had kept their word. And part of me knew he wouldn't ever either.

Who wanted to fight an angel?

When the blond man was finally out of sight, I ran to Víctor's hiding spot on the way out of Coloma, keeping to the shadows that I knew so well. If anyone did see me, that would only add to the rumors: one more person in Coloma who had caught sight of Salvación. Still, I was willing to risk being seen in order to make certain the blond man had truly left.

Once I was on the open fields outside of town, I took off my mask, crossing the river on the newly constructed bridge. I hiked up the forest to Víctor, sly as a fox, rapidá como una coneja, enjoying the trees whispering around me and the night songs of crickets and frogs.

Víctor shifted his rifle as I came closer to where he crouched between two large boulders. From far away, he was just another rock among the foliage. No matter how quiet my approach, he always seemed to hear me at the last second. It was good practice, making sure nobody could sneak up on my brother. If I couldn't do it, there wasn't a person in the world who could.

He moved fast like a rattler: one second, he was still crouched, and the next, he had his rifle in front of him, his finger inching toward the trigger.

"¿Loli, eres tú?" He squinted in the dark. His whole body relaxed as I came closer. "I almost shot you this time."

I scoffed. "Who else would know you were up here?"

"I don't know—someone pissed off at you, someone who happened to run across me on their way into Coloma, someone who just spotted me at random?" He set the rifle aside and sat facing in the direction the man had gone. There was nothing to see out there, though—just stillness, just night, animals roaming around on four legs instead of two.

SALVACIÓN · 31

I sat next to him, leaned against his shoulder the way we'd done when we were little kids. "You mean pissed off at Salvación?"

His expression was far too serious. "I think we should stop this."

He moved to put on his sombrero. It was wide-brimmed and had been one of Papá's favorites. Víctor had been so happy the day Papá gave it to him. Even after it'd gotten tramped by horses and almost lost in two or three rivers on the way from Sonora to Coloma, the sombrero had made the journey with us. I imagined he even slept with it, and chuckled.

"I mean it, Loli. I'm not laughing."

"If we give up, who will keep Coloma safe?" I pulled a piece of cheese out of my pocket and unwrapped the slivers, handing half to Víctor, who gladly took them. The only thing bigger than Víctor's heart was his stomach, and food always settled his thoughts when he brought up quitting our vigilante mission.

"Let the grown-ups be in charge of protecting Coloma. Let Papá. He's the leader here," he mumbled through a mouthful. "That's their job."

"The grown-ups are too busy making Abuelo rich off sal negra to realize danger is already here." The Treaty of Guadalupe Hidalgo changed everything for Alta California, yet no one was acting like it, only acting like we still had time when we didn't.

"You saw what Papá did today. He let the man go—a man who threatened to kill Mamá, me, and everything we're doing here. He let him go like nothing happened. No. Salvación is the answer, as she's always been."

"That's exactly what I'm getting at," Víctor said as he stood, shouldering the leather strap of his rifle. "Un día, soon enough, it won't be *one* man against us." He paused to point at the fields below. "It'll be an army. Then what? You going to take them all on in the dead of night, your sword at all their backs? Salvación is a fairy tale that parents can tell their niños about. The reality is much different. You're not an angel, Loli. And neither am I. We're flesh and bone and everything that can die."

I wasn't sure what would happen in the future. But I knew that I didn't necessarily want to go up against un ejército. I *was* one girl—one girl who wanted nothing more than to keep the people she cared about, and all of Coloma, from getting hurt and having to fight greedy Yankees for the sal negra. Abuelo was already greedy enough.

But sal negra was a miracle that also needed my protection.

Víctor bringing this up again was a stray bullet rattling inside of me. Could I stop? I wasn't so sure, not when everything in my body told me I was meant to do this.

Wasn't protecting magia worth my life in the end?

The blond man had made me doubt, though. I'd felt the same sense of facing death only a few times before, on the journey to Coloma. Yet even that journey, especially at the start, had been filled with food and the luxury that came with land and wealth and a good name.

"You remember the first day you saw the sal negra?" I asked as we started down the mountain, toward our casita at the edge of Coloma. I bit the side of my lip.

"How could I forget? I'd never seen someone with wounds like that."

"The bear threw that man around like a rag doll, this way

and that, and he was battered almost beyond recognition. He could barely breathe. If he hadn't been one of the miners in Coloma, if he hadn't been near enough to Mamá, he'd be dead. But we'd arrived that same day. Mamá had just chosen the spot where she said she'd be healing the sick. She'd just gotten the sal negra from the mines, healing herself to show the others, and she helped them apply the sal on the man's skin without even gagging. She believed she was sent to Coloma for a reason, and she found her purpose here. The man was healed and survived." As I remembered the moment, pride overcame me. I smiled.

Víctor rubbed at his face as if he didn't want to hear any of this.

I continued, "Es magia, magic, a miracle: something strange and inexplicable that we are destined to be a part of. And you don't think magia is worth protecting? You think we should turn our back on destiny?"

He stopped, so I did too.

"No destiny is worth wasting your life," he replied. "You are my little sister, Loli de La Peña, and you're worth more than any miracle. And so is Mamá and so is Papá—I only wish you'd all see that. All I do is to protect you all. Trust that I'm protecting you now by putting an end to this."

I nudged him with my hip. "Stop with the dramatics! We're not going to get killed." I patted the pouch at my side, recognizing this was a losing conversation. "One injury, and I would just take some sal negra and be healed. Plus, sometime soon we'll go back to Sonora. Now, I'll race you home?"

He stared at me longer, his piercing gaze forcing me to look away first. Only when I did, he took my arm and pulled me backward, sprinting toward home. I ran after him, yelling as the wind blew in my face. We moved in almost total darkness, but the route was familiar to us, so it didn't matter. I leapt over tree roots I knew like my own knuckles, dodged the boulders that sat on the mountain, grabbed on to the trees that lined the way downhill so I wouldn't slip at the drop-offs.

Víctor waited for me at the foot of the mountain, huffing and trying to catch his breath. He took off his sombrero again, pushed back his hair, then donned the hat. "Loser," he said, teasing.

I shoved him and he laughed as he fell. "You cheated!"

He moved to stand, still fighting to catch his breath. "I *won*."

I was about to knock him down again when a flicker of light caught my attention. I paused. Víctor noticed it as well. It was like a torch moving in the distance, a light dancing along the horizon that couldn't be an animal. It was moving too quickly.

"¿Qué es eso?" I pointed to the oncoming light, my nose twitching. It was a person. Had the Yankee already made good on his promise? Maybe he had another revolver stashed somewhere nearby and was back to take his revenge on Salvación.

The light drew closer, and then a horse came into view, small and fast, and I suddenly wished Papá were with us. The rider was not the blond man but someone in a dress lurching over the horse as if passed out, long hair down and flowing loose. Fingertips wrapped around a torch, but just barely.

And then the rider fell over, snuffing out the light.

CHAPTER 3

I scolded Víctor as he simultaneously held the woman's legs off the ground and kept the reins of her horse firmly in his grasp. "Hold her up!"

"You want to trade?" Exasperation cut through his words. It wasn't like lifting the woman's shoulders was easier when her sagging head bobbed left and right.

"We're almost there," I replied.

Víctor growled at me and lifted the woman higher, continued to pull the horse along. The horse, to the blessing de la noche, followed us without complaint. El pobre seemed exhausted from the journey, even going to its knees, and had refused to stand back up when we reached the rider, but we gave the animal a bit of sal negra and it seemed all right now.

I focused on what little strength I had left after carrying the woman from where she'd fallen near the river. I knew we'd have to explain to our parents what we'd been doing outside. They'd forbidden us from taking to the night as Salvación—

more than a few times—and we hadn't listened. But we couldn't let the woman die to hide our secret.

When we finally made it home, I knocked on the front door with an elbow. The sal negra hadn't woken her up, but I hoped that the sal we'd covered her in would keep her alive. We needed Mamá to figure out what was going on. Mamá would find a way to save her.

Papá opened la puerta a sliver. I could tell by his posture that he surely held a pistol, prepared for anything, waiting for the day someone would try to take Abuelo's sal negra claim.

This was not the day, though.

"¿Loli? ¿Víctor? ¿Qué hacen? What are you kids doing outside? Get in." His voice was stern but worried too. He opened the door wider and finally seemed to take note of what we were carrying.

Immediately, relief flooded my body and a weight lifted from my very bones. The warm light spilling out of our home promised safety from whatever ailed the woman, and the comfort of Mamá and Papá being there to help us now.

"Miriam!" Papá called, taking the woman's legs from Víctor, who led her horse to our barn. "Rápido. We need tu ayuda."

Mamá appeared, drying her hands on a kitchen towel, a scowl on her face at being rushed. Her posture changed, loosened as she took in the scene and realized a scolding wasn't what the occasion called for. Inside our home, Mamá wasn't the prim señora she made herself out to be in public either. She was wearing pants, a loose white blouse. Her hair was pulled back in a ponytail and she wore no makeup. Mamá's eyes narrowed and her eyebrows furrowed in concentration, the way they did when she was preparing to work with sal negra.

She looked me up and down, her nostrils flaring, displeased that I was dressed as Salvación. Still, she didn't mention it or bring up that I'd gone out against her wishes—again. "What happened to her? Did you do this?"

I stepped back. That was a blow, a shot to the heart. "No, of course not. She came riding into town. I don't know what's wrong, we just happened to see her."

Víctor appeared next to me, back from the barn. He doffed his hat, and his curly hair stuck to the sweat at his neck. "She's telling the truth," he said, as if I needed him to defend me.

Okay, maybe I did—but only sometimes. Usually, it was Papá who came to my aid.

"We tried to help her," my brother explained, "but we didn't have enough sal negra to wake her up. As far as I can tell, though, está viva. She's breathing."

"You did the right thing," Papa said. I grinned at his words. Mamá glowered at my father but didn't argue. It felt good when Papá said I was right. When he took my side over Mamá's, it felt like vindication.

With Víctor vouching for what we'd been up to, Mamá didn't waste time in giving my brother a new task. "La mesa— prep the table, Víctor, rápido. Clear it so we can set her down, and then I can investigate her injuries."

Víctor rushed over to the dinner table, blowing out and removing a dozen candles. Because the woman was, well, a woman, Papá and Víctor had to leave the room out of respect. I'd helped Mamá before when Papá couldn't. And I was already rolling up the sleeves of my mother's old blouse to help her now.

"Are you all right?" Papá asked as he walked past me, his

eyes searching for something in my face that might tell him otherwise.

"I just want to help her survive," I said, voice shaking.

Papá nodded, then went out for more sal from our hidden stash behind the house. The rest would be up to me and Mamá. We laid the woman down on the kitchen table. I set a pillow Víctor had brought us under the woman's head, wondering why the sal negra hadn't woken her up yet.

Víctor rushed in again and left a bucket of sal negra by the kitchen doorway. Would more magia wake the woman? And what type of injury didn't respond to sal negra?

The woman's face was so dirty from her ride and from falling off her horse that I wasn't entirely sure she was Mexican until we removed her shawl. Gently and meticulously, I took a wet cloth and washed off the grime. The shawl's elaborate needlework was of a similar pattern to some of Mamá's pieces, a design I used myself when I was Lola de La Peña. It made the woman feel familiar to me. It could just as easily have been me or Mamá on the table, a thought that didn't sit right. Who did this to her? Tears clouded my eyes as I worked, and I blinked to keep them at bay.

As Mamá had taught me, I searched for an external injury first, any sign of blood that needed stanching. But I couldn't find any wounds at all as Mamá took off the woman's gloves. The moment she did, both of us took a step back. The stranger's fingertips were stained red just like Mamá's were stained black. It was almost as if she'd clawed her way through red salt mines.

"Dios mío. What is that?" Mamá asked. We exchanged a look.

SALVACIÓN · 39

I moved to touch the poor woman, but Mamá slapped my hand before I could make contact. I flinched and didn't reach for the woman again.

"Did you touch her skin?" she asked me.

I looked at my hands. "No," I replied. "Why?"

"It doesn't feel right," she said. One thing I knew by now was that Mamá's feelings could be magical themselves. "Take Víctor and fetch más agua limpia. I want to wash her. See if that helps."

I didn't want to leave Mamá, but I did as she asked.

I found Víctor standing with Papá outside, explaining what had happened tonight.

"Agua," I said, flicking Víctor's arm. "We need to fetch water—fast. Help me."

Papá followed us. "And you said she came out of nowhere?"

"Yes," I said.

Víctor grabbed four of the dozen water buckets we kept near the riverbank and filled them. They weighed some thirty pounds apiece, so Papá carried two back, and Víctor and I each lugged one. I lifted mine with both hands and made my way to the house, hardly spilling any water.

At the front door, I hesitated. "Pa," I said. Did he see the fear in my eyes? I felt a slithering underneath my skin, a prickling at the back of my neck, fear creeping under the surface, warning us.

"What is it, Loli?"

"There's something really wrong with that woman. Something that feels magical but in a terrible way."

"¡El agua!" Mamá called from the kitchen.

"Go," Papá said. "We'll talk later."

I carried my bucket into the kitchen, slipping on a wet spot, barely catching myself. My calf hurt, but I ignored the pain and brought Mamá the water she needed.

Quickly, she took the bucket from me, and I noticed that she'd covered her mouth and nose by tying one of our kitchen towels on her face. "Cover yourself," she said, pointing to a stack of dish towels and handing me a silver bowl of salve. "Rub the sal negra salve on your hands and arms and do not touch her skin."

I snatched a towel, tied it over my nose and mouth. With shaking hands, I rubbed an excessive amount of salve all over my wrists and forearms.

Mamá was focused on the problem at hand, as good a curandera as I was a vigilante. "She has no wounds, but look," she said. The woman's skin had a slight red hue not just on her fingertips but all over. "I think the salve is the only thing keeping her alive. The sal you and Víctor used on her surely helped as well. I think washing her skin and reapplying a layer of sal negra might help even more."

Mamá set the pail on a chair and went to her herbs, plucking here and there until she had gathered a handful. Then she threw the herbs into the bucket of water, mixing the water with a silver spoon.

I nodded, ready to work. "I'll wash her arms and hands."

"Make sure to get under her nails." Mamá handed me one of the sponges she used for cleaning wounds.

I toiled side by side with Mamá for an interminable hour. We rubbed the herb water into the woman's skin, making small circles with our sponges. It was a laborious operation, but we had the patience for it. As we worked, the red tinge faded, her skin transforming into its natural hue.

When we were finally done, the woman breathed in heavily, which I took for a good sign.

Mamá must have thought so as well. She stopped, wiped off the sweat on her brow with the back of her arm, and watched for the woman to react.

"I'm proud of you," Mamá said without looking at me. It was a compliment she rarely doled out. This encounter and all it implied had frightened her.

Mamá brought out more salve of sal negra. I rubbed it on the woman's hands with a fresh sponge, gently working it into the skin as mamá had done for so many in the last three months. The more sal negra we applied, the more at peace the woman seemed.

But when we were done, she didn't wake up.

"We should discard the dirty water and bathe ourselves in the river."

And so, while the woman slept, and while Papá and Víctor waited patiently on the porch, we went to the river. The water was teeth-chattering cold, but my fear was icier yet, and so I made sure to take a long soak.

Dawn broke above the horizon. I wasn't sure whether to welcome the sunlight or dread it, but my eyes felt heavy. All I wanted to do was curl up in my bed and sleep.

But there was still work to be done.

We moved the woman to the living room, setting her down on the floor rug as comfortably as we could, a pillow behind her neck. She was younger than Mamá, but older than me, with long dark hair full of knots. I tucked a wisp behind her ear. Large silver earrings shaped like nopales dangled from her earlobes. Her lips were thin, her mouth slightly agape, her eyes large and eyelashes long.

What would have happened if we hadn't found her when we did?

"Why isn't she waking up?" I asked aloud.

"I wonder—" Mamá paused, so I grunted for her to continue. I wanted to know what she made of all of this, even if it was disturbing. "I wonder if they're battling, sal negra and whatever made the woman's skin red. We might be waiting to find out which one will triumph over the other. We should get her to a bed soon."

Papá and Víctor stood by. Mamá went over to Papá, who took her in his arms. He kissed her forehead. I'd always admired their love and their closeness even when they were so different. Maybe that was why their relationship worked. I didn't know. I didn't know what to make of love yet. But seeing them together always made me feel safe.

I moved closer to Víctor, someone else who made things better. He put his arm over my shoulder. "She'll survive," he told me.

I nodded, but I wasn't so sure.

"You two should go rest," Papá said. "Sleep. You've had a long night."

"We'll talk about your punishment later," Mamá added.

"Miriam," Papá interjected, "is there really a punishment for saving someone's life?"

They stared each other down till Papá gave Mamá a small grin to pacify her. Every time I'd been in trouble, he mentioned how I was doing a good thing. It was just one of the ways he was always there for me.

Mamá relented. "Fine, go rest."

I yawned, nodded. Víctor and I left our parents in the kitchen. But even when I was in my bedroom, the safest place in the world, I couldn't sleep. I changed into my sleeping gown. But my mind kept going over what had happened. I kept seeing the woman riding in the dark, kept watching her fall, kept seeing her give a sigh of relief, kept remembering that she had not yet woken up.

There was a knock at my door. "Can I come in?" Papá asked.

"Yeah," I said.

He opened the door and stepped inside. His shoulders sagged, like he was enormously tired, but his eyes were wakeful, alertos and wide open. He stood leaning against the doorframe. "Are you okay, mi hija?"

I exhaled loudly, considered lying.

But I never lied to Papá, had always believed that if I did, he'd see straight through me and wouldn't take my side anymore with Mamá, wouldn't stand up for me when Mamá got angry over my vigilante outings. I valued Papá's trust above all else.

"No, Papá. It's been a strange couple of days."

He nodded, though he didn't know the half of it—didn't know about the blond man, of how he'd spooked me by saying he'd come back, his voice full of conviction. "It'll be okay, as long as we have each other." He smiled then. It was forced, but I appreciated the gesture. I loved him for always trying to make the best of things, out here in the wilderness.

I nodded too. "Is Mamá okay?" It was never my mother at

the door asking me how I was doing, but my mind always went to her anyway.

I saw the debate in his eyes, but he wasn't one to lie to me either. After a great sigh, he said, "No. Whatever's happening to the poor woman, it has your mamá's mind running. Just make sure to rest. I need you and Víctor with your eyes peeled and your ears open for any danger."

"What about you? Are you going to sleep?" I already knew the answer, though I wished he would rest too.

"Don't you worry about me," he said.

"It's my job as your only daughter to worry."

"It's your job to—"

"—protect this family," I said. "I know you and Mamá think you need to guard Víctor and me, but on the way here from Sonora, we grew up, Papá."

He knocked on the doorframe, chuckling. "I know, mi hija. And so does your mamá, whether she cares to admit it or not. Now get some rest. I love you, ángel."

He left before I could bring up Salvación, but every time he called me an ángel, it felt like his secret way of telling me he accepted what I was doing, accepted me. I was the Angel of Coloma, and he was proud of me. It was also this pride that made it impossible to stop.

I flung my sheets off in one motion, got out of bed, and grabbed my guitar from a corner of my room, where it had stood leaning against the small wooden desk in front of the window. That same one I so often climbed out of. It had once been Papá's guitar and had miraculously survived the trip from Sonora to Coloma. I got back on the bed, sat cross-legged, and strummed a tune Papá had taught me, the strings familiar under my calloused fingertips. I sang a song Papá used to play for Víctor and me when we were little, in this way begging the world to let the woman live, to help her wake up.

Debajo de un árbol grande, there upon the grass
Where dicen que las flores crecen, on the graveyard brass,
Debajo de un árbol grande, in el verano breeze
El zorro llora a la noche, where you fell on your knees,
Debajo de un árbol grande, which still remembers you,
Mi amor que tanto quise, remains forever true.

Had the sal negra finally met its match? Would the woman soon be a memory too? I wondered what Salvación could do about it all. Was this even our fight? Everything depended on the slumbering woman.

Whoever had wielded something powerful enough to cancel out the sal negra would be coming to Coloma. When they did, if they became a problem, Salvación would have no choice but to protect the town, whether Víctor wanted to help me or not.

CHAPTER 4

When the smell of tortillas de harina cooking on the open hearth woke me up, la guitarra was still in my hands, my sword still at my side. The house was warm from the cooking flames and I rubbed the drool from my mouth. Then the memories of last night jolted my brain, the images vivid and overlapping.

Where did the woman come from? Did she threaten Coloma's peace? But most important, what had made the woman's skin red?

I sat up, setting the guitar down on the floor, then got out of bed and ran my fingers through my hair. I was eager to see if the woman was awake, but the insecurities of the night before had resurfaced. Finding the woman was the beginning of something important. We didn't need to fear this woman—what scared me was what her arrival meant, what had chased her to Coloma.

I left my room and walked the long corridor to the kitchen.

Mamá had the fire going, logs crackling in the hearth, a comal hot atop the flames, and a towering pile of tortillas beside her. It was definitely more of them than usual, as if she'd gotten lost in her thoughts and didn't realize she'd made enough for ten people instead of four—five, if our guest regained consciousness. I hesitated. In front of the hearth, with the flames casting shadows on her face, Mamá seemed even more tired and frayed, like don Álvaro before his sight was returned to him. When she looked this frail, I couldn't trust myself to talk to her without crying, so I pivoted to the woman sleeping under a blanket on the floor nearby. Her collarbone rose and fell, and her breathing was peaceful at last.

Apparently, she needed more rest, still needed to fight. Maybe another dressing of the salve would be enough, or perhaps keeping her alive would always be a battle.

"She's all right," Mamá said.

I approached the hearth, needing to know what Mamá thought more than I wanted to avoid her. I kissed her on the cheek and said, "Hola, Mamá. She hasn't woken up at all?"

Mamá settled a tortilla on the pile and moved on to prepare more masa. Her fingers worked fast, despite the heat of the comal, as if this were the only thing keeping her mind from running like the antelope. "I don't think she will for a while. I've never seen anything like the stains on her fingers. When you were collecting el agua, I saw something. Her skin was eating itself and healing at the same time. It is a miracle she's alive." I was about to say something when she added, "I don't know how she's alive."

I knew. Salvación had made it happen, but I couldn't mention that to Mamá. Ever since they first discovered that Víctor and I went out and helped the people of Coloma, my parents had been explicitly against it and said that we'd only get ourselves hurt. They said to leave it up to Papá. Only, we hadn't ever stopped. Yesterday they found out. Now I didn't want to bring it up and risk them barring my window.

"Sal negra is a miracle," I replied with a shrug, leaving the topic of Salvación behind.

Mamá sighed as if she knew secrets hidden behind my tongue, as if I were a constant disappointment and she couldn't understand why I'd brought this whole other bad on top our family—like we didn't have enough to worry about with the impending arrival of the Yankees.

I thought she wouldn't bring it up, but I was wrong.

"Te dije to stop getting into trouble." The way her words came out, it was as if they pained her. "El Demonio is among us now, and it's more important than ever for our family to stay safe and united. We didn't survive the trip from Sonora just to die. I won't lose you or your brother to something you can control." She said *you*, specifically talking about me, like she was blaming me for endangering my brother, and he wasn't responsible for his own choices.

I was suddenly unsure if she kept herself busy with worry about the woman or because she was frustrated with me.

"He is the third man we drove out of Coloma in two weeks," I said, pulling the pouch filled with sal negra from the pocket of my gown, needing her to understand why I would never stop. "Each one more dangerous than the last."

I had done the right thing: what she and Papá had failed

to do. And now we had our sal negra and didn't have to worry about the blond man.

She took the pouch with a slight quirk at her lips. She needed the sal to feel better after a rough night. The sal could heal injuries, but it didn't prevent new ones. She was always in pain from working with the rough material. She quickly opened the sack, taking a pinch of the sal and sighing as she tasted it.

"Just being near the woman, I felt something terrible happening inside my body. Como un hueco, an emptiness I don't even know how to describe."

I chortled. "You're talking about it like the tinge of her skin was alive."

She paused, studying my face, then waved the conversation away. "Ya no te preocupes. The sal negra will do its job like it always does."

She quickly put her finger in the sal again, then licked it clean. In a mere moment, she relaxed. Her posture improved. Her eyes brightened. She breathed in.

"It's good not to have to worry about that man anymore—" she started.

"More will come, though," Víctor said, appearing out of nowhere and cutting into the conversation. I might not have been able to sneak up on Víctor, but it was only because he moved like the wind—silent and hidden in plain sight.

"Of course they will," Papá chimed in, entering the kitchen. He'd been outside already. Perhaps watching the house? His hair looked like he'd been swimming en el río the way he often did when he needed to clear his mind, the way he did when troubled and only the cold mountain water could settle him.

I rose and practically ran to him. Where Mamá was somewhat derisive toward me, Papá had always loved me more than he loved Víctor. Now he took me in his big arms and twirled me around, exactly the same way he'd done when I was a little girl in pigtails.

"We'll keep our heads down, remember our mission," Mamá said as she worked on flattening a tortilla in between her hands, tossing it gently to stretch out the masa as she talked. "We use the sal negra to help those in need. The sal is a miracle not to be misused. This has been our way since we arrived at Coloma."

She didn't bring up her own papá—the fact that he was planning to make a killing on the sal negra. I didn't bring it up. Neither did Papá or Víctor.

The four of us, we had our own plans for the sal negra.

While the men Papá had hired mined the sal negra for Abuelo, Papá and Víctor, and one of Papá's closest friends, Beto, did it for our own stash. Every week, we sent wagons back to Sonora, laden with the sal for both Abuelo and us.

It was ours to use to help the poor in Sonora. And this was the only thing that gave me hope Mamá would one day leave Coloma. I hoped that if she knew she could continue to do her sacred work at home, she'd be okay with leaving the sal negra claim.

Papá set me down and got into a fighting stance. We'd always been this way, practicing sparring whenever we could. He pretended to have a sword in his hand, got his feet into position, and danced along the floor, jabbing here and there, attacks I dodged fluidly, of course. We laughed and continued until I caught Víctor staring at us with something like jealousy in his expression. It made my cheeks burn. I knew that sometimes my brother felt about Papá the way I felt about Mamá—unappreciated.

"I'm tired," I told Papá, who grinned and nodded.

"It's been a few tiring days."

"It's been a few hellish days," Víctor muttered, moving to Mamá's side.

Mamá kissed Víctor's forehead before saying, "We knew this endeavor wouldn't be easy, that mining for sal negra would come with perils—from the mines themselves threatening to bury us to the people who have taken over Alta California showing up to try to take the claim from us. And there are still plenty of dangers; we saw that in the Yankee yesterday. But we can overcome our fear."

The only fear we all seemed to share was that mining sal negra would somehow cause the death of people we loved.

"At some point, we might have to stop mining," Víctor responded. Mamá froze. Papá and I waited for the eruption. "What's in the ground belongs to the earth and the earth alone. It doesn't belong to us. We didn't create the sal; we don't even know where it came from—"

"A miracle needs no explanation," Mamá murmured in a way that implied Víctor was being blasphemous, almost as if he'd stabbed her through the heart. She expected things like that from me, but not from Víctor, her golden boy.

"You need a break," I said, coming to Víctor's aid. "You're always so tired. We've sent enough sal negra home to last us a few years."

"I signed up for this. I made a promise to the spirits when I answered the call. I am doing what must be done for the good of the people of México."

But we weren't in México anymore. Not since the Treaty of Guadalupe Hidalgo had been signed, and it was only a matter of time before the new owners came knocking on our door for our abuelo's claim.

I took Mamá's hands in mine and turned them over so she could look at her palms. The sal might have healed her, but there were still small marks where sand had dug into her skin—scars that would never fade.

The only way I would ever quit being Salvación was if Mamá gave up her calling and we went home to our hacienda, to the pampered life we had before and to my tutors and teachers and other girls.

"You signed up for this?"

She pulled her hands away, taking a step toward Víctor as if she needed protection from me. "Sometimes doing what's right takes sacrifices."

"You're working yourself to death. You might be okay with that, but I'm not. And neither are Papá and Víctor. It's the reason—" I didn't finish my sentence, my throat squeezing shut. I didn't want to bring up Salvación. But I'd become Salvación *for her*. I did everything just to keep *her* safe.

Mamá asked Papá, "What do you think about all of this?"

He responded by grabbing a tortilla right off the comal, caliente and everything, and stuffing it in his mouth. He never wanted to argue with Mamá, even when he knew I was right.

"You're going to burn your throat," I scolded. "Te van a salir ampollas."

He sighed roughly, spat out the hot tortilla into his hand, then replied, "I agree with Loli and Víctor."

Mamá crossed her arms, her disappointment in Papá showing in her eyes.

He stood straighter. "What I mean is, I think that we need to leave before something truly terrible happens. Spend a week mining day in and day out, then take what we find y vámonos. It's too dangerous here now that this land belongs to the Yankees."

The woman moaned then, cutting through the family conversation.

We all turned her way.

"We came here to help people," Mamá said, eyes on her charge. "As long as Coloma exists, I'll be here doing just that."

Her words quelled our conversation, made our words pointless. Víctor and I exchanged a look. Just last night he'd told me he wouldn't be assisting Salvación anymore. Could I protect Coloma and Mamá's work alone? The thought made me tired, and exhaustion made me want to simply go back to my room and to sleep.

"Loli, I need you to go into town and get some herbs from Luisa. Rapido, por favor," Mamá said. "Let's see if a good tea will coax the woman awake."

I didn't spend another word arguing my point. The woman's health, and all the answers that came with it, were too important. I went to my room and changed quickly, putting on the dress that bothered me the least and high-heeled boots I dreaded.

"I'll go with you," Víctor said, grabbing his hat by the front door and following me out of the house when I was ready.

The town was abuzz when Víctor and I arrived. Every group we passed was talking about how the man who caused the commotion yesterday had spent all day at the cantina and then went missing even after paying for a month's stay at an inn.

"I bet it was Salvación," one man said to another. "El Ángel de Coloma to the rescue once again."

The other man scoffed. "I don't believe that one woman could scare away a man like him, who shot four men and threatened the La Peña family all in one day. Doesn't make much sense to me."

The other man waved his hand. "Salvación is invincible. No sabes nada."

Víctor hit my arm softly with the back of his hand, calling my attention back to him. When we were far enough from earshot of the men, my brother said, "You shouldn't show that you care about Salvación."

I shrugged, focused on making sure my boots didn't get stuck in the mud. I hated to be in these heels and my dress: I couldn't walk as fast in them or get close enough to eavesdrop on people without hitting them with my skirt.

When we entered La Magnolia, Luisa's shop, it was warm inside. She always had a fire going with wood the men collected and exchanged for her famous cured meats. Merchandise was piled on shelves, and the middle of the room was relatively clear, allowing lots of people to come inside at once. Today there were only two men admiring the mining gear, and my brother and I went up to the counter without having to wait.

"Hola, doña Luisa," I said, walking into Luisa's bony out-stretched arms as she walked out from behind the counter. As always, she wore an elaborate dress decorated with pearls. Her high-heeled shoes were a favorite with young women. I loved that she never seemed to look her age, even as she was all wisdom.

She gave me a long hug, then pulled Víctor in for one so tight he couldn't talk through it.

Doña Luisa was one of a very few women in Coloma, and we had known her since our days on the road. We'd been in the same caravan, along with her husband, who died en route to Alta California. After burying the husband, Papá took Luisa into our group for the remainder of the expedition, and he and Beto protected her. Now Luisa owned and ran this successful shop, making money supplying the miners, gaining a reputation for her meats and cheeses. She was an old woman whom everyone loved, and just that would have been enough to make her famous in these parts.

Mamá had taught Luisa how to make a medicinal tea with sal negra, which many miners drank regularly, always fighting to restore their exhausted bodies. My mother also taught her which beneficial plants to harvest, the proper mix for brewing herbs. In return, doña Luisa often served us hot tea, of which she always had a fresh pot.

Sometimes I'd see Luisa foraging at first light in the prairie alongside the river. She looked beautiful among the bees and butterflies that flew over the plains.

In the shop, she seemed as tired as Mamá. The only difference was that Luisa's eyes tended to smile, while Mamá almost never smiled, not even with her eyes.

"Hola, Loli, Víctor, how is your mamá doing?"

"She's fine," I said, looking around the shop. There were rows of mining gear set across tables around the room. Axes, leather gloves, and hats hung from hooks on the walls. Near the register, there were also dried goods like beans in massive sacks half as tall as me.

"Did you hear about what Salvación did?" she asked, grinning.

Sometimes I thought Luisa knew all about my secret since Salvación was one of our favorite topics of conversation. But if she did know I was Salvación, she never let on.

"Seems like everyone is talking about it. Can't say I'm sorry about that man disappearing. What he did was outrageous. Coloma owes your mamá—she sacrifices so much for us."

How interesting that someone outside the family saw it too. There were a lot of people who expected someone like Mamá to do what she was doing and not complain, because that was a woman's role. But she was certainly making sacrifices, even some she didn't quite understand. One day I'd probably be married off and leave the family, and our relationship would never have amounted to anything. I might never even see her after the wedding. The idea soured my mouth.

I knew girls back in Sonora whose mothers seemed to love them dearly and think of them as their whole world. I might have wanted to count Mamá among them before we arrived in Coloma. But Mamá's calling had utterly consumed her, and here I was, same as ever. I'd never come first again, or even second to Víctor.

"She is amazing," I murmured—amazing at everything except being my mamá.

It wasn't like she hit me, as other mothers did to their children. She hadn't ever hurt me physically. And it wasn't like she'd sold me away to be married. But sometimes I saw her with Víctor, how she kissed his forehead or his hand, how he was the one person she did really smile with, and . . . I didn't know. Maybe that was why I'd become Salvación, really, to gain her approval again, her acceptance, or a spot in her heart. Only I had driven her further away. Now all I had left was Salvación, the way Mamá had her sal negra.

"I need yerba buena tea and the usual," I said as Víctor occupied himself with Luisa's newest inventory of pistols and revolvers, muskets and rifles. I rolled my eyes at him, then realized that maybe we needed more of those. Or could my sword suffice?

I still had the man's heirloom revolver, hidden in my room. Did we need greater firepower? And why did I have the sense we needed to prepare for something more?

Luisa nodded and dug around her store for a while as she talked more about Salvación. She filled two large jugs with tea and passed them over to me. Then she handed me some matches, two wax candles, and ammunition—the bullets Papá usually used to hunt the game that he then brought back to Luisa to trim and smoke.

"Gracias," Víctor said, putting the ammunition in his pocket as he approached. "I also want this." He set a two-barrel musket in front of Luisa. It was the kind of weapon that wasn't used to kill deer or other game in this area. This weapon killed men at close range.

I waited for Luisa to ask us what was going on. What would Víctor possibly need a gun like that for? But she didn't.

Instead, she said, "That one's on the house," and gave Víctor a slight nod of understanding.

Before I asked, he also took the tin jugs from me because they were heavy, while I grabbed matches and candles since I didn't want to alarm doña Luisa, though I knew Mamá didn't really want them.

She'd wanted the ammunition.

As we were walking out, Luisa said, "Loli, Víctor, both of you be careful out there. Things seem to be getting more dangerous."

Again, I was never sure if Luisa was onto me or not, but I grinned, nodded, and continued home, hoping that by the time we got there, the woman would already be awake. Whatever happened, if we did end up leaving Coloma, *when* we left, I needed to be sure that Luisa was going with us.

When we arrived back home, a man had just tied his horse to the hitching post and was approaching the front porch.

Víctor and I exchanged a glance, got off our own horses, hitched them, and raced toward the house. Beto, Papá's friend and right-hand man, came around la casita only when things went wrong. I wondered what had happened now and why life couldn't slow down.

The whole way here from Sonora had felt precarious, and we were never sure when the next danger would arise. I'd been naive to think that once we got here, things would be different. So far Coloma had meant more of the same. There were times back in Sonora when I'd hoped to enjoy freedom and fun, but not like this. I never knew how tiring and stressful the life of a vigilante was, but I was learning all about that now.

"What happened?" asked Papá, ignoring us, his full attention on Beto, who had stepped onto the porch.

Mamá appeared in the front doorway. We made eye contact, but I couldn't read her expression.

Beto held his black sombrero in front of him, shifted it in his hands. He didn't even say buenos días, which meant he didn't think it was going to be a good day at all. "Well, I think you'd better get to el centro, fast. There's word of a large caravan approaching, perhaps not friendly."

Papá turned first to Mamá, standing behind him. Her tired bloodshot eyes told me she never did get any rest. We wouldn't have answers to any of our questions until the woman woke up. If she ever did.

"Go investigate," she said.

Papá sighed deeply, as if he'd been hoping she'd tell him to stay home.

I went back to my horse, unhitched the satchels of goods from town, returned to the group, and passed the bags over to Víctor, who gave me a quizzical look.

"I'll join you," I said to Papá.

He took one look at me and must have seen the sheer determination in my eyes; he didn't argue. "I'm letting you come only because I need you to ride back here and tell your mamá if something goes wrong."

I nodded.

Mamá came out of the doorway and kissed my cheek. It was a rare gesture, especially when we'd been in the middle of a disagreement.

The tightness I'd felt in my heart for the past two days was unsettling. First the man who ran off with our sal negra, then the woman unconscious in our home, now the alarming caravan. What in sal negra was happening?

I hugged Mamá tight even as I struggled to breathe.

When I passed Víctor, I whispered, "Take care of her."

"I always do," he said. "Take care of Papá."

Papá and Beto were already a quarter of a mile away. I

jumped back on my horse and clicked my tongue twice, urging Carisma to go fast, to catch up.

On the way to town, we had to pass our claim on the outskirts of the town center, a half mile from our casita, which was the house closest to the river. We rode past the glade where Mamá healed the sick. The line there seemed to have doubled overnight. I'd almost forgotten that there were others waiting to be healed, waiting and surely disappointed that Mamá wasn't at her station yet. They seemed to brighten as we approached. More than one face fell as we rode past them without stopping. The snakes in my stomach recoiled.

We kept going, passing doña Luisa's store. Even though I'd just been there, a different feeling suffused the air—not a chill necessarily, yet more than static.

Beto dismounted, took his horse's reins, and walked over to the steps of an inn, where a man whose face looked as if he'd seen an army of ghosts stood waiting. I recognized him as one of the men who helped take our haul of sal negra back to Sonora. He worked for Papá, not Abuelito.

"Tell them what you saw, Manuel," Beto prompted.

Manuel focused on us for the first time. "There are maybe a hundred men coming this way. They have horses and guns. Saw them dragging animals—dead animals and live ones—behind them. Rode all night long to make it here to deliver the news in time."

"Which way?" Papá asked.

"Across the river, beyond the ridge." Manuel pointed in the direction that I had sent the blond man; the unconscious woman had come from that way as well. Nothing good seemed to come from there.

The string of bad omens sent shivers down my arms. I approached and whispered to Papá, "I wonder if they're looking for her?"

"Who?" Beto asked.

Papá shook his head. "No one. Let's see what's going on. We need to meet them at the bridge before they get into town, or we might not be able to push them back if they're not friendly. We do what we usually do when groups arrive: see what they want and then check them for disease if we can welcome them into town."

"And what if they aim to shoot us and take the sal negra?" I asked. "Is it wise to meet them out in the open? Should we draw them in, take the high ground, attack them from the mountains?"

Beto seemed surprised that I was arguing with Papá. Even Beto, Papá's greatest friend and ally in Coloma, knew me as a helpless señorita. I was as good as Papá with a sword, and I wanted the men to listen to me, to heed what I was saying not as Loli but as Salvación: the Angel of Coloma. I wasn't dressed like Salvación, though, so I was just Lola de La Peña.

Papá grunted. "No. We don't know if this is an enemy or a friend—"

"It's fifty men." The people who had arrived here before, they'd come in smaller groups: five, sometimes two or three. Fifty uninvited men was an army.

"And if that's the case, we'll have bigger troubles. All two hundred souls in town would die if they were to attack. We speak to them first, see what they want, then act. Even if they wanted the sal negra, I wouldn't risk your life or Mamá's for it."

"Tell that to Mamá," I replied, taking Papá's forearm.

He patted my hand as he liked to do when he didn't agree with me. "Mamá feels the same way. Stay here and let me do my job."

Papá led his horse away, Beto following. Neither of them gave me a second glance as they trotted toward a gathering of men on horseback. There were only about twenty horses in town, and it seemed like they were all collected in front of the cantina.

The horses kicked up dust, clouding the town much like my thoughts were clouded. I had a choice: go home or keep going. Once the dust settled, I whispered in Carisma's ear, "Vamos, amor," and chased after Papá and Beto, my cheeks burning with embarrassment.

When I caught up to our riders, a few of the men glared at me. I glared right back, unafraid. "She shouldn't be here," said one, his tone condescending.

I was about to respond when Papá spoke. "She stays." Then, "By my side at all times, ¿entiendes?"

I nodded, feeling the men's eyes on me, taking me for a weak girl, someone worth less than they. I hated it. I wasn't weak—and I wasn't wrong to trust my intuition. A caravan of men was not good news.

At the bridge, Papá at least proved that he sometimes listened to me.

"I don't want to be so close to town!" he shouted at the men behind him. "We'll meet them in the field, a little farther away."

I felt exposed out here in the open, though, and thought we should move into the mountains, stop them before they neared the town. We could surprise them from where Víctor liked to perch. Even if I said something, the men at Papá's side and Papá himself wouldn't listen to me.

When we got to the spot where the woman had fallen off her horse, the dry grass and dirt were noticeably altered. They were black, as if scorched by fire. They seemed stained like the woman's fingers were.

Upon the horizon, the grass before us was endless, tall stalks swaying in the soft summer breeze, the hills hiding whatever was behind. I wished everyone else would stay away and it would just be us and sal negra and magia, and not a care in the world. Especially during the day, when the sky was an endless blue and there wasn't a cloud in sight, we were in paradise. But beyond the ever-beautiful day today was the caravan.

We waited for minutes, staring out into the rolling green grass, then for what felt like an hour, during which time the men grew restless and unfocused while I kept my gaze straight ahead.

A shimmer and the lifting of dust on the horizon gave the caravan's approach away. The first thing I noticed was how all rode on horses or wagons, a whole line of them. I swallowed the frog in my throat. Usually, horses meant one of two things: riders who were wealthy or riders planning on fighting. Perhaps Papá was right. Trying to fight them would only get us all killed. Their horses were tall and strong, muscled differently than ours. I could tell because of the animals' stature in comparison to their riders.

But what if we chose not to put up a fight and they really were here for the sal negra? What if they tried to take it away from us? How would we stop them? Would it be safer to simply let it go?

Mamá wouldn't ever let it go, though, and protecting the sal negra was protecting her.

"You think it'll be a gunfight?" Beto asked, resting his hand on the grip of the revolver at his waist. The thought made me feel unsteady, and Carisma swayed with my uncertainty.

"I don't know," Papá replied thoughtfully. I had no doubt he'd been up all night even after the rest of us dozed off, watching over us as he'd done all the way to Coloma. Papá was a good fighter, a great shot. But a lack of sleep wasn't a good way to start any type of fight.

Still, the caravan wasn't the only thing that bothered me. I was examining more scorched earth below the hooves of our horses when Papá's hand landed on my shoulder.

"I want you to go back to Mamá, tell Víctor to get his rifle ready," he said. "Ready your sword as well. I don't know what these people want, but we need to be ready to defend the sal negra."

"What about the line? Those waiting to be healed?" If something bad was coming, we needed to make sure everyone in Coloma was safe first.

Papá blanched as if he hadn't given a single thought to them. He likely hadn't. His worries lay with Mamá, Víctor . . . me.

"Gather them up and take them to la casa." To Beto, he added, "Go with Loli and help round up some men to guard the house."

Beto tipped his sombrero to us both in acknowledgment. I nodded once and rode off with the wind, my hair flowing behind me in the summer breeze.

"Más rapido, Carisma," I coaxed my horse, feeling the need to hurry ever present.

"I'll gather the men," Beto said when we arrived back in town, sliding off his horse. Like the man who stole the sal negra from us, Beto was a natural on horseback. He didn't even need to lead his horse anywhere; his horse followed close behind him as he approached a burly man who seemed like he could hold his own in a fist- or gunfight alike.

Meanwhile, I rushed to the waiting line of people. Their eyes lit up, and as I scanned their faces, I knew that I couldn't let them in on what was happening. I couldn't take away an ounce of hope. Sometimes that was all people had to hold on to. Though there was also the fact that I had never been a liar. I might hide the fact I was Salvación, sure, but I'd never openly lied about anything.

I had to do it now.

"¡Hola, todos! Thank you so much for your patience," I started before catching my breath, trying to explain everything while explaining nothing at all. "So . . . change of plans! We're actually going to be healing people en mi casita. Mi mamá hurt her foot, so she can't come out here today. We'll go to her, though."

Those at the front of the line exchanged worried glances. Mamá didn't have a hurt foot. It didn't even make sense considering that sal negra could heal it easily. But no one in line pointed out the absurdity of what I'd said.

A tall woman approached me. She didn't look sick or injured, and I supposed she must have come with someone in line. "I can help you," she said.

I wanted to hug her but kept myself composed. "Thank you," I said simply. "Anyone who can't walk, I'll take you on my horse." Some of the people in line seemed to relax at the words. They'd already been through so much to get here. It wasn't fair to ask them to go farther, but it was what we needed to do.

Many faces remained afraid and tired, and I knew I was putting their lives in danger by asking them all to move, to wait a little longer, especially without much of an explanation. If nothing else, Mamá could heal a dozen people by the time the caravan arrived at our location—if it came to that.

The woman helped me, and together, we moved the six dozen folks from where the line usually was to my home.

Víctor soon approached, flagging me over. "What's going on? What happened?"

"Ask me later," I said, heart racing. "First help me get everyone inside, safe. Tell Ma."

He left without arguing after a moment of searching my face.

I led a woman with a broken arm inside. She winced with every step up the porch but was brave, steadfast. She was the first I brought to Mamá, who was already waiting at the couch with tea and salve.

I didn't see the sleeping woman anywhere. "Is she—?"

"No," Mamá answered curtly, then went to work.

I left to help others along with Víctor. Mamá didn't speak to me again.

She had on that look she got when she didn't want to be bothered.

"Loli, a little help here," Víctor said, coming out with half a dozen cups of water in a cart after we'd helped the last few people inside the house.

Our casita was overcrowded and noisy as everyone gossiped among themselves. There were injured people on the floor, groaning in pain, more on the few chairs we had. I could barely walk around them. The room smelled like blood, but something else too. Water boiling in the kitchen made it warm inside, and it gave off the smell of sal negra. Knowing that we had magia on our side was the only thing that helped my uneasiness.

I took half the cups Víctor carried and tiptoed my way around, following him to Mamá's side.

She added a spoonful of sal negra into every glass of hot water. "We need to act fast, heal these people in case they need to run."

Víctor and I nodded and took our glasses, handing them out, helping heal everyone in the house as quickly as we could.

Afterward, while those in the house rejoiced, I stood stuck, not knowing what I should really do. Should I go back to Papá? Should I stay here and wait to see how things played out?

Several people took their leave, giving Mamá hugs and thanks before they started their journey home, wanting to waste no time.

"Should we tell them to wait until morning?" Víctor asked me.

"No," I replied. "It's dangerous here now."

Beto arrived then with the men he'd wrangled. The weight of having to protect the house lessened, and I felt like I could finally take a full breath. Only I was still worried for Papá. I didn't want to leave him alone. I waited until Mamá was turned around, then slipped out the front door.

"I should go with Papá," Víctor called after me as I headed toward Carisma. Part of me knew that Víctor being at Papá's side was what society said was the natural order of things. Víctor would go to battle if need be. Meanwhile, I should stay with Mamá, forget about a brewing war that for all I knew Salvación or the woman in our home had played a part in starting, sit in some hiding place, and wait until I knew if I'd live another day.

But that just wasn't us.

"No," I said firmly. "I need to be there." I placed my hand on his shoulder. I tried to soften the fact that I wasn't really giving him an option. "And Mamá needs the protection of the best shot in all of Coloma. Aim true if it comes to it, Víctor."

In a way, Víctor had always been brave. He didn't go guns blazing into battle. Not like Papá and Mamá and me. But he would always be there when needed.

Víctor nodded, deep in thought, scrunching his features in the way he did when he was trying to weigh my words. He had to be considering if staying behind was worth losing face with Papá, who already seemed to favor me.

Then he pulled two things from behind him. One was my sword, which I'd almost forgotten. He hadn't planned on leaving me behind, then, as I'd done to him. The other was a pouch of sal negra the size of the one my father gave to the man yesterday.

"Don't do anything that might get you killed," he finally said. "At the first sign of real danger, ride away. Forget everything and make sure you stay safe. This isn't one man you're dealing with. This sounds like an army."

I grinned, taking the items and setting them into place. "That's what I told Papá." Then after a pause, "Salvación would never leave, though. You should know this."

"You can't hide behind your mask forever, Loli. I know you think you can, but one day you'll need to make a choice. And I hope you choose the path that means you get to live the long, beautiful life you deserve, hermana mía."

I shrugged to wind down the conversation, making my choice more than obvious. I'd lived life as Lola de La Peña. It was filled with dresses and makeup and gossip, a life of bliss

SALVACIÓN · 69

for some girls. But having him say this to me made me realize that although we were planning to leave . . . I wasn't sure that was what I wanted anymore. I had transformed into someone I wasn't sure could be changed back.

"Lola de La Peña wouldn't ever leave either," I told him. He read the sincerity in my words and gave a small chuckle, lips quirking on one side. I kissed Víctor on the cheek and tipped his sombrero. We laughed. "Te quiero, big brother," I added, meaning the words with all my heart.

"Love you, too, Loli," he said.

There wasn't enough time to go inside and say goodbye to Mamá. I unhitched and mounted Carisma, goading my horse on to meet Papá and the others where I had left them at the outskirts of town . . . where the woman fell off her horse, where the Yankee rode away. Had all of that really happened only yesterday? My whole being felt exhausted.

To my sheer horror, the men in the caravan were now in sight. Fifty strong men with horses and guns and wagons that carried who knows what could easily take over Coloma. There were three riders up front. They broke away from the group, the rest of whom seemed to fetch up except for one of the wagons, which hurried behind the three horsemen.

I glanced at Papá, worried about him, but if he was afraid, his stern face and loose shoulders didn't show it. I didn't understand how he could mask his fear so easily. But then again, he'd been in the war. He knew what a battle looked like; perhaps he didn't think there was a concern here at all.

They seemed to be Mexican, at least, which was a relief. I'd been expecting Yankees, the man to come for the heirloom weapon and take revenge. The men weren't bandidos either. Two of them had a few more gray hairs than Papá and well-kept beards. The third, a boy about my age, wore a wide-brimmed sombrero like the older men, but his skin was golden underneath. He'd had his share of sun compared with the other two, despite being much younger. All wore the same outfit, like an army uniform: sombreros and vests in an unusual blood red; white button-down shirts; black riding boots, shined and perfectly clean as if they hadn't just traveled across a harsh Alta California landscape.

Their clothing was too pristine for any of this to be real, and I considered that I might be dreaming. When we arrived at Coloma, our party had had to spend a whole three days washing our clothes clean of grime and dirt and blood. But these men's clothes didn't seem like they had seen a single hard day on the road.

Where had they come from? "Who are they?" I asked, wondering if perhaps we'd been wrong and Papá and Mamá did know the men from back home.

"No sé. I have no idea, Loli," Papá replied, the bridge of his nose scrunched up as it was whenever things weren't going his way. "You have sal negra on you?"

I patted the pouch at my waist. "Siempre."

Papá said, "Good."

I touched the sal negra again just to feel it near me as the three men came closer and closer until they were upon us. I didn't focus on the man leading the other two, but on the boy to the right who was around my age.

He was handsome, much too handsome, with sharp brown eyes and strong arms and a round face. He led his horse with ease, and you could see in the posture of his horse that it trusted its rider. I couldn't say the same of the other two men. I might immediately have fallen in love, had the boy not stared back at me with such distrust, as if I'd personally caused him injury. The man who seemed to direct the others had gray hair and an easy smile. He dismounted, gave the reins of his horse to the boy, then approached us.

"Are you the leader here?" the man asked, his eyes drawing in on Papá, who nodded once.

When the man walked forward, we all moved back and reached toward our weapons, but he only stretched his hand out to Papá. The hilt of my sword at my back felt cold, my hands clammy with anticipation.

"Brother. Mi hermano," he continued, which seemed to relax Papá's hold on his pistol grip. His use of familial words didn't make me feel any better. Víctor and I, as Salvación, had been protecting Coloma for months. *We* were siblings. To call someone a brother whom you didn't know—it felt like a trick of some kind.

But the stranger had chosen his words wisely: Papá was not one for needless confrontation. "My name is Damián Hernández. And I'm the man who has come to you—and to all your people—with the proposition of a lifetime, one that aims to make Alta California a free state."

Papá's face was unreadable, as was señor Hernández's. I was unsure what either of them would say next.

Papá's eyes were downcast. He was too tired to be alert. Mining for sal negra was backbreaking work, and even our wealth back in México hadn't protected us from having to do it ourselves. That was what he'd given up, a life of luxury for a life of this, all for his love of Mamá. When we left Sonora,

I'd thought it was romantic. Now I knew that Papá did it out of his duty to Mamá, who had gone as far as saying that she would be leaving with or without us.

I wasn't sure Papá had ever wanted to be in Coloma, but I did know that he was terrified of what the Treaty of Guadalupe Hidalgo meant for Alta California, when his one goal was to keep Mamá safe throughout all of this.

Hernández was very different from Papá, and I wondered what his goal was. He was Papá's age or older, but his face wasn't withered away by life. It was smooth and relaxed. He wore good riding pants and a fine shirt made of bleached cotton, both expensive. His horse's saddle was somewhat new and made of high-quality leather adorned in lavish rose designs. His horse was strong. At least a foot taller than Papá's horse, or any of the others in Coloma.

I didn't see any women at all among their group—or children either. The boy was the youngest. The rest were all grown men Papá's age. They also wore fine clothing, but their backs were hunched over from riding too much, and their faces were hard. It was obvious they'd seen better days no matter what they wore, unlike the men at the front. Did any of them have families? If they didn't, it only made them more dangerous. They had nothing to live for but their own desires and greed. It would make them reckless.

"And we brought a gift to show our good intentions!" Hernández said, signaling to the rider of the wagon. It approached, and Hernández opened the back flap of tarpaulin, letting us look inside.

It was food—a thousand pounds of meat, more food all at

once than we'd seen in a long time. It could feed several families for a whole year. Papá licked his lips, taking it in.

I wasn't sure what to think. On the surface, it seemed like a peace offering to get in our good graces. But the act didn't sit right with me. Perhaps I was being too judgmental. Perhaps it was a sincere offering.

Yet nothing good ever came to us from the direction these strangers had come, and the twisting in my belly still wouldn't go away. I didn't want their meat and preferred that they leave.

Papá sighed, then shook the man's hand. I knew he might not have a better choice, yet it still felt like he had given up a part of himself when he did. With that handshake, he was welcoming Hernández as a guest instead of marking him as a threat.

"We're hoping that you might allow us to stay in Coloma for a short time. Perhaps I can tell you about my plan, and we could find a way to work together to keep this beautiful land a part of our permanent history."

I could see the wheels in Papá's brain whirring in the way he gave a small scoff, the way he opened his eyes and shook his head. I wasn't surprised when he spoke and didn't say what I wanted him to say. Papá was like me: he'd always put whatever Mamá needed or wanted first.

"You and your men are welcome in Coloma—"

"Papá—" I interjected, going closer to his side.

He put a hand up to stop me. Señor Hernández lifted an eyebrow, examining me, but didn't say anything, as if he wasn't in the mood to deal with someone he likely saw as una niña.

"—as long as you follow our rules for a safe stay," Papá

continued. "There will be no violence. Your men will keep their weapons in their belts; they will not incite any fights or they will be asked to leave. We'll also need to do a physical examination for any type of illnesses any of them might be carrying. I hope you understand."

Hernández nodded, smirked smugly as if he was used to getting his way. "That's all fine, hermano." He whistled low. The boy rode closer to him, eyes never leaving mine. Somehow the boy's horse still walked where he wanted it to go, ending up at Hernández's side.

"Spread the word to the men: we've found our next place to stay."

The boy tipped his hat and rode off.

This was a different kind of line than the people who came to Mamá for a miracle, but one that also trailed off into the horizon. These were soldiers, I didn't have a doubt about it, coming to us for help—or for something else I wasn't entirely certain of. But as I watched the boy ride off, I fought between wanting to see his face at a closer distance and never wanting to see it again.

CHAPTER 5

I gritted my teeth on the ride back to town. We should have sent Hernández and his army away. Even if they weren't here for sal negra, it was too dangerous to let them stay. Even if they didn't know about the healing salt yet, it would be impossible to keep it a secret. Forcing them to move on was what Salvación would have done. But Papá had invited them; perhaps the meat was too tempting to say no to. Or he was taking an interest in what the man was offering: Alta California for México? Another war?

Papá and Hernández were already deep in conversation, like old friends, leading us. I rode behind them, thoughts afire. Señor Hernández looked back to me once—or so I thought, but he was just looking at the boy, who had his horse right behind mine, the rest of the men, theirs and ours, following in tow, the wagons clicking along at the tail end.

I didn't like that the boy was staring at the back of my head, but at least he didn't see my glare or how unhappy I was made by all of this.

The invitation to stay wasn't cowardice on Papá's part. I didn't have a name for it.

We headed to a courtyard at the center of town meant as an open area for celebrations. Papel picado hung from pillars, making it the most colorful place in town. So far, the center hadn't been used much, not when the only time we ever had a party was when a new deposit of sal negra was found in the mines and Abuelo gave the men bonuses. I didn't miss Sonora, but I did miss how our rancho in Sonora was always filled with color and laughter. Everything here was new—which meant raw, unrefined. Everything here was hard. The papel picado was a reminder that we were here only for the sal negra, magia, and any other joy in life had become irrelevant.

Beto swept his eyes from Hernández to Papá, as if waiting for a signal to draw his weapons. But Papá had fought in the war and came out of it less keen on fighting. He didn't talk about his experience, but sometimes he would have nightmares. Sometimes I heard him crying out at night. Avoiding a confrontation made sense if I thought about who Papá had been and who he was now.

There was no sign of sicknesses among Hernández's men, who joked around and whispered together. I didn't spot the symptoms of cholera or dysentery or typhoid fever. They seemed like men who had the strength to fight, with knives tucked into tough leather boots that looked like they could trample, Colt revolvers at their sides. All the men were too clean and too well-dressed. Coloma was a place filled with people whose fingers were stained by sal negra, faces covered with dirt. Our people toiled countless hours a day for a dream of riches—Abuelo's promise to them. Were these men coming to take this all away, now that the hardest work was done? We had our own salt reserve waiting for us back in Sonora, but what about everyone else?

I grew more uneasy as the boy continued to stare at me, his eyes boring into my very soul as if he could see all the secrets I hid away, as if he already knew I was the biggest threat to them all. It made something swirl in my blood, but it also made me feel seen in a way I normally wasn't.

It was my job to protect this place, the people's interests, Abuelo's promise to them, as much as it was my job to protect Mamá. Even riding among the men of Coloma, I felt alone in this mission.

It was odd to realize that I didn't fully trust Papá as I had my entire life. He'd given me a choice, after all, to stay in Sonora, managing the household instead of leaving it to our caretakers. I'd chosen to follow Papá and Víctor. Until we arrived in Coloma, I hadn't believed Mamá's calling was real, that she was feeling the pull of magia from hundreds of miles away, but I did think that Mamá needed the journey, needed to see it all with her own eyes before being able to wash away the idea from within herself.

Then the miracle turned out to be true.

Papá ordered food to be brought for the men. Many, although clean, appeared exhausted. Once we arrived at la plaza, the laughter ended. The men sat, and they seemed to relax, seemed to find the idea of being here freeing. They'd made it, their bodies said. And I wasn't sure they ever intended on leaving despite señor Hernández saying it was a temporary stop.

None of them was smiling anymore, not even the boy—not that I'd seen a smile bless his face yet, however that might interest me.

I stayed by Papá's side, an argument on the tip of my tongue if he tried to send me away.

"Alejandro, take the horses to the river," señor Hernández said. The boy moved, eyes still on me.

"Loli," Papá started. "Help him." He put an emphasis in the word *help*, as if he meant "watch."

My cheeks reddened, my argument melting in my mind, the words scrambling. I didn't want to be near the boy; he made me feel something strange, like butterflies of death swirling in my stomach. I wanted them to send the boy to the river by himself, except there was something about the look he gave me. He wasn't to be trusted, and the only person I trusted to watch him closely was myself.

I nodded and turned to the boy. His expression remained blank.

I patted my side, where my sal negra was safe, and below that, where I hid my pistol with a single shot on a belt on my thigh underneath my dress.

"Let's go. Vamos." I signaled with my chin in the direction of the bridge.

We each grabbed two horses, started toward the river.

Alejandro whistled, and the rest of the horses joined us. I'd never seen a more extraordinary sight—a whole herd following one boy. How had he learned to do this, and was this why he was at Hernández's side?

I stared, my mouth ajar as we rode off, the horses following Alejandro.

"Horses just like me," he said after a while, probably in response to my constant staring as we continued to ride and the horses continued to follow. He was acting like it was no big deal, but it was. Horses didn't just like anyone. You could make a horse listen to you, with enough force. I'd seen men do terrible things to break a horse. But that wasn't what Alejandro was doing. The connection that he had with horses; it couldn't be learned. It was special.

It made *him* special. The way Mamá's calling was special. No matter how many horses followed and trusted Alejandro, though, that didn't mean I should, too, not when his boss made me feel insecure.

"I see. Well, let's get this over with, I have more important things to do," I said in my most ladylike voice.

He chuckled. "Like what? Your makeup and hair? There's nothing out here to do except—"

I recalled what I look like today. Sure, I had a dress on, but I also had dark circles around my eyes, and my hair was up but messy. I wondered what Alejandro would think if he saw me really done up like a lady.

"Sometimes," I responded, cutting him off, reciprocating his obvious disdain. "It's better than whatever you are doing here, though, I'm sure."

He snorted as if sensing my test. I wanted him to give away their ill intent. Then I could easily convince Papá to kick them out of Coloma before they ever brought up the sal negra.

When we reached the river, we dismounted and let all the horses go. I'd never seen so many horses together. Another thought occurred to me then: If they stayed until winter, would we leave regardless, or would we try to stay? If we stayed, I didn't know how we were going to feed all these horses, let alone all the newcomers, even with the game they'd brought for us. Food and game would become scarce in the winter when it was difficult to travel and difficult to grow food in our gardens; shelter for so many horses, almost impossible to build. Sal negra wasn't food. It might have been magical, but what sprouted from the ground when it touched soil were blue flowers, not corn or wheat or anything that would fill the bellies of the town's suddenly inflated population. Unless there was a plan and a way to get more goods to Coloma, it'd be a tough time.

My only hope was that these men were honest when they said they were only passing through. If señor Hernández really did have a plan to make Alta California a free state, then Coloma was only one of many stops he had before making a go at it all.

I stepped toward Alejandro until we were face-to-face, eyes drawn to each other like lightning to water. "Señor Hernández really thinks he can take back Alta California?"

He shrugged and took a seat on the grass as we watched the horses. He picked at the grass, broke it apart into thin strands, and then threw those strands away.

I joined him. "I highly doubt you don't have an opinion."

He looked toward the horses drinking their fill. "I'm here to protect my employer. That's what I get paid to do."

"You mean señor Hernández isn't your father?" I'd assumed it.

Alejandro snorted again. On closer inspection, he didn't look anything like the older man, and I wasn't sure how I ever supposed the idea to be true. Alejandro was large chested while Hernández was lankier; Alejandro's cheeks were rounder, his eyes larger and a darker brown . . . so brown you could get lost in them. Alejandro's hair was almost black, where Hernández's was bronze, gleaming blond in the sunlight.

The horses came and went, nestled together. They seemed free and happy out here near the river, which was starting to be overshadowed by the mountain as the sun worked its way down. I didn't want it to get dark. I didn't want Hernández's gang to still be here when it did.

"Is your father one of his men?"

"My father is dead. My mother is dead. I'm alone. But I take care of myself. And señor Hernández gives me work, which keeps me fed and safe."

Alejandro's face grew more solemn, like he'd been struggling with the weight of that reality for a long time. I'd never been alone. I'd always had Víctor, and Mamá and Papá guiding us, raising us. Even when I couldn't stand them, even when I felt like they held me back, they were there with me, always with me.

I pitied Alejandro, but still didn't trust him—or any of the newcomers.

"We should get back soon," I said. "I have someone to protect as well."

Alejandro stared at me as if wondering why I'd been among a group of strong men, but finally nodded. I noted that he hadn't said Papá didn't need protection from his employer.

Once Carisma had her fill of the river and Alejandro's horse had, too, the two of us started toward la plaza, the horses following Alejandro the moment he headed off again.

"How'd you all get so much meat anyway?" I inquired, trying to get more information out of him.

"Just some we came across."

"Stole, you mean?" You can't stumble across things in the wildness of California.

The boy shrugged. "Is there such a thing as stealing out here?"

I gritted my teeth. "Of course there is," I replied. I didn't want to be next to him, so I fell back with the other horses, took a look at them. They were well fed. Had Hernández just found them too?

I trailed Alejandro as we approached Papá and señor Hernández. My heart began to race, eager to make sure Papá was all right.

When we arrived, the men were stripping down in a tent they'd put up in the square, and Beto was standing in the doorway, surely checking them for any sign of illnesses that were too dangerous to have in town.

"The boy's the last one." Beto pointed over to us when we approached.

Alejandro seemed uneasy at the fact he'd have to be checked as well. Perhaps they'd never had to do this. Alejandro looked to his boss, who only nodded. The boy seemed to grit his own teeth now and I almost laughed. It made me feel like we were too alike, both angry at what was happening. I knew my reasons, and I wondered about his.

The boy jumped off his horse, took off his scarf, and unbuttoned his shirt. I looked down, felt my face flush red as I fought not to look.

Papá cocked his head in the direction of our home. Hernández was looking intently at Beto and Alejandro, as if afraid that Beto might find something there. But it didn't seem like it so far. All that was underneath Alejandro's shirt seemed to be a perfectly golden torso that made me want to stay and stare.

I took Papá's hint instead and pulled Carisma back, inch by inch, until no one was really paying attention, and headed toward home, passing the horses that followed Alejandro as if they were chicks trailing a hen. I was unhappy to leave Papá behind in case he needed me. But if he'd wanted me to go, it was because he felt safe enough or wanted to keep me safe. The hoofprints as I passed by the way I'd just come seemed like a bad omen. It was strange to notice how many animals could make such large tracks and so much mess, even when Alejandro was a strange boy who could make ethereal creatures love him, but now I didn't know . . . I didn't know. Maybe they really had come for reasons other than sal negra.

The peacefulness of home was so welcome it almost made me forget about the past few days. Beyond our house ran the river; I could hear it if I stayed silent enough. I looked down at my clothes, recalling the way Alejandro had gazed at me as if to say no one who wore a dress belonged in the wilderness. Like the dress was diseased flesh. It made me realize that I'd been too hard on myself.

I didn't like wearing a dress. I preferred to wear pants, but there were lots of girls back in Sonora who had loved the gowns and the makeup and who felt at home in their bodies. There was a time when I did, too, and wanted to fit in with them—and there was nothing wrong with that. If I had confessed that I was Salvación, would Alejandro have judged me so harshly?

I reconsidered the way I judged myself when I wasn't Salvación, the girl that Mamá and Papá wanted me to be in the eyes of everyone else. That girl wasn't less kind for it; she was just a girl being a girl. I might not have liked the dress myself, but I wouldn't have been rude to anyone just for wearing one.

"You're back!" Víctor called from the porch when he saw me. He was in the middle of mixing sal negra with water for a man with a giant blistering gash on his arm, as if from a bad burn. "You-know-who is awake," he mouthed, which only made me jump off my horse and race inside.

Only I didn't get far. Mamá stopped me at the doorway. Her expression was so serious, eyes narrow, I knew at once that even though the woman was awake, that only meant more problems for us.

"What is it?"

Mamá took in a deep breath, still considering her next words. Finally she said, "The woman said she's here looking for a woman known as Salvación in Coloma. She said she'll only speak to the vigilante others have described."

My mind raced as I took in the words. Someone wanted to see *me*? Salvación me? This hadn't ever happened before, and I wasn't sure what to say or expect.

"Are you sure?" I managed. But of course she was sure. There was no way Mamá would bring up my Salvación persona lightly if she could avoid it.

"She has a portrait of Salvación, Loli, and she looks exactly like you."

I transformed into Salvación as quietly and quickly as possible, preparing to talk to the woman. Part of me was thrilled that Salvación's story had spread. Another part of me wasn't sure I'd live up to the expectations. No one except for Víctor and sometimes Mamá and Papá had seen me in my costume. What if I looked ridiculous? Without the cover of darkness, what if I was only a fool?

Still, I needed to know why the woman was here and wanted to talk to me, specifically, and what more I could do to help her. The mystery of it all was too tempting. I hadn't become Salvación for attention, but here was a stranger from somewhere else who had heard of me. I'd never felt particularly important before, always been fairly ordinary in Sonora. I kind of liked being something more. I kind of liked the idea of being valued.

I quietly exited my room and found my way to Mamá and Papá's room. The woman was seated by a fire Mamá had started. She held a blanket tightly at her shoulders and stared at the blaze as if stuck in a memory she saw playing out in the flames. The way her shoulders drooped, she seemed more tired than Mamá—but alive. Alive! My relief almost made me forget that there were other things at hand to worry about.

"I heard you wanted to talk," I said, trying to make my voice sound older. "Who are you, and why have you come searching for me?"

The woman gasped, pressed a hand above her heart, and couldn't hold back tears. Her tears couldn't hide her pale skin, her tired eyes, the lines that gave away her age, or the sunspots on her hands. Still, the sal negra had healed any blemishes and scratches on her skin.

"Eres ella. You look just like her," the woman said, having dropped the blanket and now holding up a piece of cloth. She flipped the fabric to show me a charcoal drawing someone had made of Salvación. They'd gotten my nose right, my small chin, my wide forehead. There were also features that they'd gotten so very wrong. They'd given Salvación more and longer hair, a skinnier face instead of round cheeks.

"My name is Isabela Fuentes, señora Salvación." I could tell calling me a señora didn't quite sit right with Isabela. In the daylight, my real age showed. But I was more interested in who Isabela was than what she thought of me. We'd known some members of a Fuentes family on our way here, but she didn't resemble them. Still, I couldn't stop thinking about how in the world anyone had drawn *me*. Who could it have been? We'd only sent, what, five, six people away? Or had someone else seen me, perhaps someone passing by, on one of those nights?

I didn't say anything, but waited, trying not to speak so my voice didn't give away my age.

"I have thanks to give to the two young people who found me, and the woman who healed me. I've come with a warning and a desire to help Coloma. To help you, ángel."

I had heard that twice now. One too many times for it to just be a coincidence. The woman's eyes were bleary from a lack of sleep, the usual whites of her eyes red, her posture bent, which made me believe her.

"Go on," I said. "I am listening."

"I've heard there is sal negra here. The fact I'm alive is evidence of it. But there is also sal roja in the mountainside."

Sal roja? Was that why her skin had been tinged in red?

"What does it do? And what does it all mean?"

Tears swept her up like the current of a river sweeps away a fallen leaf. She cleared her throat before saying, "Where sal negra heals, mends, makes plants flourish, makes soil fertile, sal roja is its opposite. Mi abuelita used to talk about how for everything good, there is an evil. Sal roja is sal negra's reverse.

Where sal negra is vida, sal roja is death. It ingests life and turns it into nothing." By the time she was finished speaking, she sounded more angry than sad and her tears were gone.

Death. The word alone made me sweat, made my heart speed up, my eyes narrow. "Where is your abuelita now? Where do you come from?"

She focused on the door. "Está muerta, along with everyone I ever loved, probably everyone I've ever known. There is a village a hundred miles away. We'd been hoping to build it out into a town before the Treaty of Guadalupe Hidalgo. We were just getting ready to go back home when they arrived."

Her words made my arms prickle. "And how did you escape?"

"They gave me all the sal negra that we were given. My people all chose to save me since I was the best rider still alive and they believed I had the best chance of making it here, to you."

I needed to know everything. "How much are we talking about here? What is the formula?" I asked, starting to ramble. "How much sal negra is needed to combat how much sal roja?"

"One speck of sal roja touched my body. And all our sal negra and more from the woman who lives here was used to save me."

I took a step back. A single grain of salt! It couldn't be true. But again, the woman's eyes, her look—here was someone else who could speak with her eyes, and her eyes told me that she had seen too much death, had mourned too many she loved.

I stepped forward. "What is your warning?"

"There is an evil man coming who I believe is *your* opposite. Where you are an angel, sal negra, he is a demon like sal roja."

El Demonio. Mamá talked about him all the time as if he were a living, breathing entity. The nuns who taught me back in

Sonora did too. *El Demonio is going to come and steal you away if you keep swearing. El Demonio is going to wash your mouth out with soap if you keep talking back to me. El Demonio knows when you think dark thoughts.* What were the chances that this was finally el Demonio making his way to Coloma? It brought a chill to my spine to think that there might really be something that malignant in the world. Then again, I'd never believed in magia, so maybe it was the same. I wouldn't fully believe in something demonic until I was face-to-face with it. I wasn't ready to battle something like that, though.

"A man has already arrived," I realized out loud. "With what could be called an army."

They newcomers had been so lavish, carefree, and had so much meat on them. It didn't seem natural to me, not after all the sick we'd healed, all the people who had barely made it to Coloma in one piece for the chance of a miracle. And then there was the boy, Alejandro. I picture his nose scrunched up, his eyes scanning us. What did it all mean?

"Then there is not much time. This man seeks to destroy Coloma, taking with him all the sal negra and sal roja for himself. He wants to take over all of Alta California."

"He said he wants to protect Coloma, wants Alta California to become its own sovereignty. He brought Coloma food—a lot of beef."

The woman's voice rose. "Those are lies! How do you think he came across all this food? He stole it, from my people, from countless others, I'm sure."

"Do you have proof of what you're saying? A lie slips off the tongue as easily as the truth. Especially around these parts, and folks around here, they're not going to believe you without proof."

Her face contorted, as if I'd struck her. "I nearly died trying to bring you this message. Everyone I left behind did. My town is gone. The sal roja is in Hernández's possession. And Coloma is next. Look me in the eyes, and you will see if I'm lying. I came to *you*, Salvación, because I thought you'd believe me. I thought I could trust you. Was I wrong?"

The name—his name. She spoke his name even though I had not. It was enough proof for me. The woman wasn't lying. I felt it in my gut, though I wished my gut were wrong. Her words made my stomach twist. Hernández was with Papá at this very moment. I wasn't sure what to do. Nor was I sure that Papá and Mamá would believe the woman's story.

Papá had let wolves into our den. He had let el Demonio invade our space, our home. It was like inviting in death itself. It was as Víctor had come to fear. Salvación might be up against foes that we would lose to for the first time.

But I wasn't ready to admit defeat. I never would be. Not as long as I was breathing. I stood tall as I asked, "How do I stop him?"

"With the sal negra he carries, it's practically impossible to kill or injure him. You need to make sure he doesn't get more sal roja. He has an ancient relic, an amulet, which whoever first discovered the sal must have created. It allows him to find sal roja. Destroy it and destroy his chances of waging a war over everyone in his path."

CHAPTER 6

A nger burned through my body, hot as a blazing fire. It was what I always felt when up against someone who threatened the safety of Coloma. But this time there was something else there, something new crawling underneath my skin: a hint of fear. Perhaps more than a hint.

It was from this fear that I was determined to draw my strength.

I didn't have a choice but to be strong as a galloping horse, swift as the smallest zorro; I had to outfox Hernández if not outwit him.

"How do I get the amulet?" I asked the woman, fortitude settling into my huesos. I had made up my mind in an instant: I would do what the woman said. I didn't want to imagine what might happen if I didn't stop señor Hernández.

If a single grain of sal roja could almost kill the woman, what would more of it do? Would it destroy the entire world? Would Hernández continue until all of it was under his rule?

It might have seemed like a far-fetched idea. To some, I might even have been overreacting. I could easily see Víctor telling me to wait and see what happened. Papá would want to talk, Mamá to ignore the issue altogether. But I had seen miracles over and over across the past three months. I'd always thought that something so good must have an adversary, an equally terrible thing. Here it was, and I wasn't going to give it time to breathe.

She shrugged. "I don't have a plan for retrieving the amulet. *You* were my plan." Her voice was tired, quiet, as if she still didn't feel like herself and she needed more sal negra. "Getting to you was all that kept me on my horse, Salvación. My life was spared so I could warn you. And now I can finally rest, knowing that you will help." She nodded to herself more than at me. "Puedo descansar." Tears flowed down both her cheeks.

I didn't want to imagine what evil she'd seen. I'd endured nightmarish sights on our way from Sonora to Coloma, ones I wish I could erase from memory. It wasn't fair, to live with these things, and I hoped that she found solace someday.

In my mind, I agreed: she'd done her part in this, survived to tell her story. I couldn't expect any more of her, and it wouldn't have been right to do so. She'd delivered her message, and now it was my turn to act upon it, learn what I could about señor Hernández, and stop him.

Still, if neither of us had a good plan to do it, we needed Víctor. *I* needed my brother. I wasn't ever good at figuring out things that required more planning than action. My brother and I had come up with the idea of Salvación together one night, tucked under the starry sky, looking at the moon, wondering what was out there and what it was that had made us.

We'd figure out how to stop Hernández together, just as we'd done with everyone else who came causing trouble round these parts.

When I didn't reply, Isabela settled herself on the wooden chair by the hearth again as she asked, "What will you do?"

"I'm not sure. Not yet, anyway." I glanced at the small window in the room. Back in town, señor Hernández was with Papá, who had no idea he was dancing with el Diablo.

She laughed a little. "You doubt yourself?"

I shook my head. Of course I did, but I couldn't tell her that. Not when she trusted me to stop Hernández.

Instead of calling me out for it, she said, "It means you're afraid of failing. That's a good thing. It means you'll try with all your heart, and that's all I'm asking."

"I promise I will try," I said. It was what I could offer. I wanted to run all the way to town, dressed as Salvación and everything, and warn Papá. But I couldn't go and do that. To Isabela, I added, "You still need rest. Close your eyes, sleep—this family will take good care of you. You can trust them. I'll come back soon." I pulled out a small container filled with sal negra that I kept on my Salvación disguise at all times and held it out for her. "Take some."

The woman nodded, reached out, and used her fingers to take a bit of the sal negra. She put it on her tongue and seemed to immediately relax. Before I moved on, she held out her hand to me. I took it without hesitation.

"You're everything I was expecting. Gracias, señora Salvación." If she only knew I was a señorita, would it make a difference in the way she saw me? Of course I believed it would; otherwise, I wouldn't wear a disguise.

The sentiment should have made my heart burst with joy. But her faith was a reminder of everything we stood to lose if I failed, which only made something writhe inside my veins— something hot and burning and wrong, a feeling I was growing tired of.

I left the woman to rest and headed back outside to plan my next move.

There was no time to waste, but I needed one thing before going to find Víctor.

I went to Mamá and Papá's library at the far end of the house. I pulled the plain wooden box out of its hiding spot at the base of an old wooden mirror in one corner of the room. Papá's pistols were inside, the ones that Abuelito had given to him for the road, which I knew, despite my being his favorite, would one day be Víctor's. I needed those particular weapons for no other reason than luck.

Abuelito was the best shot in Sonora. He could shoot a rabbit right through the heart, hit any mark that was asked of him, outgun any man who came looking for trouble—and to that end, for whatever reason, according to Papá's stories, trouble always came knocking. Abuelito said it was the pistols that aimed for him. That all he had to do was point, and the pistols would do the rest. Before finding out that magia was real, I'd thought he was lying. Part of me, I guess, still did. But I hoped the pistols would do the same for me.

Before I could pull them out of their box, a voice behind me said, "What are you doing?"

It was Mamá, her voice harsh. She rarely saw me dressed as Salvación, and there was something dark in her tone, like she didn't really understand me at all.

"Papá is in danger. I need to be ready," I told her, not stopping.

Instead of smiling in understanding, her face contorted with anger, her lips thinning.

"Those are not yours to have. They're Víctor's. And Papá can take care of himself without your help, Lola de La Peña." She said my full name like I needed a reminder of who I was. Mamá had this way of making me feel as insignificant as possible. But ever since we arrived in Coloma, ever since I became Salvación, it hadn't hurt as much as usual. It became a revelation. This was who Mamá was, in her heart, inside the very thing that gave people souls, and this was what our relationship would be like no matter where we were or in what other ways we changed.

I didn't back away, as I had for so much of my life. Every time that she'd asked me to just sit in the chair at the head of the line instead of letting me help her, as if she wanted all the glory of sal negra to herself. But I didn't want to be that person anymore.

I knew I might not be as strong as Papá. But sometimes you didn't need to be strong, you just needed to be smart—and *that*, I knew I could be. "The woman said that señor Hernández is not here to help us, but destroy Coloma with what she called sal roja, another type of magia. He came with horses and food and men he says will help make Alta California México again, but it's not real. None of it is. He's telling lies. We have to stop him before he finds more sal roja. We have to steal an amulet from him that lets him locate it."

Her mouth fell open into a wide and round O. I wasn't sure what to make of it, though I should have figured she wasn't about to say anything good.

The words sounded more foolish said aloud. I knew it sounded like a fantasy. But hadn't she sounded the same when she told us about sal negra?

"You are not doing anything." She yanked the box from me, her face flushing red. She pulled my mask off next, which had taken me seven tries to sew right. And suddenly I *was* just Lola. "You are a child—*my child.*" I wanted to tell her that she'd never treated me with the kindness I thought all children deserved. "And you won't go riding off to fight grown men who will not hesitate to hurt you, to kill you. I will not let my child go off to die, no matter what she thinks she knows about what's going on. You need to realize that you don't have the freedom to dictate what your place in the world is. The world decides that for us."

"That's not fair," I replied, still gripping the box with shaking hands. "You decided my fate when you brought us to Coloma. And now there are no teachers, no church, no society here to tell me what to do. The woman, Isabela, came to me because she trusts me. I'm not going to let her down."

"And you believe everything people go around saying and that you should trust her just because? There are liars out in the world, Lola. I know you like to see the good in people until they show you otherwise, but people will cheat you faster than a jackrabbit runs."

How could she say this to me when everything I'd become since leaving Sonora was because of Mamá? With everything that was going on, sometimes I felt like Mamá acted as she did and said certain things just to keep me in whatever rightful place she thought I belonged—perhaps the bottom of her zapato.

"But—" I didn't know why I argued in the first place. "You

just told me to dress up as Salvación to talk to the woman." Maybe Isabela's kindness and admiration had given me some kind of strange strength to speak my thoughts. Mamá had made up her mind already, though. She wasn't going to let me out of the house. Especially not dressed as Salvación, not if she could help it. Only she was wrong. Sometimes people were too tired, too worn out to show you the good in them. It didn't make them any less so. And then there were different degrees of good. I didn't doubt that Mamá was a decent person, even a good person considering how she had helped heal so many for nothing in return. But it didn't make her a kind mother.

She glared at me. And beneath her angry gaze, I wondered if she hated me, even a little, even if she also loved me.

"That was different," she said. "I needed to find out what the woman knew. What she was here to say. Everything she told you only makes me want to keep you safer."

I stopped trying, I could tell Mamá wasn't going to be swayed.

"*You* have to go warn Papá, then," I insisted, anger burning in my throat. I hoped she'd listen. Once she left me alone, I'd run away, do what had to be done.

"I'm not going anywhere. I meant what I said. You and I have other work to do: the work that brought us here. Go change out of that ridiculous outfit and back into your dress and come help me."

Tears burned in my eyes, something else aflame in me now—an invisible wound, the way only Mamá could hurt me. When would Mamá realize that I could take care of myself? I had driven away more bad men and protected Coloma more than anyone else here. Including Papá.

Still, I couldn't say no to her. I went to my room; changed out of my Salvación outfit; grabbed the heirloom revolver that Mamá hadn't a clue about, hiding it underneath my lightest dress, knocking my guitar over on the way out of my room and not even caring; and went back to helping Mamá and Víctor heal those still in the house. I went back to pretending I was an ordinary girl instead of the Angel of Coloma.

As I worked, I tried to talk to Víctor, but Mamá separated us, which kept us from talking. She made him fetch water. She made me hand out bowls of oats. It was as if she was trying to keep me from influencing him, like he couldn't make up his own mind. She thought I was a tiny demon whispering evil into his ear, when evil—real evil—had taken the form of the man who was with Papá.

By midday, we'd barely spoken a word to each other, but had seen everyone head back home, to wherever home was, healed and alive. We gave them sacks of sal negra for the road and mushrooms and the blackberries we grew in our garden. I was exhausted from wearing the high heels and dress and trying to breathe in at all, with the air so thick with heat that you could see it radiating from the ground, like a mirage. Back when we were traveling from Sonora, I'd seen things that weren't there when our water ran low. Then we'd found el río. By the time we boiled the water, dark shadows had been flying and birds dancing on the ground for hours.

We used the free time to clean. We'd never had so many people in our home before. Their footsteps on the land around our house were a reminder of all the good we'd done. But it was also a mess. When we were done and the sun was starting to find its way toward the horizon, the three of us settled in to wait for Papá. Mamá had her needlework and was sewing in the rocking chair on the porch. Víctor was beside her, throwing rocks at one of the nearby trees, and I was simply biting my nails.

The strong gallop of Tornado, Papá's horse, accompanied by the song of los grillos and ranas around our home, announced their approach like fanfare.

Mamá rose, ran to meet Papá, who barely waited for his horse to halt before jumping off him and meeting Mamá. He picked her up and twirled her in the air, fanning her dress out. She hadn't changed into pants like she usually did, and I believed it was to teach me a lesson and set an example. Papá kissed her on the lips. They were so rarely like this that both Víctor and I laughed.

"See, he's all right," Víctor said. "Salvo y sano."

But *was he* safe and sound?

"You didn't see the men. It's an army, Víctor."

He sighed but didn't say anything back. He knew what I'd told him, what I saw, and I'd corner him earlier to tell him what Isabela said. Wasn't that enough?

My stomach went sour when Papá kept smiling, laughing. Was he drunk? His steps were unsure. Mamá exchanged a look with us. I had expected him to come home wearing a grim expression. I expected him to come home, telling us that we had to pack, leave Coloma—or that we were at war, to ready our weapons, to sharpen our blades. But he was happy. That couldn't be.

"We have to tell you something, Edgar," Mamá said, holding Papá by the shoulders as if to steady him in place.

"I have a lot to tell you as well," Papá replied, his words a

SALVACIÓN · 99

tiny bit slurred, as if his mind was foggy with drink. He didn't wait for Mamá to go first, which he normally would have done. I didn't expect anything good to come out of his mouth. "We're going to take back Alta California."

Mamá shook her head. Even with all she knew and sensed of the world, she understood that there was no escaping the Treaty of Guadalupe Hidalgo. Alta California was lost. Unless . . . the plan was to use sal roja to take it back.

I stood from where I waited on our porch steps. Víctor watched me approach Mamá and Papá, but he neither called me back nor joined me.

"Señor Hernández is here to kill us," I said, wanting Mamá to get to the point faster. "The woman we saved; she told us that much." We should have been acting, not standing around talking, and definitely not getting drunk and making the man who threatened all of us our friend.

Mamá told me that Papá would handle it. She had stopped me, and now this was the result. By the look of it, Papá had gone and made a deal with el Diablo.

"I trust him." Papá said the words as if they were final, as if because he trusted Hernández, my own trust in Isabela, who was still a guest in our house, was misplaced. I knew he wanted me to feel the same way as he did, but I didn't, and it was as if cold air hit the back of my throat.

I coughed and glanced at Víctor, who had finally stood and started our way. I needed my brother to help me save Papá from this. He hadn't even wanted to remain here. He wanted to go back to Sonora. We all did except for Mamá, understanding how dangerous it was for our family to stay.

When I turned back, Mamá was handing Papá a small water

tin that I was sure was mixed with sal negra, likely to sober him up. He took a drink and said, "What proof do you have that *this woman* is telling the truth?" Then he sloppily wiped away the water from his beard. Mamá refilled his cup—he obviously needed a second dose of sobering up.

I hoped the sal negra would do its job quickly and bring Papá back to his senses.

Unlike with Mamá, though, I believed I could sway Papá with the right words. "The fact she was on the brink of death and almost died getting here to warn us, maybe? She isn't lying. She said Hernández by name before I ever mentioned him."

"She could be an old lover of his."

"One that arrived on the brink of death? That doesn't bode well for señor Hernández any more than the truth."

Where he was happy when he rode up, he sure as hell was something else after I confronted him. Papá didn't normally get angry or frustrated, but now his neck became red, his eyes glared. It was all so strange.

It only solidified my belief that señor Hernández wasn't planning on helping Coloma, but on hurting us, tearing us apart and then unleashing sal roja on us when we weren't paying attention.

Even when Papá's face was flushing a brighter hue of red by the second, I would not turn my back on what I believed. Coloma couldn't afford it.

"I know she isn't lying," I said more adamantly.

"But you don't know or understand. I've seen señor Hernández's plan. He's going to make Alta California Mexicano once more. Make this our permanent home; one that no one can take from us ever again. And we will be safe for however long we stay here. No one will come to take away our claim. No one will threaten our family again."

"But we took it from those who lived here before us," I replied, repeating words that Papá had often told us. "You taught me that. You taught me that it hadn't been right. You said the only reason you're here is because you followed Mamá's calling."

Papá flinched like I'd betrayed his trust by telling the truth, but he didn't take it back. What could he say, after all? I didn't believe that all of a sudden he wanted ownership of Indigenous lands that had never been México's to begin with. We were here for the sal negra, to follow Mamá's feeling. That was all. The plan was we'd return home one day: leave, not make this our permanent home. I didn't want that. As much as I valued the freedom I had as Salvación, there was something out here in this wilderness that should never be broken the way people do to things.

I shifted my eyes to take note of Mamá's expression. If what Papá had told me in confidence one night bothered Mamá, she didn't show it. Her face was stone, as if she were in her mind, thinking things through, instead of in the moment with us.

And then it occurred to me: my worst fear of all.

"Did you tell him about sal negra?" My voice already seethed, my posture already tightened, and I found myself for whatever reason searching for where I'd left my sword on the porch. I didn't need it around Papá, right?

He didn't reply at first, swallowed hard before looking me straight in the eyes and saying, "Yes. And I promised him help from our claim, sal negra for his men."

I scoffed. Mamá let out a sound of disapproval. And suddenly Víctor took my arm as if holding me back.

I didn't recognize the man in front of us. Was he so scared of living in Coloma after only a few months, of the life that Mamá brought us to, that he was willing to sacrifice everyone's safety in exchange for something so far-fetched as señor Hernández making Alta California Mexicano again with magia that destroyed instead of created?

Just when I thought I would have no help, Víctor finally came to my aid. "Let's all talk to the woman, Isabela, see what she has to say. I want to know the truth."

I squeezed Víctor's hand, still upon my arm. "That's right," I said, pointing back to the house. "She'll tell you everything and you'll see it in her eyes that she is not a liar and you'll take my side. You'll see how much she suffered because of that man. He is no señor. He is el Diablo, Papá."

Papá focused on Mamá. I knew she hated that I was Salvación. I knew she hated a lot of things about me, but I'd always done right by the people of Coloma. Sometimes when we walked through town, we heard people talking about Salvación and they always said good things. Mamá would huff and pull us away, but occasionally I'd catch her half-smiling as she did, seemingly proud of me.

When she didn't come to his defense, Papá exhaled loudly, as if sometimes, when I wasn't playing the part of a lady, my existence felt too hard to deal with. He nodded. "Let's go talk to her, then."

We entered the house, headed toward Mamá and Papá's room. Only there was something wrong. The food we set outside her door earlier was still sitting there. She'd never grabbed her meal, never eaten. It had been hours.

I exchanged a worried glance with Víctor, trying to judge whether he knew anything about this. He shook his head, understanding me.

I knocked on the door, but no one answered, and then I opened the door and saw why. The window was open and Isabela was gone. I wasn't the only one who liked to sneak out, it seemed.

"No," I mumbled, racing into the room. She'd fled. It made me doubt her words for a minute. She was afraid, though. I'd just told her that the man who destroyed her world and murdered everyone she loved was nearby. I wouldn't have stayed either. As quickly as my anger had come, it left me. The woman was still doing what she thought was right, still trying to survive.

I regrouped my family.

As Papá walked away, he said, "She left because she knew she would be found out as a liar. Forget her."

As if it were that easy. Forget her. Forget the task she gave you. Forget Salvación. Forget Coloma. Forget and do as I say.

I felt a sense of dread and desperation taking me over. Without the help of my family, could I figure out a way to stop señor Hernández? As confident as I was as Salvación, I depended on having a home to return to, a father who not a couple of days back had likely saved Mamá and me from another bad man.

"Mamá," I pleaded, hating how my voice was desperate.

But Mamá had never taken my side, and in my heart, I didn't expect anything different.

Papá waited to see what she would say. "Did you talk to the woman?" he asked when she didn't say anything.

"She would speak only with Salvación." She lingered on the name Salvación, drawing it out, as if it were a dirty word that she wanted to wash away with soap or burn away with fire. Papá scrunched his nose. "Lola de La Peña, promise me you are not going to go looking for trouble as Salvación anymore. We let you run around freely without consequences for too long. If I catch you playing vigilante again, you'll be even less happy with me than you are right now. ¡Ya basta! This stops today—never again."

It was a promise that I'd made a dozen times, one I never kept. What made him think that this time would be any different?

"But I'm telling the truth. Why would I lie?"

Papá didn't respond, perhaps because he didn't have a good reply—or he didn't want to hurt me with his answer. Either way, there was something cruel in Papá's eyes that had never been there before, and I understood something I never wanted to realize again: Papá would not always be on my side.

"Let's talk about this tomorrow, Lola. Go to sleep, get some rest. Tomorrow a new beginning is coming our way."

I didn't know what else to say. I had to save Papá from himself. I had to stop Damián Hernández.

But how do you stop a killer when you aren't one? How do you stop a killer who has convinced everyone else they're a savior?

I didn't know the answer, but I intended to figure it out.

CHAPTER 7

Coloma was abuzz with news of our guests and why they were here, the cattle they'd brought with them, and the wealth they presented us with. Now I was with Mamá, who had decided she wasn't letting me out of her sight, so I didn't try to do anything she and Papá would deem foolish. Either at her own behest or Papá's request, she had dragged me to a market day the residents of Coloma had put together for the newcomers. The day was as solemn as my mood. The weather had shifted overnight, and dark clouds approached us as the winds shifted from the heat of summer to the chill of early autumn.

The weather brought a bad omen with it.

Regardless of the day, and how el viento shifted the papel picado every which way, la plaza was full and lively for the first time ever. Vendors were reeling from the wealth the strangers had brought with them and their willingness to spend it. Even Luisa was out, happily going from stranger to stranger with her teas as they exchanged them for money. Everyone seemed to be smiling except me.

Señor Hernández brought everyone what they'd been hoping for. All these men with pockets full of coins and rare things to trade for sal negra: Didn't the people of Coloma wonder where they'd gotten it all from? What harm they'd done to get it? I imagined them robbing Isabela's people for it all. Who else had they taken from?

It made my heart clench that Luisa didn't seem to care, as long as these new arrivals also spent their coins on new boots and hats and pants and mining tools. I wondered if Abuelo would be against this. Obviously, Papá had not yet told him about his agreement. Would Abuelo be happy about sharing the sal negra?

Then again, I knew the answer. Did sanctity compete with money?

Seeing how elated everyone was, I wished señor Hernández's intentions had been noble. But I knew they weren't, and it was only a matter of time before these men wanted to collect their coins anew.

My eyes drifted from Luisa around la plaza. I found myself searching for one face. Alejandro's. I didn't spot him. Disappointment filled my bones, and then I felt frustrated that I was disappointed. Why was I even looking for him?

I remembered the horses. How they'd followed him. Like Mamá, he was magia, and magia drew people to it like a river draws the thirsty.

He was a river I wanted to drink of. I wanted to be drawn in by him, but he wasn't here to fill that need. It was strange to feel a hollowness because of a boy.

"Lola de La Peña, pay attention," Mamá warned, clapping her hands in front of my face, bringing me back to the center of la plaza and pushing a handful of small burlap sacks into my hands the moment I turned her way, the same sacks we often filled with sal negra for the long and dangerous journey home of those we healed.

As I was trying to ensure I didn't drop any of the burlap, a man slid by me, bumping my shoulder.

"Hey!" I called after him, utterly annoyed. But it was as if he didn't even hear me.

It wasn't someone I recognized from town. They were dressed too nicely, their clothing as clean as my dress.

"Stop him! Thief! He's a thief!" doña Luisa said, trying to follow him. But she would never catch him.

She was crying where a moment before, she'd been the happiest that I'd seen her since we arrived. Her pain made my stomach sink. I felt like she was speaking directly to me.

I was in my dress today. Even so, without thinking twice about it, I started after the man. As I gave chase, I bumped into people who regarded me as if they had no idea why a lady of my standing was acting in such manner. It was thrilling, acting like Salvación during the day, not having to pretend so that I could do good.

"Lola?" Mamá called out from behind me, her voice fire and fear. "Stop right now, señorita!"

I ignored her, grinning and running. The man who had stolen from Luisa was dressed in fine cloth, had his hair cut well, and was obviously one of señor Hernández's men. I could use him as an example that Hernández's men weren't who they seemed to be. They weren't here to help us. But I had to catch him before he escaped in order to do that. It would be a small win, but a win, nonetheless.

My feet hurt with the heels, which stuck in the mud. If I kept having to fight for every step, I'd never catch up to the man, so I took the moment to take the botas off, remembering the spot where I left them, right outside the cantina steps, close to where I'd confronted the man who stole sal negra from us.

Without my heeled boots, I ran much faster, not caring if my stockings got dirty.

"Come back!" I yelled.

The man glanced at me quizzically, then went back to his task of fleeing.

He headed toward a group of perhaps thirty people who were standing around and clapping. I couldn't see who was speaking. I didn't care about any of them. Or I wouldn't have if the man wasn't heading right for the group. He must have thought he could lose me in the crowd. He thought wrong.

I pushed through the line, following the thief. He'd miscalculated it as an exit route and gotten stuck, unable to get through the next row in front. I pushed the man into the center of the circle, grinning at my victory as he tripped.

I stepped forward and approached the man, pushing him down after he tried to stand and taking back la doña's belongings from him. "You stole these!" I said it as loud as I could. Making sure everyone around me heard and understood. I saw what he'd taken for the first time: food, a blanket, things Luisa would gladly have given the man had he simply asked. A knot tightened in my stomach.

The knot only got tighter when a voice asked: "What is going on? ¿Qué pasa aquí?"

I met the gaze of none other than señor Hernández, realized that he was the one who had been speaking and that I'd interrupted him.

Before I could reply, Alejandro stepped up next to me. My breathing hitched at the sight of him. The hollow feeling disappeared, and for some reason I felt safer with him nearby; for some reason I actually felt that he was standing beside me to protect me.

"It sounds like this man stole something from one of the vendors and señorita La Peña took it upon herself to return the goods."

There are some people who can say a million words with their eyes. They can show when they're in love by the way they look at you, coyly and selflessly. They can smile without moving their lips. They can feel at peace by simply being. Señor Hernández's fury showed through his eyes. He may have spoken calmly, but there was nothing tranquil about him. His eyes told me that nothing good would come of this encounter.

The thief bowed, pushing away the food and blanket he took from doña Luisa toward señor Hernández.

I took them. "This is doña Luisa's." I hugged her belongings, as if doing so would keep them safe and might protect me from this situation in some way as I realized that I wasn't Salvación, nor could I act like it without my mask, without my disguise, without my sword. I could have run around in stockings, but everything I did as Lola de La Peña would be scrutinized. This man might have been a crook, but I didn't doubt that señor Hernández was a different kind of bandit, much more dangerous than a simple thief.

I was sweating from the chase, and there was a new expression in señor Hernández's eyes now that only made my perspiration worse. Confusion? Or something close to it as he focused on me more than on the man. I seemed to be the piece that didn't quite fit, and the man's scrutinizing gaze on me made my blood run cold.

Alejandro took another step forward, almost as if shielding me. I knew that it couldn't be the case, but it still felt that way. I couldn't stop wanting to stare at him.

"What do you want to do?" Alejandro asked señor Hernández, drawing the man's attention to himself.

Señor Hernández glanced about him. The commotion had drawn more people to us. All eyes were on the center of the circle. People whispered, asking one another what was going on. All were waiting to see how señor Hernández reacted. Some were whispering my name. I only hoped that señor Hernández would react badly enough to stop people from taking his side. If he showed his true colors, I believed that the people of Coloma might no longer see him in such a positive light.

Then, to my surprise, señor Hernández let out a hearty laugh that almost seemed natural. But I could see his eyes. I was close enough to see that they weren't laughing; only his lips did. It was an act, as was everything else about him.

"There were not many places for us to stop. And not everyone with such great hospitality as yourselves," he said. "Sometimes being exhausted makes you do cruel things." He lifted the man to his feet. In a darker tone, he added, "Things that you will not repeat."

"Ye-yes, señor. Boss. I—I promise."

The past weeks helping Mamá with the sal negra, I'd seen

plenty of scared people. I could recognize the fear of death. This man was as scared as they had been. He was visibly shaking, teeth chattering. There was something in the way señor Hernández seemed to hide his true feelings underneath a smile that made a chill run up my spine.

"Then you can go," señor Hernández replied.

The man walked away. "Th-thank you!" he said.

He bumped into Alejandro on his way out of the circle. If I hadn't been as close to them as I was, I wouldn't have heard Alejandro whisper in the man's ear. "Corre."

Run.

And the man did. He sprinted away.

Señor Hernández clapped his hands, drawing the attention of all back to him and away from the fleeing man. It was almost as if as he went, the whispering of the people in the crowd followed him away.

Señor Hernández tilted his head at me, trying to assess me. "You're señorita Lola de La Peña."

I wanted to say I wasn't Lola but Salvación and confront him.

Before I did anything stupid, Mamá arrived. "Perdón," she said. "Lola sees an injustice and can't seem to think straight. I fear this place has made her a bit wild."

A few in the crowd chuckled. I opened my mouth to reply, it was such a cruel thing to say, but Mamá, like señor Hernández, spoke with her eyes. And her eyes weren't asking me but telling me to keep quiet. I realized then that even though Mamá hadn't sided with me in my argument with Papá, she didn't trust the man before us either. She *knew* I was telling the truth about the woman's warning. She had been the one to heal her, after all. And in her eyes, she wanted me to keep playing the role I'd always played and keep myself alive.

"La doña is like family," I said, feigning shyness now. "I don't know what got into me. I'm very sorry, señor, for interrupting you." The apology felt like hot coals in my throat, and I hated speaking it.

I bowed, something I loathed just as much as my apology, then made to leave, Mamá giving a small curtsy and following behind me.

"Wait," señor Hernández called. It wasn't a question or a request. It was a demand.

As we turned back, I first met Alejandro's gaze. His eyes were narrowed, his eyebrows kissing at the center of his forehead as if everything he was witnessing was troubling. He took a visible gulp. He shook his head just barely as if warning me that I had to play the part everyone wanted me to.

"We really must be going," Mamá said, her voice sweet as honey. "We must get to the line of miracles. There is God's work to be done in Coloma."

What would be el Diablo's response to hearing the word *God*?

Señor Hernández stepped forward. Mamá tensed next to me.

"I only wanted to invite your family to a celebration I'll be having tomorrow night," the man said. "We'll have plenty of food for the entire town. There is lots to celebrate. Including the valuable work that I hear you yourself, señora Miriam de La Peña, do on behalf of everyone."

"¿Una fiesta?" Mamá questioned. "Alta California has fallen, señor. Are you sure you don't only celebrate defeat?" And then both adults were staring at each other, speaking with their eyes.

I hoped Mamá's didn't say anything that would get her in trouble. The last thing I wanted was for her to end up as someone he considered a problem.

He clicked his tongue as if chastising Mamá. "One lost war doesn't mean anything—"

"The Treaty of Guadalupe Hidalgo does, as much as I wish it didn't."

"It's a piece of paper, nothing more." Hernández took a step forward, and Mamá flinched back. He almost seemed to smirk as she did so. Mamá reached toward her skirt as if she were going for her hidden weapon.

Her motion made me reach for my pistol too. It was strange, to be face-to-face with someone who wasn't white, who was Mexican, and still feel imminent hostility. The hair on my neck stood straight. My head tingled with anticipation.

"I'm not sure the Yankees who have been traveling to Coloma in search of sal negra would agree with you. Soon we'll be flooded with them. And you and your fifty men will be outmatched."

He shook his head; meanwhile, I watched as Alejandro gulped again, standing by, listening to Mamá and his boss start to argue. "They are not as strong as they think they are. There is still plenty to do. I believe señor de La Peña understands that the only way you'll keep healing folks around these parts is by making sure you can still live on this land."

And there it was. Señor Hernández had found Mamá's one weakness. She would not defy Papá's wishes. For he had left our hacienda behind and the comfort of having a big home with a lot of land and many animals and servants who tended to our every need, none of whom had dared to travel with us on our journey from Sonora. We were alone here—we were all we had. When Papá had chosen to follow Mamá, I knew it meant Mamá felt that she owed him everything from then on.

She didn't.

But even señor Hernández seemed to know that the reality of things didn't matter. All that mattered was what Mamá thought to be true.

"Perhaps you are right, señor Hernández," Mamá said, deflating and taking my hand. I squeezed her fingers, trying to let her know that I was here and on her side.

"That's the spirit!" He raised his arms high, signaled to everyone in the crowd. "We're going to make history together. It's only fair that we show you full well what we have to offer. Tomorrow night, we celebrate, and when the full moon arrives, we'll strike!"

There were words Mamá wanted to speak. I could tell in the way her body was stiff.

"Señora La Peña and señorita Lola, will you be there?"

"We'll be there," Mamá said on our behalf.

My head whirled. Una fiesta. A party meant lots of people would be in one spot with plenty opportunities for a distraction. It might be the perfect time to search for the amulet. Find proof that would make Papá stop trusting señor Hernández. And if nothing else, make it that much harder for the man to find sal roja.

"Good," señor Hernández said with a half grin, "because your family are my honored guests."

Mamá gave a slight bow, then squeezed my hand back. I expected her grip to be harsh, demanding, but it was soft.

Alejandro and I exchanged a strange glance as Mamá led

me away. It almost seemed like his eyes were telling me to tread carefully or I would end up in the same place the thief was bound for. I glanced the way he had gone. I could see him off in the distance, still on foot, still running. He wasn't going to be able to outrun anyone without a horse.

CHAPTER 8

The moment Mamá and Papá excused me from dinner, I hurried to my room and started changing into Salvación. My heart fluttered as the reality that the day was nearly done settled. I'd likely be too late to stop what I feared was going to happen tonight—

Still, I had to try.

I sneaked out my window and made straight for the shed, where Víctor hid his extra rifle. The door opened with a squeal at the hinges. I expected someone to come chasing after me, but there was no one even after several minutes. I waited a few seconds longer before going inside. There was a trapdoor hidden on the ground, leading to an underground bunker in case we ever needed to shelter from a storm. I entered, grabbed Víctor's rifle, feeling the need to ensure I had more than two weapons, and closed the door before rushing off.

On the outskirts of our land, I thought of going back and getting Víctor. But Víctor hadn't talked to me much the last few days. I wanted him sano y salvo, so I hadn't pushed it. I'd never forgive myself if something happened to him, and neither would Mamá.

I found fresh hoofprints in the center of town leading away toward the bridge. I couldn't risk following on Carisma—a horse would be too obvious—so I proceeded on foot, staying in the shadows, looking behind often to make sure there was no one watching me.

I ran on steady feet, my heart beating fast and loud as I followed the tracks. At the very least, I didn't have to run in the high-heeled boots, in the constricting bodice and vestido that were both so uncomfortable. My pants felt as incredible as always, my shirt loose, allowing me to breathe deeply as I kept going. I had my Salvación mask on, hiding my eyes from view. My hair was hidden underneath my poblano hat. At least if anyone saw me, I wasn't going to make the same mistake as in la plaza. No one would recognize me as Lola de La Peña. No one would unmask me unless they caught me— and I was not one to be easily captured.

At the bridge, they had veered left, into the forest y la montaña. There were mountain lions and osos in it, which meant no one ever roamed alone and at night. My sword, pistol, and Víctor's rifle might protect me against them, but a bear could just as easily thrash my body beyond recognition. Going back was not an option, though, not when just outside the line of trees, at least two dozen horses were waiting for their riders.

My throat tightened as I bypassed the horses and trekked through the trees.

A sudden noise above stopped me, the trees swaying in the warm summer air, an owl nesting, singing its song in one of them. Papá once said that bears live in the trees. That they were up there, you just couldn't see them. I tried to forget the fact, ignore that I wasn't ready to be mauled to death by a bear, and continued on, focusing on following the shoe tracks visible in the light of the moon.

There was firelight ahead. I stopped before reaching it and hid behind a cluster of trees and a massive boulder. Despite everything I had done and all I had achieved as Salvación, it hadn't made me any stronger, any faster. I was still made of flesh and blood and needed to be careful.

I took in the scene—the fire, the men, none of whom I recognized. The man in the middle of them all. They had stripped his clothing away, built a fire, and now struck him with flaming branches.

I covered my mouth with both hands to stifle a scream. I felt bile rise in my throat. I shut my eyes and took deep breaths, trying to make it find its way back down.

This far from Coloma, no one would hear the man screaming. At least they wouldn't realize it; to them, the man would sound like a wolf howling to the moon. They had caught the man, and he would not escape señor Hernández's wrath.

I'd seen terrible things during my time in Coloma—injuries that went beyond what would have been reparable without sal negra. But nothing like this.

I hid in the shadows, unsure of what I should do. Víctor hadn't come with me. I had his rifle, but he was the better shot. A few men, I could perhaps have handled on my own. But this wasn't a few men. At least two dozen stood, watching as señor Hernández repeatedly struck the man who had caused the scene with one of the burning branches.

The man was bleeding from his head and a cut lip. His face was covered in dirt as if he'd been dragged through the valley. His hair was disheveled. His shoulders slumped. His eyes were downcast. He was crying and begging señor Hernández for forgiveness.

I had sal negra on me. If the man held on and I could find a way to give it to him ...

I wanted to save him. Despite the fact that he was a thief. Was that enough to sentence this man to death? But he had done something worse than death—he'd embarrassed señor Hernández. And now Hernández was showing him what that embarrassment cost him.

It was all my fault.

If I hadn't pushed the man into the crowd ...

If I hadn't given chase like Mamá had beckoned ...

If, if, if ...

So many what-ifs—and no way out of this.

Alejandro stood to the side of the circle. He was pacing, gnawing on the skin of his thumb, watching señor Hernández have his fun. "He's learned his lesson," Alejandro finally said, surprisingly speaking up. I willed him to do more, to stop what was about to happen. Perhaps his boss would listen to him.

Señor Hernández didn't glare at Alejandro or tell him he didn't know what he was talking about. I didn't think it was out of respect, but the opposite. He didn't think Alejandro was a person to fear, someone to respond to.

Señor Hernández shook his head at the boy after a moment, adding, "He made me look like a fool. There is no lesson to be learned here—there is only the beginning of the end of a life."

He pulled something out of his pocket. I pulled Víctor's rifle from my back, set it upon my shoulder, took a single step forward, a branch snapping below my foot. Only Alejandro seemed to notice. Luckily, he turned my way for only a moment, likely thinking it was nothing more than an animal, before his attention went back to his boss.

The man, oh the poor man. I couldn't see what Hernández was doing to him. But when I heard the man yelling, it made my insides shrivel, it made me want to hide. I focused even when my eyes watered from the sound. I had Hernández in a shot, but then Alejandro moved in my way. If I pulled the trigger, I'd shoot the boy. I lowered the rifle, silently asking Alejandro to take a few steps away, and saw as the thief tried to crawl away on his hands.

The man's shrieks became violent, the pitch of them deafening. They made my stomach twist and tortured my mind. I let go of the rifle and put my hands over my ears.

Alejandro turned away from the scene, my way. He didn't seem to notice where I was, but we were staring right at each other as the man died. Alejandro's chest rose in a deep breath, as if willing himself to keep it all together.

I tried to peer around Alejandro, to figure out what was killing the man. I couldn't see anything from where I was.

Then señor Hernández lifted something into the air. "Witness the power of sal roja."

I moved my hands over my mouth again before I gasped too loudly.

This time, Alejandro seemed to know that there was someone hiding, watching them. He took a step forward, squinted into the darkness.

I tried not to worry about him, even as I calculated how fast I could reach for the rifle at my feet and pull the trigger. I wouldn't shoot Alejandro. I knew I couldn't. All I could focus on was the sal roja. What it could do.

I'd seen the sal roja at work only once before, with the woman. This was evidence that there was more. That she wasn't lying. There really was sal negra *and* sal roja. Sal buena y sal mala.

The screams soon faded. Only then did Alejandro move and I saw clearly that the man's body began to disintegrate, as if the sal roja had funneled its way to his heart and then was eating the man every which way, seeming to suck the man's blood and bones into itself, devouring the man from the inside out.

On the ground, the man was nothing soon enough.

I watched, eyes wide, unblinking, and stunned. It was frightening to see just how horrible sal roja was, how horrible Hernández was.

There was no body to bury, no body to hide. The man was nothing now, and in his spot, no flowers marked the start of life. The forest floor was blackened.

If the woman hadn't had sal negra on her, the same thing would have happened to her. What would happen if the sal roja were everywhere? What would happen to Coloma and all its sal negra? It was another sign that señor Hernández wasn't here to help anyone. He was going to get what he wanted, mine all the sal negra and sal roja he could find, then move on, leaving Coloma and its people in ruins. Worse, perhaps he'd make us all disappear too.

Was that what he'd done to Isabela's town?

I glanced at Alejandro once more, found him looking

straight at me. His eyes were wide, unblinking. I wanted to touch his face, comfort him. No one should ever see this, be a part of something so awful. He seemed to want to say something, call to me, ask for help, ask for me to get him out of this. But he didn't. As he'd done with the man earlier, he mouthed, "Run."

I ran through the dark, trying to blink the tears away from my eyes as the events of the night played through my mind.

CHAPTER 9

How do you stop el Diablo when you're only human? Back home, my bed felt too comfortable compared to the woods. When I blinked my eyes, when I breathed, when I stared at the wall, all I could see was the man disappearing into nothing—dying as if he had never existed. I kept envisioning Alejandro's hollow expression. How many times had the boy let his boss go on doing horrible things?

He should have tried to stop Hernández. He should have argued harder.

In my heart, I knew that if I wanted to stay alive and out of trouble, I should forget what I had seen. I should lock it away in the depths of my soul like Alejandro must have. But when I closed my eyes, when I had them open, every waking moment, I heard the man, the way he sounded as sal roja devoured him. There was no trace of him afterward, nothing to bury, nothing to mourn.

But I wasn't going to do nothing. I needed to find a way to

stop el Diablo before he unleashed sal roja on all of Coloma—before I became nothing too.

One question kept coming up in my thoughts: the woman had called me an ángel; the man who stole sal negra from us earlier that night did too. But I wasn't an angel. I wasn't invincible. With sal roja, did I stand a chance against señor Hernández?

I kept remembering Isabela. How sal negra had saved her life. She said she'd used all of her town's sal negra to survive. I understood it now. I should have gone after her.

It was vexing that complete strangers trusted me, while my family thought of me as a little girl. But I wasn't a kid, not anymore, not since we traveled here—not since I became Salvación.

I didn't think I was a grown woman either. I wasn't like Mamá or any doña I knew.

I was somewhere in between being a little girl and becoming an adult.

As much as I wished I knew what to call that, I didn't—just like I didn't know how I would stop señor Hernández. One thing I was certain of was that we needed more sal negra to have a fighting chance against him.

And I had to act fast.

As Lola de La Peña, I wasn't allowed to mine. I wasn't allowed anywhere near our claim. Which meant that it was time to convince Víctor to take my side and stay on it. As much as I hated having to bring him back into this world, the fact of the matter was that he couldn't stop being Salvación as much as I couldn't.

I stopped by the kitchen on the way to his room, opening up the package that Mamá kept tortillas in. I quickly warmed up four, and then prepared them just the way Víctor liked, with a little bit of mantequilla and a pinch of sugar.

I knocked on his bedroom door.

"Yes?" Víctor called out.

"It's me, open up."

He hesitated, then I heard movement on the other side of the door. He opened it slightly.

I filled the view with my face. "¡Buenos días!" I said, holding up the plate of tortillas so he could see that he should fully open the door. "These are for you."

He kissed my cheek and took the plate. "What you want?" he asked, chewing and leaning against the doorframe.

I scoffed at the idea I had just bribed him with food. "Why, señorito La Peña, what would make you think I want anything at all and haven't simply done a nice gesture for my favorite brother?"

He raised both eyebrows, took another bite. "You really want me to answer that?"

I chuckled, though I couldn't hold the expression on my face as the burning man's image took over. The way his body contorted. The sound of his scream as he vanished.

I closed my eyes tightly, tried to shake it all off. Tears fell when I opened my eyes again, and Víctor stopped eating. "I saw something yesterday."

"Hey, it's okay, come here." He pulled me into his room, sat me on his bed, which was perfectly made as usual. "When? I thought Mamá was constantly watching you."

"She wasn't watching me at night," I mumbled, staring down at my hands. I didn't know why the memory made me so ashamed. Then again, I hadn't saved the man the way I thought

Salvación should have been able to. What if I wasn't a hero? I didn't want to be an innocent bystander. I didn't want to be the type of person who stood by and watched terrible things happen. Maybe the girl who left Sonora would have, but I'd changed.

He paused. "You went out by yourself?" He shook his head. "You shouldn't have done that, not with all of señor Hernández's men here. What were you thinking?"

"That I didn't have a choice," I shot back. I knew that going alone into the night wasn't wise, but if Víctor hadn't told me he didn't want anything to do with Salvación anymore, then I wouldn't have been by myself.

Víctor rolled his eyes at me. "Of course you did. You should have stayed home."

"You should do this. You should do that. That's all I ever hear from you, Mamá, and Papá—meanwhile, I'm the only one who was out there trying to save a man's life. And it's—"

"Yeah?"

"It's my fault that he died, Víctor. I did something wrong when I went out with Mamá yesterday."

Víctor went quiet. "What did you do? What did you see?"

"I saw señor Hernández murder a man from la plaza with sal roja. And it's all my fault."

Víctor sat back, rocked a little, whistled, all while holding a rolled-up tortilla in his hand, suspending it just above his plate. "Lola, you saw what now?"

I repeated my words, adding, "A little outside of town. That boy, Alejandro, was there, as were about two dozen of señor Hernández's men. He simply . . ." I paused, trying to figure how gruesome a picture I should paint for my older brother.

SALVACIÓN · 127

"He sprinkled, for lack of a better word, sal roja on the man, and the sal roja devoured the man's body completely. There's no trace of him left."

"No evidence, you mean?" He searched my face as if trying to figure out if I was telling the truth.

"I'm not making this up, Víctor."

"I didn't say you were."

"You implied it," I replied, my cheeks growing hot. "Just a few days ago, you were out there with me. You know I'm not a liar. You know I wouldn't make this up. I didn't lie about Isabela."

He finally set down the tortillas, pushing them aside as if this conversation had taken away his appetite, as if he'd seen what I saw. "Loli, I know." He rubbed at his face, his eyes, and then focused back on me. "I wish you were. This is exactly the kind of shit that I was scared would show up on our doorstep. It's here. We didn't get out in time, and now we're stuck." He sat back on his bed, looking toward the window near the corner of his small room. We could see the rest of town from here. Coloma was everything we swore to each other to protect, for Mamá.

"We can't abandon Coloma now." I understood him, I did. It would be easier to pack up our belongings and head back to Sonora. He could live the life of a rancher. I could go back to my dresses and makeup and friends. But it wouldn't be us anymore. I saw that so much clearer after last night. It would be haunting to try to forget who we'd become. "Víctor, I need your help. I really, really need you. I don't think I'll survive this alone. And I do intend to do everything I can to stop him."

He nodded, ran his hand through his hair, and then his

face froze in that look he got when he was out as Salvación. There was work to do, and Víctor was ready to see it through.

"What's your plan, Loli? I'm assuming if you brought me estas deliciosas tortillas, it's because you have a plan."

I grinned. For the first time since I saw the man die in the forest, I felt some hope, however small, that we might be able to stop the disaster I knew we were in the midst of.

"You know the fiesta we're going to tonight?"

"The one señor Hernández invited us to?"

"I know Mamá and Papá said we don't have to go, but—"

"You want to go after the amulet at the fiesta?" he said skeptically, as if this idea were the worst he'd heard.

"Do you have a better plan for stopping him? Isabela said that was the way, and I think that we should listen to her."

"She also ran away instead of helping us."

I shrugged. It was true. At first I didn't understand it. After seeing what had happened to the man in the forest, I did. "Isabel told me that she'd done her part, delivering this message to Salvación." I shook my head, trying to make sense of it all. "I don't agree with what she did, but sal roja, it's unlike anything we've ever seen, Víctor. It's death itself. If señor Hernández had seen her, she'd be dead, just like the man from la plaza. I don't doubt he would kill us for what we know too. If we can get the amulet, though, we can have the upper hand. He can't get his hands on more sal roja."

"But we don't know how much he has right now. He could have enough to destroy Coloma and the rest of the world already."

"Why would he want more if that was the case? Why wouldn't he simply kill us all and take Coloma?"

SALVACIÓN · 129

Since Víctor didn't reply, I went on.

"I think he's here for the sal negra too. Isabela said that she used all of her town's sal negra in order to survive just one grain of sal roja. That means he can't walk around with sal roja; he might be el Diablo, but he's wearing a man's skin. He isn't immune to sal roja . . ." My mind wandered. "Dios mío. He's just a man. How do you kill a man who is a murderer when you aren't? How do you stop a man who can murder you with a grain of salt?"

"What are you talking about? You're not making any sense now."

"Just hear me out. How?" I asked again, smiling, because it was all starting to come together.

"How, Loli?"

"You beat him with his own weapon. We need to get our hands on the amulet *and* sal roja. If we can do that, we'll simply have to leave sal roja someplace he might just happen upon it. He'll be gone without a trace if he doesn't have any sal negra on him to protect him. But if we're going to use sal roja, we're going to need a lot more sal negra before señor Hernández's fiesta."

Víctor crossed his arms, thought on it, and nodded as he processed the idea. "That could work if we were able to get close enough to where he sleeps. We could leave sal roja on his bed, and he might not have a clue. When he lies down to sleep, he might not be able to act fast enough."

"That's right!" I stood to pace back and forth excitedly. I liked the idea of beating him at his own game. Of not having to bloody our hands. "He's staying at the new inn. I'm sure he keeps sal roja in his room. If you can cause a distraction en la fiesta, I can sneak in, find the sal roja, leave some on his pillow, find the amulet, take it, then come the next morning, it'll all be over."

Víctor laughed. "You're making it sound easy."

"It won't be. I know, but all we need is to have enough sal negra on us, as much as Isabela had on her when we do this, and we won't have to worry about the sal roja, at least."

"Good thing we have our very own claim, then. And we've just hit a pocket filled with sal negra. ¿Hermanita? Can I ask you a question now?"

"Yes, you most definitely can."

"Do you want to go mining?" He stood, reached out his hand to me.

I took it. "I thought you'd never ask."

In a lot of ways, even though Víctor and I were brother and sister, we had lived two completely different lives.

Víctor was a caballero; he worked with Papá, hunted, mined for sal negra. He did all the hard labor and was expected to know how to ride his horse well, was expected to take over the ranch when Papá passed away, and know how to raise our live-stock, how to lead. I was expected to do none of those things. Yet I did them anyway.

It was odd to me, to be expected to live a life that offered less than I had to give.

I could mine sal negra. I could hunt. But Papá wouldn't have me do any of those things. He had in Sonora, where our rancho was far enough from anyone else's and our land so vast that no one would ever see me.

It had never occurred to me that Papá's love and acceptance

depended on how much I went along with him. He accepted me because I didn't argue with him. It didn't feel right to realize that he might not like me if I were my own person.

Víctor had outgrown a need to please our father years ago. He didn't always do what Papá wanted. He didn't always act the way Papá thought he should. I had never admired my brother as much as I did in that moment, realizing all of this.

Despite all our differences, Víctor and I worked well together. We hadn't in Sonora. We'd never had a reason to stick together. We spent our time with different people: Víctor with the young men in our area, me with the young women.

When we first arrived in Coloma, things were different. We were scared and only had each other. We feared the people we met here, who had since become well-known, familiar, and like family to us. We were terrified others would arrive the way Hernández had done. With men and guns and a plan. The people here, and in a way even my family, had no plans. We wanted only to survive and live a simple life, to help others survive. We wanted nothing for ourselves. It was the way Mamá raised us.

Everything changed one day: we saw a gruesome thing the day we became Salvación. We saw a man dragged through the streets of Coloma by a man who wanted to rob him. That night, Víctor and I stayed up and Papá and Mamá had no idea. Our parents stayed up as well. They had their shotguns out, ready to shoot anyone who came to do us harm.

Víctor and I, we didn't sit around waiting for trouble to find us; we set to planning how to make sure that trouble stayed away. We decided that we wanted to be Coloma's angel. And I convinced Víctor to let me pose as Salvación. He was reluctant at first, but part of me always thought that he didn't want to put himself in so much danger. That he was more okay with me being the actual face of this as long as he was safe.

The first night we went out, the first night we fought back, it felt exhilarating. It was more than just that, though. It was almost as if the sal negra sang to us afterward. It was almost as if sal negra had brought us here just like it'd brought Mamá. It was as if we'd arrived at our destiny.

It was almost as if it stuck with us, became a part of who we were too.

Despite the connection I felt to sal negra, I had never been mining for it. I had never seen where it came from, really.

It felt good leaving the entire world outside and entering the place where magia came from. I was smiling even though life right now was chaos, even though there was so much at stake. I checked behind us once, and when the coast was clear, followed Víctor as he led the way inside the mine.

It was dark, but we had lamps. As we went farther into the mountainside, their light flickered. I wasn't sure if I expected the sal negra to glow or sparkle or something like that. But it was plain. The salt was earth.

The story goes that there used to be water covering all the land, that the earth rose from the depths of the sea and became solid ground, bringing about all its wonders—trees, birds, and insects. Which is why if you dug in some places, there was crystallized sea that has turned into sal. All la magia came from the ocean, from water, long, long ago.

For years, the sal was only white and it did nothing for us. Then sal negra was discovered here by Mamá, changing everything. Here was sal, dark as midnight, that healed all those who ingested it.

Víctor lit all the lamps in the small cave of our claim to sal negra. The sal negra itself was sleek black and so shiny you could see your own reflection on it. The mine wasn't deep, yet there was sal negra in every direction.

I felt the sal negra enter my pores. It refreshed my tired body.

There was life here. But there was nothing breathing here. A phenomenon like sal negra is hard to describe. There was nothing like it except sal roja.

I wondered where the sal roja was, and whether if we dug a little deeper, we would uncover a deposit. Would it kill us the moment we struck it?

There were dozens of men mining sal negra in the mountains—what would happen if one of them were to uncover sal roja by accident? Would we even know about it? Or would we simply assume that the man had packed up and gone home to México, not realizing sal roja had killed him?

I shivered at the thought, taking in the sal negra in front of me.

Víctor handed me leather gloves about two sizes too large for my fingers, then a few tools, something pointy and a large brush. "Chisel away, then brush down into the bucket." He kicked a bucket so it slid and landed right at my feet, below a large formation of sal negra.

I had never realized how tedious mining was.

In Sonora, we'd had everything handed to us. Here, we had to work for it. No wonder Víctor had changed so much.

Like Mamá, Víctor and Papá were working themselves to the bone.

Guilt tore at me—I had tried and had managed to help so many people in Coloma, but here was my brother, right in front of my nose, who needed help as well.

There was an odd feeling to mining sal negra, moments that made me recall what Papá had once said: sal negra belonged to the earth itself, not to us.

Most important was the question of whether we should keep mining it.

Was the sal roja a way to stop us from pulling any more sal out of the earth? If the other miners knew about sal roja, would they go home? Would they deem it too dangerous to mine the mountains, not knowing if the next deposit they hit would be their death?

A stream of questions got all tangled up in the passageways of my mind. All I knew was that without sal negra, we didn't stand a chance against señor Hernández. And so, for now, we mined. We pulled sal negra from the earth. I would worry about the larger questions after this was all done.

We worked quietly but quickly so as not to draw attention to ourselves, with calculated use of the small pickaxe and the brush, until we had filled half a bucket with sal negra.

I only hoped it'd be enough.

We carried sal negra on our horses, riding not toward home but to the spot where I always met Víctor, high up in the mountains. It was the safest place we knew to hide the sal negra until we needed it. Not many people ventured into the mountains, but we knew the road like the back of our hands and made the trek with only moonlight to guide us.

"Mamá would kill us both if she knew that we were planning to use this much sal negra in one go."

I snorted. "She'd *kill me* and blame *only* me for the idea."

He didn't say anything back; he knew it was true. She would blame me. Víctor and I were both Salvación, yet somehow, everything associated with the vigilante would always be my fault, as it usually was. Somehow, I'm the one they didn't want out here. But if we pulled this off, I'd be the reason why Coloma was saved.

We set the sal negra pails down on the ridge, stared at them. I was sweating. Summer was warm. Not as humid as Sonora, but something about the lingering heat made it easier to stay up this late at night, though it didn't take away the tiredness that resulted from doing so.

"I don't think she'd kill you. Maybe yell at you. But she wouldn't kill you."

I snorted. "I'm not sure that's any better," I mumbled.

"You think it will feel strange using that much sal negra?" Víctor asked, arms crossed at his chest. He kept blinking as if he were ready to fall asleep.

This was a good question I hadn't considered. Would so much sal negra affect us? It was the reason Mamá used so little of it when healing the sick. Not much was needed. And if we used more than needed, would it mean we'd die? The plan was to make it into a salve, rub it on our bodies, constantly rub it on our hands, and hope it was enough to combat any accidental encounter with sal roja tonight. Mamá had never truly told us how she came up with the amount of sal negra to use. Perhaps she'd simply known because of her intuition. Perhaps she'd tested it in some way. It was a precaution, one that could save our lives but could also, for all we knew, kill us just the same as sal roja.

I was willing to take the risk.

"I think it's more dangerous going in without it to Hernández's quarters or to the fiesta. I'll feel better knowing that the man won't be able to harm either of us using sal roja."

Víctor nodded as he removed some brush from the base of a large boulder, his usual hiding place for his extra rifle, where we hid the bucket of sal negra. We'd have to return before the party to apply a salve of it to our skin.

"It'll be here when we need it," I said, my mind on the party, toward whether Alejandro would be there or not.

"We should go back home and rest." Víctor swayed on the spot. Just watching him made my eyes heavy with drowsiness.

I nodded, went over, and hugged him, grinned in the dark. There was something special about being out here with Víctor again. It made me feel whole. We hadn't been born together, but we'd shared a womb. We had in our veins the same magia that made Mamá special.

There are things you fight to protect. Self-preservation, of course, is still there. But so much of what I did was for my family, for Víctor. It was nice to see him doing the same for me, especially when Mamá and Papá so often hesitated.

"Víctor," I said, stopping him as he started heading down toward home. "If something happens at the party and I'm caught, you had no part in this."

He smirked and didn't reply. Then he ruffled my hair, the way he used to do when we were back in Sonora—only more gently this time. "I am Salvación as much as you are," he said.

"I've hidden up on this mountain for too long while you've been facing all these terrible people. I won't let you face this alone. I'm your big brother; I'm supposed to protect you, not the other way around."

We hugged. While hugs from Mamá and Papá sometimes left me with feelings of wanting, hugging Víctor made me feel like my brother would always take care of me.

I only hoped that we could pull this off.

CHAPTER 10

The evening of the fiesta was too warm. I stood outside waiting for Víctor, trying to catch a shooting star in the sky and wondering what the weather was like back in Sonora, wondering what else there was to discover in a world with magia.

What a dream it would be to leave and never have to worry about sal roja again.

What a dream it would be to keep traveling, exploring, but niñas like me never could, not alone.

While I waited for Víctor, I also thought about how it was a nightmare to feel foreign in your own town and your own home. And it was getting worse. Where before I walked the streets and sometimes overheard talk about Salvación and how the vigilante had scared off a rotten fellow, now there was no mention of her anywhere. All everyone seemed to talk about was señor Hernández, the wealth he'd brought with him, and the idea of a world where Alta California was still México. To me, he wasn't a hero, he wasn't even a man; he was el Diablo casting a dark shadow on everything that had to do with life in Coloma. As long as he was here, I wouldn't feel good. I'd always feel like he was going to make his move, and his move would involve the deaths of everyone I love.

Mamá and Papá, two of those people, were waiting for us on their horses. I watched them from atop Carisma, near the house. Despite my anger toward Papá, and the fact I couldn't stand to be near him, he and Mamá, when they were together like this, were something special.

Back in Sonora I fell in love once or twice—a boy from the rancho next door, a boy from my school, who said his family was just passing by, yet was still there when I left two years later. Against my will, in this quiet moment as I watched my parents, I thought of Alejandro. I remembered the boy and the way what his boss did to the man alarmed him, made him breathe hard. I thought of the way he had stood in front of me at the plaza. How he seemed protective. What was his story, or did he have a more monstrous history?

I might never know. That was one of the things about being Lola de La Peña: I couldn't ever get close to anyone. Doña Luisa was one of the only people I really talked to, and we usually spoke of Salvación or other general gossip. She was also older than Mamá. She wasn't my friend, more like an abuela. There weren't many young people here.

Could Alejandro be my friend?

Then I thought of the way he'd always seemed so scornful, like my whole existence as a señorita troubled him; like he hated anyone like me, blaming me because he thought I had led an easier life. If he'd seen what we went through to get here, he wouldn't have thought that. Many families in our caravan lost more than one person. We were lucky. We were guided by Mamá's internal compass.

Maybe that journey was what gave me the courage to become Salvación. Maybe it was why Mamá felt so protective of those who traveled such a long way to see us. It wasn't an easy journey. Life never was, I guessed. And it didn't seem like it was going to get any easier anytime soon.

I was hugging Carisma when Víctor finally came out. He gazed toward the sky too.

"It's a good sign, la luna azul," he said.

I gave a hmm. It was what Abuela used to tell us whenever there was a blue moon back in Sonora. She died right before we came to Alta California. Somehow that seemed to be the moment Mamá made up her mind. Part of me, at first, before we saw sal negra existed and it was what Mamá came to find, thought that Mamá was only trying to flee her pain.

It was something more, though.

Like Mamá, Abuela always had a special affinity toward Víctor. Where she taught him about healing and the moon and the stars, she taught me how to sew and do other needlework and said that all the other things were not necessary. I think she always believed the destiny laid before me was to get married and move away, and she'd never see me again. She used to get so angry when she caught me wearing Víctor's pants and clothing. I never understood why something so mundane as my attire could elicit such emotions.

Maybe she'd sensed, even foreseen, my future as Salvación.

"I hope so," I said to him. For some reason, the sal negra I'd slathered all over my arms and legs and torso hummed with the memory. "How do you feel?"

He grinned. "Like I could run through this entire valley and not feel a sore muscle in all my body."

I understood the sensation. Sal negra wasn't like drink, not that I'd had anything to drink more than a few times and never enough to be drunk. But it also wasn't not like drink in a lot of ways. At that moment, there was more sal negra coursing through our bodies than anyone in the world had probably ever had, perhaps except Isabela.

Without her to ask, I only hoped it would be enough to keep us safe.

I looked back to my parents. Staring at Mamá and Papá also made me feel a bit guilty. Should we have told them our plan?

I laughed at myself. Of course not.

I examined Víctor. I was unspectacular next to him, like I'd always been in Sonora.

Víctor had always had something special about him, something unique. It was hard to describe. But it was as though when we came out of Mamá, he carried the magic of the night with him, and I carried its pain, as if he were a shooting star, brilliant and glowing, and I were the night sky, a bland nothingness, a simple background for stars to shine against.

Being Salvación had changed everything, but in moments like this, I still felt inconsequential next to him, like the version of myself that Mamá and Abuela had in mind for me.

I wondered if secretly Papá did too. Sure, he taught me to

fight with a sword and to ride and shoot, but had he intended I do anything with it?

Víctor was luminous with so much sal negra on him. His skin practically glowed in the light of the moon. He was dressed in a clean off-white button-down shirt, pants like the ones that I liked to wear as Salvación. He looked like a man instead of a boy. And it made me feel sad that soon we'd be expected to act like adults.

Víctor finally grinned shyly like he totally knew I had been assessing him. "What's on your mind, Loli? What's bothering you?"

"Todo," I replied. It was overwhelming, the sense of having the whole world on my back. If we failed, what would it mean for Coloma? What would it mean for everyone? I tried to stave off having to talk about my fears, so instead, I said, "You look like you're going to this thing hoping to find a wife."

He grinned. "Wouldn't that be something! Girls in Coloma. I've been surrounded by boys for too long out here."

"So have I," I said with a grin.

"And you still haven't found one to fall in love with you."

From his expression, I could read the joke. It was true, though, and it stung. Where Mamá had Papá, would I ever find the right person to stay with me? I didn't want to think about the future. "It's not like many of them come around me with Mamá and Papá hovering all the time."

"You're special, Loli. Everyone can see it. The right person will see it too. One day. And then your entire life will change." Back in Coloma, I'd had my entire future planned. Sometimes I missed the idea of knowing that I would grow up, find a suitable husband, marry, have children, and barely lift a finger throughout it at all. I'd felt safe in Sonora. Yet I also knew that that life was never my destiny. Sal negra was our fate, and I had to embrace it.

I rolled my eyes, but he always made me smile, even if I knew he was full of it.

"Well," I said, "let's make sure we survive this whole thing first."

I had to pretend to be Lola de La Peña, solamente una niña, a girl without anything to hide, as if my life depended on it tonight.

I wasn't sure what señor Hernández would do or say if he suspected that I was Salvación. Perhaps it was vanity that made me believe that word of me had already reached his ears, that he might even have been expecting me. For some reason, I believed that señor Hernández was one of those people who saw things coming a mile away.

Did he see through me, though? He'd stared at me an awfully long time at la plaza, until Mamá had come to my rescue.

Tonight, I was confident he wouldn't, at least—not when I was prepared.

I was dressed the part of a señorita. I wore a long flowing dress made of fine fabrics we'd traded for. It was black con rosas stitched across the bottom. It was tight in the bodice and made me look more like a woman than a girl. I was sure to stand out. But that was what I wanted. For as much as I had made fun of Víctor in what he was wearing, I wanted señor Hernández to think that I was interested only in one thing in life: finding the perfect husband, and maybe I thought there was one among his men. I hoped I could pull it off. Because all this life as a señorita had never come naturally to me. Even back in Sonora, I'd often been chastised by las monjas and my tutors for disappointing them. Even when I liked the life, I wasn't any good at it. I guess that was why this change had come so easily for me.

A permanent change terrified me, though.

I got on my horse, dress and all, wearing pants underneath the layers of fabric.

When they noticed Víctor was finally outside, we rode off with Mamá and Papá, who didn't say a single word to us and I guess just expected that we'd be following them. Papá hadn't spoken much to me since our disagreement, in fact. It was like the moment señor Hernández had arrived, something clicked inside Papá that made him not think straight, unable to see that some strangers are more dangerous than others. Where the man who stole from us was one to attack you from the front, señor Hernández seemed to me one of those terrible people who would strike you from behind, when you weren't looking, when you least expected it.

Riding together, Mamá and Papá were like the wind on a summer day. They slowed as we neared town, a trot calm enough to talk again.

What was it they spoke of when we weren't around? What were they saying at that very moment? Were they planning something as well? Had Mamá changed Papá's mind after what happened at the plaza?

If they had something up their sleeve, I wasn't privy to it, and neither was Víctor, despite being the eldest. Papá, after all, must not have trusted señor Hernández as much as he appeared to, considering we were riding into town on our horses, which would make it much easier to escape should trouble arise. For whatever the reason, riding into town relaxed me. The warm wind felt good against my cheeks. It felt calming. Underneath my dress, my Salvación outfit lessened the hurt of riding. I'd never understood why women weren't encouraged to ride until I had to ride in a dress on our way to Coloma. Ever since then, I'd used pants under my clothing.

Carisma continued forward. She had made the trip from Sonora to Coloma and seemed to like it here better, the wide-open sky that was as cold sometimes as the snow atop the rim of the mountains. Where before she was stuck mostly in the stable, here, we often galloped in the wide fields surrounding Coloma. I thought that Carisma tasted a bit of freedom as well. She'd earned it on the long and arduous road.

There was music dancing through the valley, and I was surprised that the earth below our feet didn't rumble at the sound. Laughter sounded even louder. It made my stomach recoil. Hernández was not a man to be celebrated.

I had seen the woman, her eyes speaking her fear.

I had witnessed the man's death, how he disappeared into nothing.

I knew exactly how terrible Hernández was, but I was only Lola de La Peña; if I told people about it, they wouldn't believe me. They'd probably think I was seeking attention.

I also couldn't show myself as Salvación. The safest thing to do was to keep the identity of the vigilante secret and take care of this without anyone else knowing.

Everyone in town was at the fiesta. Without our current plan of action, this might have only made me upset. But tonight, it was a good thing. If everyone was here, they wouldn't be at the inn. The few women in town wore their best. Señora

Luisa was there, selling her sweet tea to a long line of revelers. She gave me a small salute when she saw me, which I returned. I'd have to grab some sweet tea later.

To my utter surprise, the first thing I did when we arrived at the party was search for Alejandro in the crowd. I scolded myself for thinking of him at a time like this instead of our plan, though he *was* already part of the plan, ¿no? I shut my eyes to refocus, knocking into someone. It was a burly man with a scowl on his lips.

"I—I'm sorry," I said, taken aback. "I didn't see you there."

He grunted at me as if he wasn't about to let me get away with what I just did. "Not yet, you're not."

"I really am sorry," I said, hoping that would be enough to be the end of it.

But when I moved to leave, he stepped in front of me. "Girls like you don't belong here with all the men."

I saw he had a cup of sweet tea from doña Luisa. Did he think she didn't belong too? I didn't think he understood what he was suggesting and where his drink had come from. Luisa didn't have a husband; she was doing all of this on her own. She was a successful business owner. And she was amazing. I wondered what the man would think of the woman who had made him his drink.

"I think you owe me something more than an apology," he said. He pointed at what he wanted. It was my necklace, the one that Abuela gave me before she passed away. It was one of the few things that we had from her, and I'd worn it today only for its extravagance—it was fine silver, etched in the form of a perfect rose.

"I can't give you my necklace when I've already offered you

my apologies," I said, backing away, fingertips guarding the
necklace. This time I searched for another boy. My brother was
here somewhere. Our plan had been to separate at the party
and come back together once we had some ideas of how to
cause a good distraction.

"I could cut your hand right off, or your fingers one by
one," the man said, still not moving out of my way. It was an
appalling thought. Made even worse by the fact that I was
dressed as a señorita, was a señorita, should be treated with if
not kindness, then respect. I hadn't done anything to this man,
yet there we were.

The music continued despite the confrontation; some men
played the drums, their beat rhythmic. Others strummed guitars.
Yet others played instruments that I had never seen before and I
didn't know the names of. I realized then that I'd lost Mamá and
Papá in the crowd as well. I searched for them next and spotted them standing with who else but el Diablo himself. Señor
Hernández greeted them with a hug for Papá and a handshake
for Mamá, which he finished off with a small kiss on the back of
her hand. I wasn't fooled by his false kindness, and I hoped neither were my parents. Where Papá's body seemed to physically
ease after señor Hernández did this, Mamá wiped her hand on
her dress when the man wasn't looking.

She was there at la plaza too. I knew she didn't trust the
man.

"Well, girl, what's it going to be?" the man added.

I finally spotted Víctor talking to some of the young men
who had arrived before us. I wasn't sure what to think of it.
He seemed so natural among them. I'd never fit in the way he
did. Not back in Sonora, and not even here considering most

people stared at me as I walked by but didn't say a word or else treated me like this man was treating me now—like scum because I surely thought I was too good and better than they were.

In this case, I ventured that I really was better than this man, but perhaps not so dangerous.

It felt strange to know that I was Salvación and that I would be treated differently had I arrived dressed as the vigilante instead of as myself. I thought about screaming, about showing myself to be who they wanted me to be. But I was Salvación, and I didn't ask others for help, I gave them the help they needed.

Someone was handing out drinks as if they were lollipops. I watched in horror as Víctor took one. But it honestly didn't seem like the worst idea.

Without a single word, I hurried over to him. To my annoyance, the burly man trailed behind me.

Víctor took a cup of alcohol, which I promptly stole away. I took a long drink, then I threw the rest of the drink in the man's face when he touched my shoulder roughly.

The crowd stilled. The man gasped angrily, and Víctor looked from the man to me. The man was at least a foot taller than my brother—a whole lot stronger too. Even if Víctor was the more agile fighter of the two, I wasn't sure he'd make it through unscathed. I'd wanted a distraction, but I had most definitely not wanted Víctor hurt.

I waited for the man to hit me. With so much sal negra coursing through me, I wasn't sure that I would feel anything.

"That was good alcohol," a familiar voice said from behind me. "What prompted you to throw it at Irvan's face, exactly?"

"It tasted like water to me," I said, keeping my eyes on Irvan. "And he said he'd cut my fingers off if I didn't give him my necklace."

Víctor tensed. I formed my hands into fists, not that I thought I could fight my way out of this one.

I turned to find Alejandro staring at me with big, tired eyes. He was smiling, so different from the other night. His cheeks looked flushed pink. He swayed a bit.

"Is that true?" Alejandro asked before Víctor could say anything.

Irvan looked away; he seemed scared of Alejandro, which didn't make any sense to me. He was so much bigger than the boy.

I'd thought before that he didn't have much authority under señor Hernández, but perhaps I was wrong. I needed to be careful and backtrack whatever feelings I thought I might have for the boy. He was the enemy, *my* enemy.

The man still hadn't looked Alejandro in the eye. "I'm sorry. Don't tell the boss."

Alejandro pivoted his head. There were so many people that it seemed like all those who saw me throw the drink at the man were back to their other usual gossip.

It was going to be harder to cause a distraction than I had thought.

His gaze landed on the man. "Leave and don't go near her again, or you're the one who won't have any fingers after tonight."

The man nodded and walked away, but not before glaring at me. It made my stomach twist, thinking that if Alejandro hadn't been here, something catastrophic might have happened.

"You didn't have to do that," I told Alejandro, holding back a grin. I wasn't sure why it annoyed me so much that he had intervened. And I wasn't sure why it could be *so good* that he had.

He chuckled. "You're welcome," he said, swaying more.

"Can I tell you a trick?" I said.

He nodded, coming close, sticking his tongue out just a little between his bottom and top lip in a way that made my stomach swoop.

Víctor tried to grab my hand, as if warning me to stay away from Alejandro, as if knowing that I was about to push someone's boundaries and they might not like it. Whenever I did that with my family, I knew that I wouldn't get much more than a scolding. Alejandro was different, yet I couldn't help myself.

"You can sober up with sal negra. It recalibrates the body and the mind. It's—"

"Magia," Alejandro finished, his eyes widening when he said it.

He was staring at me with a warm gaze. The slight upturn of his lips as he took me in made me feel like we were the only two people here. He'd always stared at me, but there was something different; this time there wasn't hatred in his gaze.

I wondered if he knew it was me hiding in the forest. If he knew that I'd seen them murder the man from la plaza. I wondered if treating me differently sudden was a ploy—one that would jeopardize everything we were trying to do. But he wasn't treating me differently. I was still so sure that when I pushed the man into the crowd around señor Hernández, Alejandro had stepped up by my side in la plaza in order to protect me in some way.

"Oh, hello, there," Víctor said, and disappeared suddenly,

SALVACIÓN · 151

leaving me with Alejandro to go grab some beef skewers that had been set upon a table. I wanted him to come back, not to leave me alone with the boy. To come back because we still had work to do tonight. I couldn't let Alejandro distract me.

Though, I admitted, he *was* distracting.

There was something about the redness of his lips, the sheen of his black hair, the way he had dimples when he grinned.

Alejandro got closer. I thought he'd smell of drink and sweat, but he smelled of something else, something familiar—sal negra, same as me. He was probably covered in it too.

"You look beautiful . . ." he said, not mentioning what he probably smelled on me as well—that I was also wearing a heavy dose of sal negra, "Lola de La Peña."

Instead of saying anything or calling me out, he brushed my hair behind my ears. The action made my breath hitch in my throat. It caught me so off guard I didn't move away. I thought of what Víctor had said earlier. There had been boys around me this whole time. But I didn't really care about them enough to let them get to know me.

"You really didn't have to help. Víctor would have taken care of the man. And if not him, Papá would have surely skewered him through the belly at some point."

He grew serious, eyes wide at my words. I guessed ladies didn't often talk about death with him. "I'm sorry, again. I don't have any say in what men my boss takes on. It's his business and his company. My job is to manage things. To do exactly what I just did. Stop problems from happening before they get too out of hand. Do I think he was really going to cut your fingers? No. Do I think that it was wrong of him to threaten you? Absolutely."

What was so special about Alejandro that had me stuck in place even when I had to go and save the world? There wasn't anything, not on the surface. I shouldn't like him. A couple of chance encounters, one in which he was full of drink and being nice to me didn't mean anything unless it was a continuous kindness.

Victor had already walked away from us. Any minute now, he'd find a good distraction, and then it'd be my time to act. Would I be able to slip away from Alejandro's side?

I wasn't sure that I wanted to, but I needed to figure out a way to shake him off.

Alejandro might have seemed sorry that his boss killed a man, but he was still working for señor Hernández. They were here to destroy us all. There was no way I could fall for someone like him, no matter what his eyes told me in this moment.

But then I remembered how he'd stood in front of me with señor Hernández, moving away only when Mamá arrived to help me. And I couldn't imagine that he might be terrible. There was something in the way he stared at me. As if he wanted to protect me. I only wished he understood that I was the Angel of Coloma. I did the protecting, not the other way around, and perhaps that was what he needed—a way out of whatever hole he had found himself in. Perhaps he needed someone's help.

"Coloma is peaceful," he said, taking it all in with a sigh.

The sun was going down. Hues of pink and red and orange stretched across the horizon. He looked beautiful in the evening glow. I wondered how he could mean it after what had happened the night before.

And I wondered how much he would have had to drink to feel it considering he had sal negra on him as well. Seeing him in such a happy state after watching a man die so violently made me wonder if drink helped forget the sound of screams. I so desperately wanted to get his screams out of my mind. The only way, though, for me wasn't drink and wasn't to numb it all away. I needed to vanquish the evil that had caused such a traumatic event. I was convinced that to make the memory of the man's screams disappear and the guilt melt away, I needed to stop it from ever happening to someone else again.

In the middle of my thoughts, I suddenly locked eyes with Víctor, who looked like he was holding back a grin. I wanted to tell him it wasn't what he thought. I wasn't standing here, flirting with our enemy. I didn't have feelings for Alejandro.

But then his face twisted, his mouth opening into a slight O as if something else was dawning on him.

He winked and it was all I needed to know. Like Mamá, Víctor had inherited the ability of speaking with his eyes. It was a strange thing that I wondered if I did too. Víctor's eyes always spoke up when he was about to do something mischievous that I wouldn't approve of. This was one of those moments.

I gave him a look to stop him in his tracks. But he didn't freeze. He didn't turn back. He came toward us, and I knew this wouldn't be good.

In one swift moment, he knocked into Alejandro, who spilled his drink all over himself and onto me.

"Víctor!" I screamed, not even faking it. I was soaked enough that surely the liquid would make my Salvación disguise wet as well.

"I don't think my sister wants to speak to you anymore," Víctor said, his face grimacing in feigned anger.

Alejandro's features contorted with confusion, though to his credit, he tried to dab at my dress to help, but I pushed him away. When I did, he shifted angrily toward Víctor, shoving my brother back in the process.

"What's your problem?" he asked, taking the bait.

Víctor's smirk only seemed to make him more upset.

When I'd asked Víctor to find a distraction, I didn't think that he'd get into a fight with Hernández's right hand. We'd just seen a man twice Alejandro's size cower before him.

Still, I took my cue, trying to refocus on the task at hand, and not be burdened with having to figure out Alejandro. I left as everyone rushed toward the sound of yelling between my brother and Alejandro. I hoped neither would hurt the other.

I became a shadow, someone of little interest as I hurried away, pretending to cry over my poor beautiful but ruined vestido, and seemingly fleeing home in distress.

I changed out of my dress in the shadow of the alley on the side of the inn, leaving it behind in the darkness to make sure it stayed as clean as possible. In my pants now, I could move easier, libremente; this is how I wanted to be now and forever. I tied my mask on my face. I'd changed into Salvación so many times that it was like a second skin to me. I was transformed. And it was glorious. I wondered if one day I would be able to be Salvación out in the open, without the mask. Maybe after all this was over, I thought suddenly, I would hang up my mask and I wouldn't be Salvación anymore at all. Would it be freeing? To rid myself of this burden. Was it a burden at all? Answering that question wasn't easy and would have to wait until this was all over. I only wondered if Mamá ever saw her calling as an affliction.

Despite what Mamá and Papá wanted, the thing about becoming Salvación was that it offered me the freedom to do whatever I thought was right without worrying about what anyone else would do at any given moment. A lot of the times it matched up with what Mamá and Papá believed. Other times, it didn't. I wasn't sure we would ever see eye to eye about Hernández, and we didn't need to. All I had to do was make sure that he was gone soon.

And afterward, maybe for once I'd be allowed to be myself.

The night was oddly cold for the middle of summer. The winds blew like the weather was changing and we'd be seeing storms soon. It seemed to carry with it a bad omen.

From the alley, I heard voices on the front of the building. I inched my way forward, taking a quick peek. There were a few men outside the inn's door. It seemed like not everyone was at Hernández's party after all. Were these men here because they had drawn the short straw, as punishment? Or had they volunteered to get in good with the boss?

I wasn't going to be able to sneak into Hernández's room through the front door of the inn. Not that this was part of the plan to begin with. I went around to the back.

Hernández and his men had taken over the town in less than a day. They had the new inn, which hadn't even been ready to the public, and now he was there, taking it over as if he planned to stay awhile. Alejandro was surely staying there, too, and many of the others. The rest of his camp was set up just on the outskirts of town, near the forest, near the mountain— near the only way out of town. They were closing us in. They'd surrounded us. How were Papá and all the others in Coloma blind to this? We were trapped.

I took a moment to consider my options. Obviously leaving or failing wasn't among them. That only left me with trying to figure out how I was going to get inside without calling attention to the men guarding the inn. Where was Víctor to cause another distraction?

I crept through the shadows. Someone was singing in the distance now, and the commotion that Víctor had caused at the fiesta seemed to have died down. I hoped he hadn't been knocked out by Alejandro or the other way around.

I couldn't worry about them now, though. I couldn't fail tonight. Not if we were to have a fighting chance to save Coloma, and the entire world.

Two men walked by, neither noticing me in the shadow of the inn. They were both tall and stronger than me, and in any other moment, they might have caught me—and then it would all be over.

I was about to come out of hiding when I overheard their conversation.

"Boss said to keep an eye out for Salvación."

The other man snorted. "He's really afraid of a mythical creature?"

"Boss isn't afraid of anything," the first replied. "And if it's to be believed, what the people of Coloma have been saying, Salvación is an angel. They say she appears out of nowhere and drives away those who aim to do harm to the people of Coloma. That's us."

I'd been right. The fools had just admitted to what I'd thought all along. They were not here to be our friends but to hurt us.

"Are you saying he *should* be afraid?" The second man sounded quizzical now, as if this were a battle to be fought between un ángel and el Diablo.

In a way, that was what it felt like to me too. Only I had never been an angel. I hadn't been in Sonora. I hadn't been the way I am now; hadn't thought of anyone else but myself. I am not invincible. I'm only a slightly better person than I was a year ago.

The man continued, "I think it's just a story they like to tell themselves. These people out here, they're miners, doing some of the hardest work there is. I'm sure many of them get fed up and simply leave without owing anyone an explanation. And then the people think this Salvación did it. If there even is a Salvación."

I tried to see if there was a window low enough for me to crawl through. The only open window that made any sense, though, was at least three stories up. I could make it, especially since I'd removed my dress, but doing so would mean taking the chance that I'd fall from the railings of the other windows I'd be hanging off on the way up. I might not die from the drop, but I'd definitely be injured, likely unable to walk, and of course, captured.

Still, I had to try. This was our best shot.

I checked my clothing, double-tied the mask on my face

so it wouldn't get loose, and then leapt. The first time my fingers caught the edge of the window above me, but I couldn't hold my grip. The second time, I didn't even reach the railings. The third, I caught myself only to fall on my butt. My tailbone hurt after that one, and I stood rubbing the soreness out of my spine, then checked to see if the sound of my fall had alerted the guards. When no one came, and they still seemed to be speaking about Salvación—a conversation I was fascinated by but didn't have the time for—I refocused, got low, then leapt, taking hold of the metal railing with all my might and pulling myself up to the first floor's window ledge. It was narrow, barely the width of my feet. I had no idea how I was going to make it to the second-floor windowsill without being able to squat into a lunge, and I made the mistake of looking down. I imagined myself in exactly this situation but in a dress. I chuckled, losing my balance. My heart slipped along with my boot, but I caught myself, my grip coming to my aid once again. Luckily, I also noticed that the window was cracked open.

I pushed through the window and tumbled into the room, which was . . .

Completely empty.

I wasn't expecting nothing. I had thought that Hernández would share the inn with his men, but he hadn't even given them a good place to rest.

It made my blood boil even more. The men following him were foolish if they thought they wouldn't one day share in the same fate as their boss's victims.

I slipped out of the room; the hallway was dark and threatening. Room by room, I checked for Hernández's living quarters. Room by room, there was nothing: no furniture, no clothing, *nothing*. It made the inn eerie, every creak the floorboards made caused my heart to skip a beat, and I wasn't sure my idea had been good after all.

I hadn't ever noticed, I guess because my family had always been a part of my life, that people were what made buildings and houses and rooms vibrant: the things we had, our laughter, the very aspect of having someone you know next to you, everything. Without people, rooms were meaningless.

Finally, I reached the room at the end of the hallway. Since there was a huge distance between the other doors and this one, I knew it was going to be the biggest room in the inn, reserved for the most important guests. I'd seen señor Hernández with Mamá and Papá en la fiesta, yet my hands still began to perspire. I was so nervous, even though I was certain there'd be no one in the room. The guards were outside.

I listened closely at the doorway. There was no light on inside. I could tell because there was no light coming from underneath the door. Still, I hesitated before turning the knob. What if señor Hernández had set a trap? What if the minute I touched it, I melted away like the thief had?

I had to trust in sal negra. I had to trust that Víctor and I had lathered all our bodies in it enough to risk this. Still, I made sure to open the small pouch of sal negra that I'd brought with me and rub more sal on my hands before opening the door. And even then, I touched the door for only a brief moment, patting it a couple of times to make sure I didn't feel anything unusual before gripping the doorknob and twisting it.

I'd been wrong. A small lamp was set up on a desk. It was dim but offered enough light for me to see the room.

I looked around. There was a bed to one side—larger than

even Mamá and Papá's, and they always said they loved to sleep like royalty; a lot of books, or what seemed like journals, were scattered every which way, on the desk, on the floor, on the bed; a revolver he'd stopped cleaning midway. The weapon on the desk, stripped into pieces, surprised me. Why would he leave it unguarded? Maybe I was the only one foolish enough to stand against him. It served as a reminder of how dangerous the man was.

Were Mamá and Papá safe so close to him?

I noticed something else then, a thin and clear container as tall as the length of my hand filled with sal roja. Another next to it, exactly the same size, filled with sal negra.

It was odd, seeing them side by side, as if this were the perfect example of good and evil. One sal destroyed. The other sal healed. Some people believed that everything in the world should have a balance to it; that was why there was new life and there was death. I wasn't sure what to believe. I hoped it was all a lie, or not true in the way it was all made out to be. That there could be peace in death. That good could win and evil could be vanquished. That it didn't have to be so black and white. Being out here and really understanding the world for the first time in my life had me believing that this could be—at least until the men started arriving, those who aimed to hurt Coloma, and Víctor and I became Salvación. My biggest fear was that we'd never be able to have that peaceful world again. Or maybe I was being naive in thinking that we'd ever had it to begin with.

I had the sal roja I needed right at my disposal. I hadn't been sure I'd be so lucky, but there it was. Something so powerful that it could destroy a man in a matter of seconds seemed so natural and tiny and insignificant. But it wasn't. It was small but mighty, and I only hoped that sal negra was mightier.

Before I used the sal roja, I needed to find the amulet. I couldn't risk someone else taking it and gaining control of the sal roja nearby. Salvación was the only one I trusted with it: Víctor and me, that was all.

I meticulously searched Hernández's belongings, careful to set everything back in its place when I was done with it. The process was slow and tedious, but considering there was no one allowed inside the building, let alone this room, I had to make the room look undisturbed, especially when I went missing from the party. There was nothing like an amulet in sight, though. The man didn't even have any jewelry or plata fina. There was nothing here of value except for the sal and la pistola and his clothing, which seemed to be made of fine linen. He really was as wealthy as he made himself out to be, I just wondered what mountain of bodies his wealth lay upon.

I was sweating now, starting to panic as the minutes went by and the noise from the party was fading. People would start going home soon if they hadn't already. I'd always been sly as Salvación, but tonight there were more people out and about than ever before.

Despite my caution, I kicked a book on the ground. It skittered loudly, opening as it went. Even though all the rooms had been empty, I was still afraid. I stilled again, sucking in a breath, and holding it in so I could hear over the beating of my own heart. Once enough time had gone by and I was sure I was safe, I went over to the book, trying to remember how it was originally positioned.

The book was the first clue that the woman was telling the

truth—one I might be able to take back to Papá. Even once Hernández was gone, it wouldn't be the end of things. His men might still want the power that sal roja was bringing them. I needed Papá to be on my side when it all happened. I needed him to destroy the company and make sure that a new leader never rose up. The only one of them that I could see being that new leader, though, was Alejandro. It made my stomach sour at the thought. I couldn't imagine he was the type of person who dragged a man into the forest and ended his life over something as trivial as what had occurred in la plaza.

Inside the book was the photo of an amulet—colored like plata and with a giant red gemstone at its center—or was it a crystallized version of sal roja? I picked the book up to examine the page closer, careful not to leave a fingerprint smudge or to bend any of the pages. Not that it might be easy to notice, the notebook was used, the pages looked thumbed through constantly. Only it wasn't a book. It was a log dating back twenty years. Whatever it was to Hernández, the page talked about the amulet, its location, its use; it seemed to track everyone whom he had come into contact with that led to Hernández finally finding the amulet.

Twenty years.

It was a difficult fact to wrap my mind around, a difficult history to understand. He had been searching for the amulet for longer than I had been alive.

Why hadn't the news of sal negra spread before Coloma then? Surely he'd found sal negra before sal roja, or it might have been too dangerous to be around sal roja.

As far as anyone around here knew, Coloma was the first place where sal negra had been found. But if sal roja had existed in other places before, surely sal negra did as well. I tried to tie the story together, but everything I thought of seemed too extreme, too fabricated.

What did it all mean?

Had Hernández destroyed every trace of sal roja and negra entirely for all these years and just slipped up with Coloma? This realization made him that much scarier and made me shiver. Someone who hadn't known the sal existed until recently somehow felt like less of a threat. But in this situation, *we* were the ones who had come out of nowhere. *We* were the ones who had stepped onto what he surely thought of as his claim—I didn't doubt that was the way he saw it, anyway.

Worse, the Treaty of Guadalupe Hidalgo surely made him feel like time was running out. It trapped him, made him more dangerous to us.

Suddenly I grew aware that I was in el Diablo's home, without any backup, with only the Yankee's heirloom revolver and my knife in hand. I took out my knife and carefully cut the page out. I knew it was dangerous to take it with me, but I hoped he wouldn't notice anytime soon. There were many other books and journals on the ground—if I was lucky enough, this was one he wouldn't look at for a while. Once loose, I rolled up the page, stuffing it gently into a pocket.

I hurried, putting the book back into place and continuing my search for the amulet. Where could it be? Where would he leave it? And then another question occurred to me: *Why* would he leave it?

I'd assumed that something so valuable would be hidden, which meant he'd likely have it in his room, because that was where I would have hidden something of my own.

But if I stepped into his shoes . . . he wouldn't have left it. Sal roja and negra, sure. If anyone messed with those, chances were they'd likely get themselves killed with the sal roja. His revolver, sure. But the amulet? He'd have it on him at all times. Hidden in plain sight.

I swore under my breath.

Our plan would have to change. Some point after Hernández found his demise at the hand of sal roja, we'd need to figure out if he really did have the amulet on him.

I rubbed more sal negra on my hands, bit at my lip as I stared at the container of sal roja. What held it all together? What kept it from eating through its container? Did it only destroy life—the soil, skin and bones, organic material?

I grabbed it and went back to the bed. I needed to put a single grain or two where it would touch Hernández's skin the moment he laid down. On his pillow made the most sense.

I opened the container carefully. Since I couldn't touch it by hand, I had to tilt the container and hope it wouldn't overflow.

I moved to get it done.

Held my breath.

Then heard a noise in my stillness.

I froze. There was someone in the inn, perhaps one of the guards. I had to hurry and make sure I didn't get caught. But I also had to take my time, do this right, so I didn't hurt myself in the process. As much as I was willing to risk my life to get the job done, I didn't want to die.

I put my ear to the entryway. When I didn't hear anything anymore, I opened the door an inch or two to see.

Alejandro stood in front of me, his eyes large, his stance ready to attack. But he seemed to be waiting for me to react.

SALVACIÓN · 165

Perhaps he wasn't even looking at me, hadn't seen me, wasn't sure *what* he was seeing.

I thought I could still salvage the situation, but I couldn't move my feet.

I was a cornered animal. I'd seen Papá hunting enough times to know what prey looked like. I was the prey in this situation, and Alejandro was the predator. He could move at any moment, and I wouldn't have a way to escape except to jump out the window, maybe hurt myself.

We stood there, he and I, watching each other, neither of us acting. It occurred to me: Was he outside Hernández's room to do the same thing I was attempting? Had he been intending to steal from the man? Or perhaps he was grabbing something for him? For some reason, I doubted that was the case. All my insides told me there was more to Alejandro than met the eye.

For good—or for bad.

"Salvación?" he said, his eyes aglow, almost as if he couldn't believe what he was seeing. He took a step forward. I took a step back. I'd never been caught like this before, and I wasn't entirely sure what to do. But he had the answer for me. "You should run."

Where before I had stood stuck in place because of fear, I now stood in place because of the utter shock of the moment.

Was Alejandro helping me? Or was he telling me he'd give me a head start? They were the same words he'd said to the man in la plaza. We'd played this scene out before, and it hadn't ended well. I didn't want to and couldn't imagine dying because Alejandro, the boy who I hadn't been able to get out of my head, had caught me.

I glanced at my clothing, trying to make sure that I wasn't

dressed as Lola de La Peña. I'd jump out of the window no matter my injuries if it meant I had the chance to get away. If word got back to señor Hernández that I had been in his room, he'd take it out on my family, I didn't have a doubt about it.

"It's okay," he continued, his voice low as if he didn't want to spook me, his hands up as if showing he wasn't a threat. Was he at all afraid of me? "I won't say a word. But you have to leave. Now."

He was talking to Salvación. He was *helping* Salvación.

When it sank in, I did what I was told. I opened the door, hurried along past him, the drawing of the amulet in my pocket, the sal roja still in my hand.

I inched past him, and his hand brushed mine as he took the sal roja from me. "This stays or he'll notice it's missing," he whispered, his expression calculating rather than cold.

It froze me, the feel of his touch. It was as if the sal negra on both of our hands connected and clicked and something sparked between us. It was electric being so close to him, and I felt a drop in my stomach, the same feeling as when you fall in a dream. Was the feeling a giveaway?

I let go of the sal roja. When our eyes met, there was an intensity there.

"Don't come back," he added. "He let down his guard tonight, but he already realized it was a mistake even before knowing his room was broken into. There'll be a trap set up next time."

I nodded once. Alejandro walked into señor Hernández's room, leaving me alone in the hallway. I ran when I was out of Alejandro's sight. Swiftly, quietly, down the stairs, where the two guards were still in front of the main door. I didn't hesitate, though, I didn't freeze, feeling this wild desire to get out of the inn as quickly as possible. I sneaked out the service door facing the alley. Once in the alleyway, I stopped and looked up while holding my side and trying to catch my breath. For some reason I'd expected Alejandro to be staring down at me and to be watching as I left. But there was no one. It made it that much scarier. La fiesta must have finally been dying down, because it was so much darker outside. I had been used to being the shadow coming for those who did wrong in the night. Tonight, I felt like the shadows were stalking *me*. I couldn't believe what had happened.

I sneaked over to where I'd left my dress and picked it up. I didn't put it on. I didn't care. I could barely think straight. I hurried out of town. I didn't stop until I'd hiked the mountain with my dress, until I got to where Víctor was supposed to meet me.

Only when I got to the top, he wasn't there as we'd agreed. It didn't make any sense. We said he should cause a distraction and then come here immediately. Had he gotten hurt? Had he simply gotten delayed? I wasn't sure which was more probable. The forest felt incredibly empty without him here waiting for me.

I was exhausted and shaking, and I gasped for breath. That was close, too close. I got away only because of Alejandro. He could have discovered my identity. He could have called Hernández. He could have stopped me—could have killed me.

Why didn't he?

"Loli?" a voice called out. I didn't know what overcame me, but I leapt up from where I was, finally letting the dress go, and hugged Víctor, crying.

"Where were you?" I shouted, still gasping for breath as my emotions came out all at once. I'd never been one to break down. Even back in Sonora, where the girls could be cruel and the boys broke hearts easily.

"I got stuck with Mamá and Papá after the fight; I had to wait them out. Are you okay?" he asked me, concern coating his voice. "Are you hurt?"

I could have been hurt.

I could have died.

I could have gotten trapped inside the inn, could have been tortured.

Instead, I'd only failed. I didn't have the amulet. I hadn't placed the sal roja where we could beat Hernández at his own game.

I shook my head. "I failed, Víctor."

He held me closer, patting the back of my head as I sobbed. "It's okay, Loli. It's okay. We'll figure out another way."

The only problem was, I didn't see any other way in front of us.

CHAPTER 11

I couldn't sleep, tossing all night until I finally picked up Papá's old guitar and strummed until my fingers felt too sore to keep going. Even then, I just held the guitar in my hands, remembering the day Papá had chosen to give it to me instead of Víctor. I remembered the look on Víctor's face. I'd laughed at the expression then, I'd thrown it in his face in Sonora, made him feel inferior because of it, but I didn't consider it all that funny anymore. I'd hurt Víctor by accepting the guitar. In that moment, I wanted to destroy it. I'd risked losing my brother's affection for a bit of Papá's. I'd never realized how much I needed Víctor and how much he meant to me. I couldn't do this without him.

I was out of bed before the sun kissed the horizon on a new day and the birds began their song. I needed air and to clear my mind, take Carisma for a run. I kept unfolding the page I took and staring at Hernández's log and the image of the amulet.

Would it be enough evidence to show to Papá and Mamá for them to take my side against Hernández?

And had Alejandro done what I hadn't been able to with the sal roja? Something told me that wasn't the case. If he were going to murder his boss with sal roja, he'd have done it long before.

Víctor wouldn't be awake for another couple of hours. I crept by his room, leaving the guitar outside his door. I wished I'd given it to him when Papá first offered it to me. Or at least offered to share it. I thought of the night before. A lot of the time that I was Salvación, I acted like the older sibling. But last night, I understood why I couldn't be Salvación alone. It was too burdensome for one person. And Víctor helped me make sense of our failures as much as our successes.

Despite how he helped settle my thoughts last night, it wasn't enough this morning. I ran out the door as quietly as possible, walked over to our stables, and fed and groomed Carisma. Then I put her riding gear on and mounted up.

I was in my dress, but still wore my Salvación pants underneath so I wouldn't have to ride sidesaddle, which would only slow me down.

I galloped all the way to the field where Víctor and I had found the woman, hoping that I could find a clue as to where she went. Something told me that she'd gone home. I figured if I could find her, I could bring her back, get her to tell Papá her story. If I had both her word and the page in my pocket, it might be enough to burn through whatever hold the man seemed to have on Papá's dream of Alta California remaining.

Papá needed to know that Hernández was using sal roja inhumanely.

Or maybe Papá already knew that Hernández was shit and wasn't telling the truth.

Maybe Papá was interested only in what the man had to offer him. Except what he had to offer wasn't real—just something to make people fall in love with his plans and take away their souls.

But Papá didn't understand how he planned to get it.

I recognized I had arrived at the right place because sal roja had burned the patch of grass. Worse, it had infected the soil around where it had originally landed and spread.

The scorch was three times larger than it was the last time I saw it. If I squinted my eyes and stared closely enough at the edges, I could see the burn spreading. Sal negra didn't affect soil in this way. The flowers that sprang up when it touched the soil didn't spread, and they were beautiful. One piece of sal negra for one flower. That was how it'd always been. But this was something strange and abnormal and wrong and I didn't understand it—and I didn't want to have to.

In a way, I was almost glad that Alejandro had stopped me from unleashing sal roja right in the middle of Coloma last night. The inn would have ended up like this. It was like a dark disease had infected the earth.

I leapt off Carisma, kissed her nose, and petted her head the way she liked. "Quédate," I said. She listened, stayed put, but watched me as if she were the one worried about me and not the other way around.

I kept an eye on my horse, making sure she wasn't getting too close to the sal roja, recalling how dangerous it was. And she kept one eye on me, neighing and stomping the grass below her hooves the closer I got to the spot. She neighed louder as I knelt in front of the scorch.

I clicked my tongue a few times. "I'm okay, I only need a moment," I told Carisma, which seemed to settle her for the time being.

I took the sal negra that I carried with me and sprinkled half the fist-sized pouch across the area that was being affected. I hoped it would be enough to stop the diseased soil from spreading farther out. If it wasn't, I didn't want to think about what would happen when it reached town.

Had Isabela known what she was bringing to Coloma? She had come to warn us, she said, but we were all at risk because she did. She never said that the only real way to make things better was to pack up and leave Coloma.

If she hadn't come here, though, I would never have known about señor Hernández and what a monster he is. If I hadn't known, I wouldn't have followed him into the forest and seen for myself, which was why it was so important that we didn't fail.

But I *did* fail last night. And even Víctor's consolation hadn't been enough, not when we were being attacked from both within and outside of Coloma. Hernández was already inside our home, already trying to claim it all for himself. And this sal roja, if it kept spreading, would eventually reach us even if Hernández didn't manage to tear us apart himself.

I stood, trying to make sense of everything that was happening, though I couldn't put the pieces all together in a way that suited me. I needed to know the amulet's location.

That was when I spotted them: tracks from a horse leading away from this spot, away from Coloma. But also, shoe prints,

SALVACIÓN · 173

from a shoe slightly larger than my own foot. Isabela must have stopped here on the way out of town, to see the spot.

My blood boiled. Was there no honor left in anyone? Was there no winning this?

I followed the tracks on foot, unsure if it was the right direction to go, Carisma behind me. I didn't get far before someone said, "You're a ways from home." The voice startled me, and I first made sure that Carisma was all right. When I saw she was, I turned to the voice.

The sun had barely begun to rise on the Alta Californian horizon, and I thought I'd be the only one out at this hour. Still, I wasn't fully surprised that it was Alejandro who'd found me, as he'd done last night, when I was dressed as Salvación. I was only relieved that I didn't have to worry about him recognizing me. Out here, I was safe as Lola de La Peña. At least I believed so. The puffiness and dark circles around his eyes made it seem like he hadn't been able to sleep himself.

He almost seemed worried about me. Like he couldn't quite explain to himself what I was doing out here alone, but I could take care of myself. Or perhaps he'd seen the scorch marks as well. Perhaps he knew what was coming to Coloma too. Maybe he even regretted not doing what I started yesterday. There had to be a way to stop Hernández.

Outside of Hernández's camp, I was in my world. Coloma was my world. And I knew and breathed this world entirely: the fish that swam in the river, the mayflies that flew nearby, the tall grass that swayed in the wind and was perfectly still in the summer evenings when everything else stopped, too, the wind that calmed Carisma, the clouds that brought the rain.

To me, Alejandro was the one who shouldn't have been

wandering all alone in a place where he wasn't welcome—at least not by Salvación.

Though he had saved me last night and I wasn't going to forget it, I also needed to know why he'd done it. He could have called the guards. He could have stopped me himself. He had let me go. It didn't make any sense unless he *wanted* to get rid of his boss. I wanted to ask him if he had done it, if he'd succeeded in stopping señor Hernández, but I also knew in my heart the answer was no. There was another game Alejandro was playing.

"I like being alone, it helps me think," I replied after a moment, having to say something as Alejandro stared. The fear from what happened last night made my hands sweat around him. Did he already know that I was Salvación? Could he see right through me?

He opened his eyes wide as if he didn't expect me to have any thoughts in my brain at all, and any good feeling I had about him left with the morning breeze.

I rolled my eyes, wishing I could shoot him in the leg and ask him to leave my home and take his boss with him. It would be easier that way. But I had thought about it all night long; I needed to be smart about this and come up with a real plan. One that didn't involve giving myself away as Salvación. One that didn't involve Alejandro at all.

"What are you out here thinking about?" He seemed genuinely curious but didn't glance my way as he asked. His face was pointed toward the sunrise, his eyes on the dark gray clouds that were coming our way as if scrutinizing them would make them vanish. I kept my position in between the sal roja and Alejandro, careful not to let him get any closer to it, trying to block it completely with my body. The last thing I wanted was to have a conversation about it. I've been many things, and sometimes, yes, I was a liar when I made promises. Back in Sonora more than here. But most of the time, lying didn't come easily for me. And for some reason, even though I didn't trust Alejandro, I found myself wanting to be honest with him.

"I'm thinking about how I want you and your boss and all the rest of you gone and am trying to figure out how to make it happen. If you have any suggestions, I'll take 'em."

He watched me as I mounted Carisma, led her away, and therefore led Alejandro and his horse away, too, from the sal roja, which if he noticed he didn't mention—probably on purpose not to draw more attention to it or himself.

After a moment, he laughed loudly, though. His laughter echoed against the backdrop of the wide valley. Then he stopped, looked back out beyond the mountain, as if realizing I had been serious. "You know, I'm surprised you ride." He examined Carisma. "Your horse is beautiful—"

"More importantly, fast as lightning."

"Doesn't matter how fast a horse is without a skilled rider."

I smirked, snorted, understanding that he was calling me unskilled. Papá had taught me to ride a horse as soon as I could walk. I was a better rider than Víctor. But Alejandro was something else with horses, could ride as one with them; I could see it in his horse's eyes.

"You want to race?" I asked without thinking much of it.

He grinned, licked at his lips before saying, "I won't go easy on you."

"Carisma is faster than your horse and I'm a better rider than you can dream to be." It was an exaggeration, but he didn't need to know that. Perhaps I *was* a better rider; I'd never see him go anything faster than a trot. But I knew I had more heart than him. I knew Carisma had more heart than any other horse alive. I'd seen it on the way from Sonora to Coloma.

He laughed, his gaze toward the scenery. "Where does the race end?"

Alta California was beautiful. Nature surrounded us—the morning light was soft and amarilla and the birds began to sing their morning melodies. There was grass as far as you could see. Tall mountains to one side, the river, winding down into another. A wide-open space you could revel in. What would happen to it all if the sal roja spread? I'd been so worried about Coloma and its people, I'd almost forgotten the land, which was just as, if not more, important.

"There." I pointed to where the line of trees started, in front of the horizon. "Do you see that one tall tree, the third one from the left?"

"To the tree?"

I nodded.

"Okay," he said.

He took hold of the reins of his horse, smiled for the very first time. It was a joyful smile, as if he hadn't had this much fun in so long. As if being next to me offered comfort. I guess, if I thought about it, his company did comfort more than frighten me. It wasn't that I necessarily trusted Alejandro, but I felt safe with him, like staying this close to my enemy meant that I couldn't get hurt, or that he wouldn't see me coming after him.

"On the count of three?"

"On the count of three."

We counted together, staring at each other's faces—one, two, three—and it was hard to remember Alejandro *was* my enemy. That he was working for the man who aimed to destroy us all. That he hadn't treated me kindly, unless you could count the time that he saved me when I was dressed as Salvación—which I didn't. Still, his eyes were bright and happy and I never wanted to turn away from them.

Suddenly, we were two young people who might have been friends or something else entirely in another life. In a life like the one I'd had in Sonora, where I was only Lola de La Peña.

Who had Alejandro been in his other life? I wondered, and then we were off.

There was only the wind brushing against my cheeks; the rush of the cold air hitting the back of my throat as I whooped; the thrill of the gallop; the force of Carisma pulling my body forward so fast that everything around us was a blur; the trees and sky and mountains all collapsed into one, and it was as if we weren't human at all but light moving at full speed.

I would be lying if I said I wasn't surprised that Alejandro kept up so well. I would also be lying if I said I didn't like it. It felt good to have a worthy adversary. Víctor stopped racing me years ago, after he tired of losing. It felt good to have someone by my side as I rode. To have someone here in this moment as I tried to come to terms with everything I'd discovered. Even if Alejandro might realize that I was the person he saw at the inn yesterday if I wasn't careful. I always wore a disguise when I was Salvación, sure, but I wasn't entirely certain that the way I walked, the way I moved, the way I was, wouldn't give me away, especially when I thought that Alejandro was one of those people who, like me, watched and paid attention to everything.

Alejandro was yelling into the sky as well. And calling his horse forward. Prisa, that was what he called his horse. *Hurry. Hurry. Hurry. Go faster, Prisa.*

"¡Vamos, Carisma!" I shouted, trying to drown out his voice.

Out of nowhere, Alejandro passed me, staring at me as he did, as if proving himself right by beating me.

Only he wouldn't win. I bowed my head toward Carisma's ears, whispered to her, "Vamos, amor. Rápido." Hurry. Hurry. Hurry.

She was an extraordinary horse. All heart and strength. I didn't care if Alejandro thought he could beat us. I didn't care if Prisa had heart too. Here was the truth: Carisma was the one who would win. He was wrong in thinking that it was what a rider had within them that triumphed in victory when it came to horseback riding.

Carisma was the victory. She was strong and fierce and had taught me much about how to survive and thrive on our way from Sonora to Coloma: the way she took me from one side to another as we crossed dangerous rivers; the way she kept her footing on the mountain range that made most men tremble; the way every day she woke up and carried me, even when everyone and every animal in our group was hungry and weak; the way she outlasted them all.

My horse had always been the love of my life, and that wasn't about to change now. I trusted her completely.

Perhaps if Alejandro had trusted his horse as much as his horse trusted him, he would have kept his victory. Inch by inch, we caught up to Alejandro, surpassed him, and shot past the tree we'd agreed would act as the finish line.

I laughed into the wind, let go of Carisma's reins and lifted my arms up to the sky until she came to a steady stop all by herself. She trotted, dancing a little as she went, almost as if she relished the victory as well.

Alejandro settled beside me, wheezing and out of breath, having lost. He laughed again, and this time it wasn't mocking—he seemed in awe of me. I could see it in his eyes, the way he looked at me not as disdainful as usual. His cheeks were flushed, his smile wide. His lingering smile suited him. Maybe it meant something more. Like he was comfortable enough with me to let his guard down. And if he had his guard down, should I take advantage of it to try and figure out where the amulet could be? Would talking about it make him doubt who I was?

"You're amazing," he said, making any thoughts of using him wilt away. Though he seemed to correct himself, cleared his throat, and reached down to Carisma, as if he had meant her, or only her.

"We're only as good as the people who push us to be better than them," I replied with a grin. He side-grinned, nodding, eyes still cast toward my horse, his cheeks becoming one shade redder than they were before. When he finally glanced up, we locked eyes as if we didn't want to leave the moment. Returning to Coloma meant that we had to face what was happening to the town, and the evil that señor Hernández had brought with him, the evil that maybe Alejandro carried inside him as well.

"There's a storm coming. By the looks of it, an ugly one. You should head home before it arrives," he finally said.

"I bring the storm," I whispered. "I'm not afraid of a storm."

He gave a little scoff, his harsh demeanor emerging once more. I swallowed down the feeling of, I didn't even know what you'd call it, relief that Alejandro made me feel sometimes. "You should be. I've seen storms out here tear wagons apart, kill livestock, sweep up children only to let them go far past too late."

"I didn't say I *shouldn't* be afraid of storms. But I'm not afraid of the world, not afraid of the earth. All it does for us, brings for us, gives us—if the world decides it's my time to die, then so be it."

He stared at me like he didn't believe me. Until yesterday at the inn, I had felt that way. But there was that moment when Alejandro saw me, before he said he'd let me go, that I truly thought I might be dead soon.

I needed to shake that feeling away, the one where I felt fragile. Salvación didn't have the luxury of such things.

Thunder rumbled in the direction of the incoming storm; it was loud and brash and I loved it. It was followed by lightning striking the ground. I'd always been amazed at lightning, the veracity of the sky, the fierceness of the wild.

It was life itself.

I wanted to stay and witness the storm up close, forget what Isabela said about Hernández, forget sal roja existed, even forget that sal negra did too.

Alejandro touched my arm, his fingertips tender yet electric like the storm. "Let's head back," he said.

I nodded, staring at his fingers still on my skin.

He turned without acknowledging that he'd touched me unprompted and signaled to Prisa, who began to gallop.

I watched the storm for one minute more. The lightning struck at a completely different place. Then another bolt hit the ground a hundred yards away from the last. It was magnificent. It was a distraction. It was also, as Alejandro was making a point of letting me know, dangerous.

"A la casa, Carisma," I said, making sure to heed her growing weariness, and then we followed Alejandro and Prisa.

It was as I stared at the back of Alejandro's head that a possible solution to my problem finally came to me—or at least the beginning of a solution, a way to fix things. If I could befriend Alejandro, If I could somehow get him to trust me, he might lead me to the amulet.

What better way to get to Hernández than through his right hand?

Then again, I could barely keep eye contact with him without blushing.

I had only one other choice. I could go after Isabela. I was sure that with Víctor's help, together under the cover of the storm, we'd be able to track her and catch up to wherever she went, offer her the protection of Salvación for coming back and talking with Papá. With Papá on our side, we'd be unstoppable. The people of Coloma might dream and admire Salvación, but Papá was the one who had befriended them. People trusted him.

Neither choice spelled victory. Neither choice made me happy. But the reality was, I didn't want to be alone. I couldn't be alone. Even as Salvación, it was Victor and me.

I glanced once more at the impending storm and followed Alejandro.

CHAPTER 12

Back home, I somehow felt better. The race with Alejandro had given me new energy, made my spirit lighter. I was seated, thinking, picking at some old bread that was staler than I would have liked.

Víctor came out of his room, smiling. Apparently, I wasn't the only one who was feeling better. I hadn't been sure exactly how Víctor would take my gift, but it seemed like I'd made my brother happy. Things were wickedly bad right now; we'd failed, *I'd* failed. But somehow Víctor, family, always made me feel like it was okay to fail.

Today was a new day to try again.

And try again we would.

"The guitar, Loli?" Víctor asked as he joined me at the table. I passed him the bread, which he tried to chew and quickly gave up on. "You left it for me?"

I nodded, also passing him some goat milk to dip the bread in. "I love you. It should be yours."

Suddenly Víctor seemed to realize something. He looked at me like he couldn't quite figure me out. "You seem . . . almost happy."

I tried to stifle my smile, tried to forget Alejandro, how relaxed he seemed around me, and stopped imagining that he was relaxed because of his run-in with Salvación. Because of his run-in with me as myself and our race. I allowed myself to imagine that he might have been happy that Salvación was going to take down his boss.

Who knew.

Víctor looked like a child today, pajamas askew. His hair was a mess. It reminded me how we liked to chase frogs and swim in the creek when we were little and we'd always be in a disarray. But we were competitive then, always had to be racing each other and competing to see who could catch more.

The race with Alejandro had started off as a competition too. But its energy had changed in a way I couldn't explain.

I unfurled the page I'd stolen from señor Hernández and passed it over to Víctor. He made sure Papá and Mamá couldn't hear us and weren't coming our way before opening it.

"Is this a picture of the amulet Isabela was talking about that lets señor Hernández find sal roja?"

"It very much is, hermano. Question is, is this picture proof enough for Papá that Hernández isn't here to help but to hurt us?"

Víctor frowned. "Papá wants things to go back to the way they were so badly, he would give up todo. Both of them believe that they won't come out unharmed from all of this. I just . . ."

He paused to look at the bread. He was picking at it, breaking it apart into little parts. "I can't stand up to them like you do."

It was in moments like these that I realized I'd never known my brother in Sonora. He was a stranger there.

"You're the strongest person I know. Remember that time en el río? Where the man who lost control of his horse almost took me down with him?" I usually tried not to talk about the journey here. It was a subject that all of us would rather forget. But right now I needed Víctor to know that that moment in the river was when everything changed between us. "You risked your life to save me. You came after me, and you pulled Carisma to safety, pulled me to safety, even when Mamá and Papá stood and watched us from shore."

He turned to me again.

"You're my sister, Loli, mi sangre."

"I know. Just like we both know what needs to be done, whether or not Mamá and Papá jump in after us. I have a plan for getting the amulet Isabela spoke of."

Víctor's eyes went wide. "What plan?"

"I'm going to make the boy fall in love with me."

Víctor almost fell out of his seat. He seemed so alarmed. When he realized I was serious—dead serious—he began to laugh. I couldn't really have stopped Alejandro from laughing at me before, not unless I wanted to possibly start a war. Víctor, on the other hand, I didn't have to worry about. I slapped his arm with the back of my hand, playfully but sharp enough he pulled away and winced and I wondered how exactly his fight with Alejandro had ended. But I didn't want to ask.

"Don't laugh. I'm serious. I think he's the way to get close enough to Hernández to find the amulet."

He grew serious. "But, Loli, I can't imagine you seducing a boy."

I flinched, stuck out my tongue and scrunched up my face. "Who said anything about seducing?"

He laughed some more. My cheeks grew red hot and I knew I was blushing. "See."

"Well then, *you* befriend him." I crossed my arms, pursed my lips angrily.

"I don't think after last night that's a possibility." He rubbed at the bruise on his chin, where he'd obviously gotten hit.

Now he was the one with the sour expression.

"Who won the fight?" I asked, curious.

"It was a draw. Papá and señor Hernández ended up pulling us apart." He ran his hand through his hair. "He can hit. Hard. But I'd like to think I would have won that fight."

"I didn't see Alejandro wincing this morning," I mumbled.

"You saw him?"

I shrugged, feigning that the encounter didn't matter at all. "I took Carisma out."

Víctor stared at me, really looked at me. "You like him."

I scoffed. "How could I? I remember him in the forest. He was there the night his boss murdered that man with sal roja. He didn't stop him."

"How could he have?"

The kettle buzzed, saving me from having to continue the conversation with Víctor. Giving me space to avoid my feelings for Alejandro.

I used the water I'd been boiling to make an herbal tea for myself from some of the flowers and other plants in the area that we got from Luisa, as I thought about how to become friends with Alejandro, ignoring Víctor. So far all I knew he really liked, though, were horses and racing. He'd even seemed somewhat partial to losing. He didn't seem to like people much. But I wasn't sure how to tie it all together and how to get him to see past the fact that my biggest disguise of all wasn't that I was Salvación but that I was pretending to be una señorita de clase alta. My disguise was Lola de La Peña.

Of course, Víctor repeated his question as soon as I sat back down. I didn't think he was going to let this one go.

"He stopped me at the inn from putting the sal roja on Hernández's pillow," I responded, ignoring the imminent question. And then I remembered something else. "But I think he was protecting Coloma. Víctor, I saw something else this morning. I saw the place where Isabela landed in the grass, and sal roja has spread there like a disease. It's killing the soil. It's spreading—toward town."

In all the excitement over Alejandro, I'd forgotten all about the scorch.

"What do you mean? And you just left it there?"

I covered my mouth before saying, "No. I poured some sal negra on it, and then Alejandro arrived and I didn't have time to do anything else."

"What are you two talking about?" Papá joined us at the table, appearing out of nowhere suddenly. I gasped without meaning to, spilling my tea. Papá chuckled as if he hadn't been angry at us for days. "Keeping secrets?" He said it like a joke, something funny to say. But he also said it in a way that made me think he wasn't joking at all.

I worked on cleaning up my mess, all while it occurred to me that he didn't like us talking. My brother and I *were* keeping secretos. But it felt more necessary than ever to do so. I wondered if Papá would tell us that we weren't allowed to be alone without him or Mamá. Sometimes parents did that, kept their children apart to keep them from plotting against them. Did Papá think that was what we were doing? Plotting against him? In a way, I guessed we were, but how did we get to this point? It made my stomach sour and I wished Papá hadn't made me spill my tea.

I gave Víctor a warning glance that told him he better not go jabbering about my plan with Papá, who wouldn't approve of my going after Hernández after he already gave us his stamp of approval for the man. And he would especially not have liked my going after Hernández as Salvación. As far as we knew, he had no idea what had transpired en la fiesta and that Víctor's entire fight was all part of a plan.

"Nothing of importance," Víctor replied, taking another bite of bread. The way he was acting, you couldn't even tell the bread was hard.

There was a glint in Papá's eyes as if he was trying to get me to open up to him like I'd always done. But I hadn't forgotten, and I wouldn't forgive Papá for not taking my side in this. It was the side of justice, and Papá, for the first time that I could remember, was turning his back on the lessons I'd grown up with. This was the first time that I truly needed him to come through for me. He hadn't.

I stood from the table, said, "We should go see how long the line is today. The miracle awaits."

I couldn't look Papá in the face as I walked out of the kitchen, out of the house. I sat down on the bench outside the door and slipped on my high-heeled boots. My dress was tight. I walked over to where Carisma was tied up and grazing by the farmstead, set her saddle comfortably on again, mounted, and galloped toward our claim, hoping that maybe I'd run into Alejandro and start working on my plan.

I didn't care what Víctor said. If he wasn't going to befriend the boy, then I'd have to do it myself. Otherwise, my only other plan involved running away and trying to find Isabela, and I wasn't sure I was ready for that yet. For all I knew, I wouldn't even have to try on any kind of charm I'd likely possessed back in Sonora and lost along the way here. It wasn't like he'd ever liked me when I was acting ladylike anyway. For all I knew, he'd fall in love with Salvación in a blink, the one who wore pants and fought and was obviously so completely like the person who I was to everyone else.

I was met with a different surprise, a less desirable one, when I arrived to where we usually healed people. Mamá was already there, waiting, face in her hands. Was she crying? I didn't even know she had already left home. I guess I should have figured, considering Mamá and Papá were always side by side lately. Almost as if Papá wouldn't let Mamá talk to us, either, the Lord forbid that the three of us conspired against him.

Still, for all the anger I felt toward Papá lately, I had softened toward Mamá. I'd always thought her to be the bad guy in all situations, the one who didn't get it, but I was starting to see that often Papá was the one who was disgruntled, who didn't like being disobeyed.

Whatever had happened that actually led to them separating today, it didn't matter. Mamá seemed miserable, sitting next to her usual two buckets of sal negra. Thing was, there was no line, there was no one waiting.

I didn't get it. Had she gone through the line itself so fast that there was no one left to heal? But I knew that wasn't the case.

"Mamá," I called. The miracle of sal negra wasn't just the sacred sal. It wasn't only magia. It was Mamá's calling to come to Coloma when she had no idea what she'd even find here. We found magia. But now it was as if sal roja was withering away sal negra's entire legacy.

"There is no one," she whispered through her tears. I could barely hear her, and I was certain she wasn't even talking to me. She covered her face with her hands, pulled so viciously at her hair that when her hands came away, a few strands were entwined in them.

I did a full circle, still on Carisma. All of Coloma was strangely quiet.

"There's something not right," Mamá continued, looking on at the empty space in front of her. She then glanced at the two buckets of sal negra at her heels. The thing about miracles is that sometimes, if you're too slow to grasp them, they disappear. I didn't doubt we might be the ones starting to disappear now that señor Hernández was promising something greater than being healed: an enduring legacy for Coloma to once again be a part of México.

Mama seemed more withered than ever. As if the only thing that kept her going was la magia she did with sal negra.

I'd always been jealous of Víctor's relationship with Mamá. In that moment, though, I felt a pang, a desire to take this gift and go with it, perhaps convince Mamá to go back to Sonora. If we left, everything that was happening with señor Hernández wouldn't be our problem and Mamá would be able to refocus on us. Maybe it'd be for the best. But was that what I really wanted? Was I willing to sacrifice the safety of everyone in Coloma, leave them to their own, just for a chance to finally be at the center of Mamá's attention?

Seeing her this way, though, I knew if we went back to Sonora Mamá would always feel like a failure. She had helped more people during these past weeks than the majority of the population who had ever existed on earth had in their entire lives. She was a hero. She might not have worn a disguise like Salvación, but she was indeed just as angelic as the vigilante was.

"I'll be back, Mamá. Don't worry, more people will come to you to be healed, I promise."

There was something like love in Mamá's eyes then. It was something I had wanted for so long that it only made my need to get to the bottom of this greater. "Loli, whatever happens next, I love you. Mas que sal negra."

Although I wasn't sure she meant it when she said she loved me more than sal negra, there was something sincere in her words and the way she said them.

I rode Carisma around town. Even la cantina was empty, which was never the case. It was hard work mining the sal, tiring work living in Coloma where food could be scarce, but where drink was the one thing you could always count on— Abuelo made sure of it.

Perhaps travelers were staying away out of fear for Hernández and his men. But could the news of everything travel that fast? And to everyone who came to us?

SALVACIÓN · 191

Perhaps I'd been wrong the whole time and Alejandro had killed Hernández himself after all.

Still, I doubted it. It felt like a bad omen. A sign that my family's business here was done. It also felt like victory. Mamá had been wrong in holding her ground against Papá. She knew I was telling the truth. But she couldn't stand against Papá. Mamá loved him more than the sky loves the stars.

But this morning, things were finally going my way. If Mamá spoke to Papá, we had a chance at having him listen to us. Otherwise, he'd be condemning Mamá to a pointless existence. If she couldn't heal the sick, what would bring meaning to her life? Surely not me.

Maybe Víctor would. But I had a theory that even he wasn't enough to satisfy Mamá after she became one of the first people to use magia. Papá's love for Mamá might be the only thing that really could make him see that he was in the wrong, that Hernández was not the answer, was indeed a terrible man, el Diablo, in the flesh.

The closer I got to the plaza, the more voices I heard. One louder than them all. Hernández. Still alive. Still breathing. My heart sank. A part of me really did imagine that Alejandro had gotten what I was trying to do, and rather than let me do something very dangerous, he planned to put sal roja on Hernández's pillow himself. It hadn't happened. He was standing in the middle of the crowd, waving his arms. The entire town was here. Except for Mamá and me and Víctor and Papá.

What would Papá think of this? I wished that he'd have come to la plaza with me so I could gauge his reaction.

"Magia brings with it a chance," he said, raising his pointer finger up into the air and whirling it around every which way to the crowd. "Only *one* chance to take back what is ours. This land was yours from the start . . . do you want your children and their children to grow old upon it?"

Agreement rang through the crowd. I gritted my teeth; this land wasn't ours. We took this land and now others had taken it from us. Before Hernández, Papá had taught me that. He said we'd do what we were here to do for Mamá, and then we would go home.

Now Papá was talking about keeping the land. Then again, he'd been letting Abuelo build out the town all along.

Hernández was riling everyone up. Getting them on his side. It made my stomach sour and tears of anger clouded my eyes. Was this the same speech he gave to the town of the woman before he destroyed it?

People in the crowd clapped, some whistled, some cheered. I wanted to tell them to stop, to shut up, to open their eyes to who this man really was. How could someone so evil speak so naturally? The townsfolk seemed happy. These were the same people Salvación had protected for weeks, now turning their backs on the sanctity of Coloma. This wasn't the way, but without the shadows I hid in, without the mask I wore, without the words I spoke that were unlike the real me, I was only a girl in a dress who rode a horse. I wouldn't be taken seriously, and no one would believe I was Salvación even if I admitted it right here and now.

I wanted nothing more than to confront Hernández.

I noticed Alejandro then, standing to the side of the crowd, watching his boss at work. He seemed bored, like he'd seen this routine before and it was exhausting. As if he sensed my presence, he immediately spotted me at the back of the crowd.

What did my face tell him? Could he see the disappointment in my eyes, the rage, the fear behind them?

I was terrified of what I was witnessing. Tears fell from my eyes. I wiped them off quickly. Not wanting to see Alejandro's reaction, I looked to the sky.

As if the skies were sad as well, the storm that Alejandro had been speaking about in the morning drew nearer. A cold wind blew through, hitting me on the cheeks and making me shiver. My dress was low cut and let way too much cold air hit my skin. Thunder sounded right on the outskirts of town.

Alejandro glared its way, concern drawing on his heavy brow. Why was everyone listening to Hernández instead of preparing for the storm? I hadn't passed any boarded-up shops. If I were Hernández, I wouldn't have been here either. The inn was new, sure, but I'd be double-checking that all the windows were shut tight.

A part of me hoped that the storm was enough to drive Hernández away. Perhaps it would sweep through his camp, leave them all wet and hungry, and unable to stay in town. Then again, Papá wouldn't let that happen. If he had offered Hernández his help, he would give it and see it through. And if the inn were ruined, I wouldn't be surprised if Papá gave the man our house and kicked us all out to do it.

It made my stomach churn thinking that at the end of this, Papá might be an adversary. Only Salvación could save Coloma, it seemed. I sat higher on my horse, any trace of pain and sadness replaced by utter rage.

"Now, go!" señor Hernández said. "Seek refuge from the storm. And be ready tomorrow to fight for Alta California!"

The crowd was in an uproar. They cheered so loud it almost felt like they really were ready to go to war. Hadn't they had enough of death? Hadn't there been enough loss? Enough orphans? Enough widows? Mexico had barely made it out of a war. I didn't see why anyone would be willing to rush back on a lie.

There were things that war did that made men different. Papá knew it firsthand. He had fought in the war, survived it, while many others hadn't. And he'd never been the same since.

That couldn't be what Papá wanted. Papá must have thought that with sal negra, they would have the advantage, use la magia to heal all the wounded and never lose a single man. In the long run, you'd win. But the question remained: What was Papá really thinking?

A rush of cold air slammed into my face, but I didn't flinch. I'd meant it when I told Alejandro I wasn't afraid of a storm, no matter if it was brought on by nature or by man. A cold drop of water landed on my nose. Then another and another, until it was almost a downpour. The crowd quickly dispersed, perhaps finally feeling some urgency to prepare for the storm.

I had a spark of an idea then. I wasn't going to give up. And I didn't want to befriend anyone anymore. We were already at war. Salvación and Hernández, perhaps Alejandro. One I wasn't going to lose.

I rode up to Alejandro. "Do you all have refuge?"

Hernández was completely fazed, as if I were the last person he thought would be asking about his well-being. It gave me greater confidence.

"The storm that is coming will be a hard one to endure," I

added when they didn't reply. I knew that the inn sat empty. That everyone in their camp should seek refuge there. "We get them every once in a while, as if el mundo were trying to wash us away from atop its shoulders. All your men should get inside the inn, stay safe, cover the windows and such." We'd seen plenty of storms on our way here from Sonora. We'd seen plenty of families lost to the wilderness. Something told me, going by señor Hernández's log, they'd likely seen their share of them too. But their well-being wasn't what this was about. It was all an illusion and a part of my plan.

Alejandro didn't react. That feeling between us from the morning was gone, chased away by the arrival of the storm. Still, he didn't take his eyes off me, either, as if he was gauging me, trying to figure out my game. I'd spoken ill of señor Hernández before, so I was sure he knew that I wasn't as worried as I made myself out to be.

The two of them stared as if they expected me to leave, but this was a chance to make a move. I had Mamá on my side as of this morning, so perhaps I could get Papá on my side as well, if I played my hand at the right moment. I couldn't befriend Alejandro, no matter how close I wanted to be to him again. It was too dangerous.

"We should seek shelter," Alejandro said after a minute of awkward silence, practically ignoring me, as if he didn't want his boss to know we'd been with each other this morning.

"You should go home, señorita," Hernández said to me. "You should seek cover from the storm before it arrives as well. I'm afraid that my friendship with your father would be no more if something were to happen to you out here." It was what I was counting on. He turned to Alejandro before I could answer, continuing, "Alejandro, take her home." The way it was a command instead of question made my blood boil more. His face flushed for the tiniest of moments. I couldn't believe Alejandro had stopped me from securing my victory at the inn. But again, I had to remind myself, if he hadn't stopped me, sal roja would be spreading at the center of town. At least this way, we had a chance to figure out how to stop the spread of sal roja before it got to us.

"I don't need a guide," I said, perhaps too harshly. Perhaps.

At the same time, Alejandro said, "She can get home fine by herself."

I rolled my eyes. Alejandro glanced away. Señor Hernández examined us both.

I wasn't entirely certain I was acting as quick-witted as Mamá always did, but I knew this was as good a plan as possible. I hoped she went home. If she told Papá what had happened, if he saw how hurt she was by it all, he was sure to be as upset as I had been. That was a good thing. Especially since I was planning to go into the storm. The storm would be my cover, same as my mask was. And maybe if I disappeared for a while on the way home, Papá really would blame Hernández for my disappearance. He was falling for my scheme, after all, and I loved it. I still thought señor Hernández could be his own downfall. Maybe I hadn't unleashed sal roja on the man, but if this plan worked the way I wanted it to and hoped it did, I could defeat him by bringing the wrath of Coloma's people on him.

This could all work out. I remembered Isabela's tracks from the morning before Alejandro found me. I knew the direction she'd gone in. I'd made a mistake coming home, following Alejandro, letting him distract me. He wasn't going to be my friend. And he sure wasn't going to be much of anything else, not now, not until this was over. I needed to find Isabela, beg her to come back and tell her story—if not to everyone in town, then at least to Papá.

Or I needed to see it all for myself.

"Alejandro's right, I'll be okay." I rode off before Hernández could say anything, not looking at Alejandro as I went, even though I could tell that his angry eyes were following me.

"Rápido, Carisma," I said to my horse, hoping that I could get home fast enough and discreetly enough that Mamá and Papá wouldn't see me.

I needed to get something from la casita.

I left Carisma far enough away from the house and approached from the back, went in the window of my room, changed out of my dress, and got dressed as Salvación. When I was ready, I crept through the hallway and knocked on Víctor's door.

He opened the door. I grabbed his arm and started dragging him out, without explaining anything. "Come with me," I said. "We're going on an adventure."

"Mis botas," he replied when I was yanking him through the window.

I froze, glanced at his feet. He wasn't wearing any shoes. He probably needed those if we had any chance of making it far enough past the storm to find Isabela. "Well, get them on. We have a storm to catch."

He quickly got his boots onto his feet, laughing as he went, confused as to what was going on but still willing to do it all with me without much questioning. "I guess I better get my coat, too, then. And why are you dressed like that?"

"No questions," I replied. "Just following."

When Víctor was finally dressed and ready, we grabbed his horse, Panchito, met Carisma around the back, and rode off at full speed. The sound of Mamá crying and Papá trying to console her echoed through the house as we left, a small victory, I hoped. Panchito followed Carisma, who led the way valiantly back to the tracks, almost as if she knew exactly where I wanted her to go. Part of me felt she did. She knew me. It always surprised me how she rode with her head high always, as if her heart were too large for her chest—or as if it were tethered to an invisible string that pulled Carisma forward.

We rode back to the field. The spot with the sal roja, which to my dismay seemed even larger than the last time I was here, despite the sal negra that I sprinkled over it. There weren't even any blue flowers on the ground. My throat squeezed and I suddenly had trouble breathing. It hadn't been enough. I hadn't thought it would be, but part of me had hoped that it would have at least slowed it down enough to avoid adding it to the list of immediate worries.

"What in the world is that?" Víctor questioned, his voice tinged with confusion and fear. "Is that the sal roja? You weren't lying, then."

"It's what sal roja does when it touches the earth, and a problem for another day," I replied, taking a moment to watch the sal. "If you look hard enough, if you pay enough attention, you can see it scorching the earth, spreading like a slow wildfire.

Gobbling one piece of the grass and soil at every blink— You thought I was lying?"

"I don't know. I guess I was hoping you'd been exaggerating," he said. "Why are we out here, Loli?" He stilled, pulled his coat tighter around himself. His clothing was unmatched—the flannel pajama pants, the loose shirt, the wool coat, his hair askew. His expression told me he wasn't happy about having been dragged out here only to be given some bad news. "You mind taking a few minutes and explaining?"

I pointed to the trail, the foot- and hoofprints.

Víctor had this way of usually knowing what I was getting at. Today wasn't any different. "That's—"

I nodded, grinned. "Exactly. If you don't think that we can befriend Alejandro, well, I think if we find Isabela, we might be able to convince her to come back with us. Talk some sense into Papá. Meanwhile, the last person who saw me was señor Hernández himself, who didn't walk me home in the storm. I won't be coming back. How do you think Papá will take his two kids missing?"

"You want us to ride into the storm? Go after Isabela in the rain and wind? And you're trying to blackmail el Diablo himself? I'm not sure that'll go over well."

I ignored his last comment. "I think if we go through the storm, we'll be on the other side of it as fast as our horses can carry us. We've ridden in storms before—"

"Yeah, and Papá said it was the most dangerous thing he had ever asked us to do and would never do so again. I don't know if you hit your head at some point and forgot what riding in storms is like, but it's not any fun—not for us, and not for our horses. You willing to sacrifice Carisma if it comes to it?"

"Víctor, we don't have time to argue. I need you with me on this." I didn't say that Carisma's life was bigger than what was at stake. I couldn't say something like that out loud. Was I willing to sacrifice my horse's life for this? I guess, but not really. The thought didn't sit right with me. It was an impossible choice I hoped I wouldn't have to make. I'd made a strange oath when I became Salvación, one that went deeper than any words I could have spoken. I needed to protect Mamá, sal negra, the whole town. I needed to. "Hernández, he has the whole town at his back now. He has everyone except for our family. For all I know, we're the only two people who will stand against him. The town needs Salvación. We have to convince them to help us. If we can convince Mamá and Papá, they can convince everyone else. And we will need an army of our own when the time comes."

Víctor glanced back toward town, then to the charred earth. There was only one way forward, and I knew he understood it. "Fine. But we can't get killed for this. What we've been doing up till now is nothing compared to who we're up against. The page, the log—señor Hernández won't stop at anything to get what he wants. We need to be careful, or this really will be the end of our family. Tell me you understand, Loli? What you did going into the forest alone, you can't ever do anything like that again. Everything we do from this moment on is together or not at all."

"I agree," I said, not giving it much thought. At the end, I'd do what I wanted. For now, I did what I had to do to placate my brother. I stuck out my hand, which he shook. "Now, let's go find Isabela!"

He nodded once. I didn't waste time, leading Carisma into

the nearing storm. She tried to twist around once, twice, more than a few times. But I convinced her to keep going each time. I followed Isabela's tracks with precision. Soon I got to the point where she had mounted her horse again. And then the soil turned to mud and the tracks became harder to follow. We slowed.

The storm ahead of us echoed across the valley. Lightning flashed in the sky as it grew darker around us and harder to see, even when it hadn't yet hit nightfall. The wind practically swept us up and blew us backward, yet we kept going.

This might not have been my best plan, but it was the one I had, and since Víctor didn't call to me to go back, I took it as a sign to go forward.

Farther down the road, as the storm intensified, the winds rocking me as I rode, I made sure Víctor was still following. Aside from me, Víctor was the best rider. Even better than Papá; I knew he would keep up. I thought of Alejandro, wondered where he had learned to ride. It couldn't have been from Hernández, I didn't think. Where did he come from? And why did everything remind me of him—the storm, the horses, the wind brushing against my face, the feel of his fingers as they took back the sal roja back at the inn? If he knew I was Salvación, what would he think? I found myself listening to the beating of my heart as the storm grew louder. I used my shoulder to wipe away the sweat from my brow.

The rainfall quickened; we were in the middle of it now. Lightning suddenly struck near us. Carisma reared backward. I fell off, rolling away from her just in time. A second slower, and she would have landed her hooves on my face and crushed me dead.

I landed hard against my shoulder, which throbbed. I immediately recoiled and tried to stand, only to be knocked back down by the wind. I ignored the pain in my arm. I had bigger things to worry about. If I hadn't been ready for it, if it hadn't been Papá who taught me to ride, if I hadn't ridden in a storm before, I would have died. I scrambled, not worrying about myself, but Carisma. Yet by the time I was on my feet, she was as small as an ant in the distance. Gone.

She was gone.

Víctor had asked me if Carisma's life was worth all of this, and now that I was watching her ride off without me, and without knowing if she'd make it through the storm, the answer was that I would have chosen her.

"¡Carisma, ven a mí!" I shouted after her, even though it was for naught.

I searched for him but couldn't spot Víctor either. Luckily my mask and hat stayed on, and because I was still Salvación—strong, brave, enduring—I held my tears at bay. I'd get through this. There was no way that my time was over. A mere storm wasn't going to be the end of me.

I moved. I wasn't even sure in what direction. The wind was too strong, the sudden gusts sending me reeling from one side to the other. I couldn't see through the haze of the rain, which was impossible to blink out of my eyes. I hadn't anticipated the storm would be so strong. I was worried for Carisma, worried for Víctor, worried for Coloma. The storm would wreak havoc on the town itself. Were Mamá and Papá okay? Had it been wrong to sneak out and not let them know where we were going. This could be goodbye to my family. Goodbye to Salvación, sal negra, maybe even the entire world.

I got to my knees, hugged myself tight in a ball, letting the rain fall over me.

Someone touched my back then. I looked up slightly, trying to cover my face from the worst of the rain, and could see only a hand. Víctor. I took it, but when I stood up, I wasn't met with Víctor's face, but Alejandro's.

"What are you doing out here?" I shouted, pulling my hand back to myself, sounding too much like me and not enough like Salvación. I hoped the howling wind masked my real voice.

"I saw Víctor de La Peña riding out here. It didn't seem like a good idea. I followed," he replied, his back to the storm. His voice was so much softer than when he spoke to me as Lola.

"We can't leave without Víctor. We need to find him!" I shouted, suddenly glad that Alejandro hadn't found me on Carisma. He would have known immediately that Lola de La Peña and Salvación were one and the same.

He shook his head. "We should go back," he called. I couldn't hear him, but that was what I thought he said. "I'm sure he did the same." Was he suggesting this because of the altercation that Víctor caused at the fiesta? Or was he afraid?

"No," I said, shaking my head so he understood me even if he couldn't hear me. I continued to search for my brother. Víctor wouldn't have left me. He was out here and he would be until he found me.

Luckily, as if the heavens heard me, his horse suddenly appeared.

"Víctor!" I shouted, jumping off the ground. Víctor approached, staring at Alejandro first. "Salvación," he said, playing his role in our charade without hesitation. "Are you all right?"

Alejandro seemed to size my brother up, almost as if he were jealous.

"I'm all right, thanks to him," I said, flipping my thumb toward Alejandro.

Víctor nodded at Alejandro, who looked out back toward Coloma again. The storm finally seemed to be easing off, its eye heading toward Mamá and Papá instead.

"We should head back now. Stay behind the storm and arrive there in time to help those in need."

It surprised me that Alejandro had any interest in helping the people of Coloma. The thing was, he likely was there when Hernández destroyed Isabela's town. He was there the night his boss murdered the man in the forest with sal roja. He knew his boss was a monster, and yet he continued to work for the man. Whatever the reason, nothing justified that.

My head told me that Alejandro couldn't be trusted. But there was something else about him that I couldn't deny. He *did* seem to care about Salvación's well-being.

By the look of it, we hadn't gotten turned around. In fact, the storm might have helped us. "I'm not going back," I said, standing tall, looking in the direction we were going. I pointed into the forest ahead of us. There was a piece of fabric from Isabela's elaborate shawl, blowing in the remnants of the storm. I grinned, and to Víctor said, "Let's go."

Víctor lowered his hand for me to take it and mount Panchito behind him. Although I was still very much worried about her, something good had come of Carisma's disappearance. I couldn't risk being caught as Salvación.

Before I climbed onto the horse, Alejandro interjected. "I can take you."

SALVACIÓN · 205

I ignored him and climbed aboard Panchito. "Just a minute ago, you were going to go back to Coloma. You don't even know why we're out here. What we're doing."

"Con respeto, Lady Salvación, I think you have forgotten that I'm the reason you're still alive."

Víctor didn't say anything. I wished he would have. It might have made my mind straighten.

"You can come with us," I said, unsure if it was the right choice, but certain that Alejandro had been helpful before. Perhaps he could still be helpful. Confronted with Isabela, he might see himself in a new light. Or at the very least, the woman could accuse him, acknowledge that he was there when her people were murdered in cold blood. And then I wouldn't want to defend him anymore. Then I'd see him for who he really was. "If you want. Or go back."

I also wasn't entirely sure he'd say yes. Inviting him might make him not want to come.

But if I had any hope of that, it was crushed instantly. Alejandro mounted his horse. "Lead the way."

Víctor asked, "You sure?"

I examined Alejandro once more. "Yes," I finally said, which was enough for Víctor. Back in Sonora, he never would have listened to me. Things had changed.

"Are you all right?" Víctor asked from in front of me. Víctor had never been protective of me in Sonora. He didn't care when kids would pick on me or when girls would fight me and call me names and I couldn't say anything to Mamá or Papá or risk our family losing face. When the nuns hit me with rulers and sticks or when my tutors flicked my hands when I got answers wrong, Víctor did nothing. He didn't care about the way I struggled every day in my dresses and heels and everything I didn't want to be but had to pretend to be. Everything changed on our way to Coloma. Everything changed when we worked together. Maybe things change when you start to grow up, to become an adult. Whatever it was that made Víctor finally notice that I was his blood, a part of what made him *him*, it made me feel like he would fight anyone and everything including the earth itself if it meant I was safe.

"Yes! Keep going," I replied.

We continued, the wind still howling around us. More lightning struck nearby, but thankfully no longer in our immediate vicinity. We rode to the edge of the forest.

Panchito refused to go in, as if there was something ominous in the trees.

We dismounted. Víctor pulled Panchito's reins toward the tree line, but he didn't give an inch. Like Carisma, Panchito was strong like the storm. We were weak in comparison. If Panchito didn't want to budge, he wouldn't.

I took Panchito's head in my arms, he swayed back and away, but I managed to pull him close. He wasn't my horse, but I knew him. "Please, Pancho! ¡Vamos!"

After a beat he calmed down, but he didn't listen. Víctor managed to pull him into the cover of the trees, but not any farther. It was still rainy and wet, but less so than being out in the open.

To my surprise, Alejandro followed us. Without a word from him or a retort from his horse, Alejandro dismounted, and they both slipped into the edge of the forest.

"It's probably best to leave the horses. Your horse isn't going to follow," Alejandro said.

I glanced back into the storm for Carisma. At this point, we could say we'd simply found her. Maybe he'd believe she wasn't my horse. I only wanted her to appear so I could know she was safe.

"It'll be a long way home if we don't have our horses," Víctor replied thoughtfully.

"If we leave them tied up and we don't come back, they'll starve," Alejandro replied. "You can leave your horse to such a cruel fate, but I am not going to."

Víctor swore under his breath, then kissed Panchito on the nose, scratched at the back of his neck where he liked. Then my brother led him back out into the open air. He seemed happy to leave the forest. Then more loudly, Víctor said, "¡Panchito, a la casa!" Off the horse went toward Coloma. I only hoped that Carisma had done the same. She knew the way home like Panchito did, didn't she?

I touched the shawl. Pulled it off and handed it to Víctor, who nodded. "Buen ojo."

Alejandro's eyes widened as if he knew exactly whom I was looking for. I wondered if I should refuse to let him come with us. What if while we were searching for Isabela, Alejandro was hunting her down? What if when we found her, somehow Alejandro managed to take her away and return her to Hernández?

But there would be three against one if that were the case, and Víctor was larger and taller than Alejandro. And if I thought about it, I didn't feel threatened. I felt an ease the way I did with Víctor being around Alejandro, especially while I was dressed as Salvación. He'd saved my life twice. Didn't I at least owe him some kind of courtesy?

"Let's go!" I shouted, and took off into the forest first.

It was still damp underneath the forest cover and hard to see with my mask. I couldn't risk taking it off, though, not with Alejandro so close. We climbed as well as we could, the soil so wet that I sank into it with every step. I was happy to be wearing boots today, slogging my way through the forest but nonetheless able to do it.

Thunder struck suddenly, hitting a nearby tree. A large branch cracked overhead and fell. When something like this happens, you barely have a warning. The warning is the branch falling already; and all you have is the chance to get away from it in the blink of an eye. Only I didn't have the chance. I stared blankly at the falling branch, and something stuck in my frame of vision and stayed still.

To my side, I heard Víctor yell. "Move!" But I couldn't move.

An arm wrapped itself around my waist and pulled me back in time. I fell on top of Alejandro. I stayed down, catching my breath. Then Alejandro cleared his throat and I stood up fast. Too fast, since my eyes blurred and the world spun. Once more he caught me. "Are you okay?" he asked, voice sincere, eyebrows questioning.

"She's fine," Víctor said almost to himself in relief, checking me over. "You're fine, right?"

I nodded. "I only need a moment. I'm dizzy." I didn't want to sound weak, but I also needed a moment to figure out where to go next.

Alejandro stared at us intently. There was something in his eyes that told me he might know who I really was. But if he did, he didn't say anything.

And I had other things to worry about besides Alejandro.

If I couldn't find Isabela, I would have put my life and that of everyone else in Coloma at risk for nothing—all just to see if Papá would blame señor Hernández if I disappeared. The trail became a slippery slope up toward the skyline.

"We should turn back," Víctor said. "If we fall from this height, it could kill us."

I ignored him—there was no going back in my mind. This climb was the most important thing. I needed to be able to pull it off, especially when dressed as Salvación. What would it mean if I failed?

Víctor stopped me, kept me in one place. I could tell he was about to call me by my name, my real name. Before he did, I said, "I wonder if we get to the top of the mountain, if we can see the entire valley and see if we can spot some sign of Isabela."

"There are no tracks to follow anymore! It's all slippery slush beneath our feet."

All around us were trees and boulders and mud. I blinked. It was the only thing short of taking off the mask that would help me see better. There was no other sign of Isabela. Víctor was right. We'd lost her tracks. Worse, the storm seemed to be picking up again. It made the trees sway viciously. It made them whistle loudly.

I lifted my chin up to the sky, screamed, hoping that maybe she'd hear me and think someone was in danger and come to help. The only thing that answered was the sky. Lightning struck another nearby tree, which caught fire before the rain smothered it. The wind threatened to blow my hat away, but I kept hold of it. I didn't just need to keep my disguise on because of Alejandro but because of Isabela too. She wouldn't come back to Coloma for Lola de La Peña.

At least I wasn't trying to hike in a dress. At least I wasn't wearing my dumb heels. The storm was wild, the mountain was wild, and in the chaos, I found myself smiling. This was the life that I desired.

A life of storms that weren't brought on by people but by nature. You can't be angry with nature. You can't swear at a mountain that she is being unfair or cruel or evil. She can't be evil. She is that from which magia comes from.

There was sal in the air. There was something out here that was making me feel strong, even if I couldn't pinpoint what I was looking for. I stuck my tongue out and let the raindrops that slid free from the trees land on my tongue. The water tasted like sal negra.

I wondered where the sal roja was hiding.

Even if Hernández wasn't the one to find it, someone someday would. What havoc would they wreak upon the world? And how could we keep it hidden from them? How could we keep each other safe?

"Salvación?"

It wasn't Víctor who said this but Alejandro. The timbre of his voice brought me back to the moment. The storm seemed fiercer. The wind hit my face, almost as if each raindrop sliced my cheek. I found the trunk of a tall tree to lean against. Víctor knelt next to me. Alejandro followed.

What if I'd led my brother, the person I loved the most in the world, out here just to perish? I covered my face with my arms as the wind knocked the forest every which way.

A blanket covered us then. It took me by surprise. I let a yelp out. But when I spun, I met Isabela's eyes straight on.

"Salvación," she said, though in her gaze I could tell that she was suddenly seeing right through me. She knew I was only a girl. The storm had washed away my disguise. I expected her to say that I needed to go back to my parents. That this was all too dangerous for someone as young as me. That a warrior woman was easier to believe in, to have hope in. A girl, well, that was something entirely different. But she didn't say any of those things. It was enough to be with the shame of it all, I guess. I didn't need to hear about how all the adults in my life didn't believe in me.

When she *did* talk, it wasn't to say anything more to me. "Alejandro, you're here." She touched his cheek.

He closed his eyes, leaning into the hand, almost as if they were related, as if they knew each other. It occurred to me then: Had the drawing of Salvación that Isabela had come from Alejandro? But how?

Before I could ask, Isabela added, "Follow me, the three of you." She guided us to where she'd built shelter in a crevice made by an overarching rock. How long had she been here? If I hadn't known any better, I'd think she had waited for us to show up all along.

She had more blankets. A couple I recognized from home that we hadn't even noticed were missing. It'd been wild days that were all a haze. I didn't know where she'd gotten the rest of them. She handed us each two of them to help us ride out the storm.

I didn't waste any time wrapping mine around me, trying to make my teeth stop chattering. Alejandro kept staring at me. As if who I was, and who I wasn't, were very obvious in this moment.

When we'd settled in and everyone seemed safe and warm, I moved to Isabela. She hadn't as much as glanced at me since she handed me the blankets. She seemed to be thinking, surely trying to figure out what was going on and what to do next. I needed to act before she set her mind on something else and convince her to return to Coloma. I hadn't traveled here for nothing.

Hadn't lost Carisma for nothing.

"I need you to go back with us," I said. "Señor Hernández has the whole town of Coloma on his side. You must tell Coloma's leaders that he isn't who they think he is. You have to tell them what happened to you and your people!" I shouted, trying to make my voice carry through the wind and the storm. My voice needed to be its own kind of storm: one that brought a flood of change to Coloma, one that washed away Hernández and his men. I couldn't be just a girl, trying to hide under blankets.

Alejandro and Víctor stayed seated but stared at me. I could feel their eyes at the back of my neck, expectant, awaiting Isabela's answer.

She only shook her head and said, "I can't go back, especially not after what I found out. You might as well give up if everyone stands against you. You are not the hero I heard stories about. You're not the hero Alejandro sent me to find."

There it was. I was right. It had been Alejandro who had described me. But from when?

It didn't matter right now. I had a choice to make. I could cower. Or . . .

"But I am." I heard doubt in my voice, in my abilities. That was why I was out there, though: a feeling and knowing of not being enough. That was why I couldn't convince Papá without Isabela.

"Please," I said. "You're our only hope."

"I once said those words to *you*. If he sees me, if he finds me, I am dead. Alejandro knows this."

I glared at Alejandro; I still wasn't sure how he knew what I looked like. He avoided my eyes until he couldn't. The moment that they caught mine, though, I felt my face soften. I wasn't mad at him, not really.

"If I'm dead," Isabela continued. I moved my focus back to her. "If I'm dead, the stories of my people will be forgotten. Gone forever. I can't allow him to get away with that. I must protect the history of my own life. Do you understand?"

I did even when I didn't want to, like I'd understood, in my heart, why she'd left in the first place.

"I want to show you something when the storm is done. For now, rest."

I wanted to argue. I wanted to fix things. By the minute, my chance of stopping Hernández grew slimmer.

Instead, I did as I was told. The storm was going strong. I sat next to Víctor. I closed my eyes, my head against my brother's torso, while Alejandro watched the impending storm. I stared at the boy as I fell asleep.

CHAPTER 13

How do you stop a killer when you're not one? You find the rage inside you that's burning to be released.

I woke up with a start. The rain was gone. Instead, sunlight seeped in from under the rock and birds were singing their morning song nearby. I was lying down, someone's blanket a pillow underneath my head. I must have been exhausted not to remember anything after I fell asleep next to Víctor. I was the only one still underneath the hedge of the rock. On instinct, I moved my hands to my face. To my surprise, my mask was still in place, though my sombrero was at my side and perhaps both Isabela and Alejandro knew who I was by now.

"You're awake," Isabela said. In the daylight of a rainless morning, I got an actual glimpse of her. She was different from the last time we had seen each other. Her eyes were alert, wide, large, and red. Her face was smudged in dirt, as were her clothes. I wouldn't have been surprised to learn she hadn't slept all night.

Then I remembered that the woman and Alejandro knew each other. Alejandro had been the one who told Isabela to come find Salvación. Everything I thought I knew about him changed. Did it make him a good person? One good deed didn't make up what I saw in the forest—or did they balance each other out? It was all dizzying and made my head hurt in about five different places.

Alejandro and Víctor both had cups in their hands. They were drinking something that seemed warm.

I was about to ask Alejandro about it all when Víctor handed me his cup. "Here," he said. "Algo calientito to warm your hands."

The gesture was so familiar that Alejandro raised his eyebrows at us. I almost held the cup back, but I was too tired and cold and thirsty to really care. I didn't even care if everyone here found out that I, Lola de La Peña, was Salvación.

Would it be that bad, after all, if Alejandro found out? At this point, maybe it would help. If he respected the vigilante, if he helped Isabela escape, maybe he wasn't so bad. Maybe he had only been biding his time to make the right move on Hernández.

"Let's go," the woman said.

I got up quickly, moving fast because they were obviously leaving me. I was supposed to be the strong one. But I was the last to wake. Still, I looked begrudgingly at the blankets as we took off.

"Where are we going?" I whispered to Víctor. "What did I miss when I was asleep? And why didn't you wake me up?" I hit his arm as I said the last words.

"Dunno," he said, rubbing at where I'd hit him. "And ouch. I didn't wake you up, because you seemed to need the rest. I have a feeling this is going to be a long day. We still have to find our way back home."

I didn't want to think of going back home. Maybe we could live like Isabela, help her. This whole thing had been my idea, coming to find her, and I hadn't much considered what would happen if we did and she said no to our request. We'd needed a plan that I didn't have.

And I'd failed at getting the amulet.

I asked Alejandro. "Why did you stop me that night at the inn if you are on our side?"

He froze at my question, sighed, and kept walking.

I almost thought he wasn't going to answer me, but then he said, "I've been following Hernández for a long time. When I was little, he was like a father to me. I looked up to him. He saved me. He literally found me, starving, alone. I'm alive only because of him. But then things changed when he found the sal roja and sal negra he'd been searching for. The amulet, I don't know, it's as evil as sal roja. It's why I can't let you have it. It corrupts people. It makes them bad. He wasn't so cruel before. He really did only want the sal negra to help. Or maybe he didn't, I don't know." He scratched the back of his head, sniffled.

"That doesn't answer my question. I could have killed him."

"I didn't let you kill him, because I—"

"You love him," Víctor said, cutting in.

I guessed Víctor understood how you could dislike someone and how they treat you, but still care about them. That was how he must have felt about Papá.

SALVACIÓN · 217

Alejandro scoffed in a way that wasn't toward Víctor, but in disbelief at himself. "Yeah. I know it sounds strange when he's evil now, but I don't know. I guess I keep thinking that maybe he'll change and see he's doing wrong—"

"He isn't going to do that, Alejandro," I replied. "Have you ever noticed how some people speak with their eyes? The eyes can tell you so much. You know what I see in his eyes?"

He turned back to face me from his place up front.

Isabela kept going, but in the same direction so I knew we'd catch up to her.

Alejandro had never been closer to me than he was right now. His eyes bored into mine, and I wondered if he recognized them as those belonging to Lola de La Peña. He took a deep breath as if preparing for my reply.

"I see someone cruel, someone who doesn't care who they hurt to get what they want. He might care about you, but look what he's done to other people."

He turned to watch Isabela walking on, but didn't move toward her.

She was mumbling to herself, not making much sense, surely playing back every moment of what had happened to her—the words she could have said that might have stopped the destruction, the things she might have done to destroy señor Hernández.

Alejandro didn't say anything. He knew I was right.

"Let's keep going before she leaves us," Víctor said, taking the lead.

Alejandro followed him without another word to me.

"Where do you think she's even taking us?" I asked as we walked, to no reply.

We climbed until we reached a ridge with a panoramic view. I stared at my feet, tired from the hike to the top. I held on to my side, pushing against my abdomen, which felt inflamed. Who had decided that we were going to climb a mountain?

I looked up only when I heard Víctor gasp. "How is this possible?" he said. I'd never seen Víctor's face grow this serious—not since Sonora, the river, the trek. Things were supposed to be different once we got here. We were supposed to find some kind of peace, but this world didn't seem made for peace.

I stood up straight and joined my brother at the summit.

Sal roja had scorched the earth as far as I could see and was eating the valley alive. There was a semblance of what might have been houses once, a town sinking into the ground, as if the earth itself were swallowing it all.

"I wanted to go back home," Isabela said, scoffing. "Salvage what was there. Start over maybe. But then I saw this."

The sal roja had spread to an area perhaps ten times the size of Coloma.

"There is nothing to go back to. There is only the scorch. The end of times is upon us. That's why I was still in the forest when you came. But I think the wisest thing we can do now is run—run to where we think sal roja won't be able to reach us, somewhere out past the sea."

"This happened so fast." I thought of the scorch back in Coloma. How long would it be until *this* was Coloma? How long would we be able to hold off? If we mined all the sal negra we had, would it be enough to stop it? If not, we would have to move somewhere else, like Isabela suggested—maybe run. This might have been a bigger threat to us than Hernández himself. It seemed like all of a sudden, things were about to get even wilder.

Sal roja permeated the air, carrying the stench of disease and death. The sal roja had destroyed everything it touched. I worried that simply breathing near it might damage our bodies.

I shook my head, straightening out my thoughts . . . Although the sal roja was responsible for the destruction, it didn't end up here on purpose. It came from somewhere, somewhere those who had made this magia hid it deep. Hernández was the one who brought it forth and created havoc. The sal roja didn't have a brain, at least not that I knew of.

"Hernández did this," I replied to no one in particular, channeling my anger where it was rightfully deserved.

"You're right," Víctor said. It was bittersweet, like the stems of the yellow flowers that grew in our backyard, to hear him agree with me. I wished that we weren't seeing what was truly at stake. "We can't let this happen to Coloma. We can't."

I nodded to him, agreed with my full heart, with every fiber of my being that we weren't going to let Hernández get away with this death.

"What part did you play in all of this?" I asked Alejandro, my voice angry.

"This was the last straw," he said, taking in a shaky breath as if he might cry. "He unleashed sal roja on everyone. I couldn't even move to stop him. He didn't talk about it. He didn't ask for advice. He only acted."

I would have been angrier at Alejandro had he not been crying. There were actual tears in his eyes, falling down his face.

"I should have stopped him, I know. When I was little, he only seemed to want things that made sense. And then, this."

"Now you see what you are really up against," Isabela said. "We can all be guilty of ignoring things we shouldn't. I did many times. But now I leave you to the ruins of my life, in hopes that you don't make the same mistakes." With that, she was once again walking away.

I didn't know where she was going, only that she wouldn't ever have agreed to return to Coloma with us. I had no help to offer her, no place to bring her home even if I wanted to. Coloma was in so much danger.

"I need to get closer," I said, running off toward the destruction instead of away from it. "I need to understand it."

"Wait!" Víctor called. I didn't stop, knowing he would follow me.

I wasn't sure how to explain it. There was a feeling, a pull like the one Mamá talked about. The same one that made her want to come to Coloma. She had spoken of the pull, but I never told her that sometimes I felt one, too, in the middle of my stomach, as if it were coming from what remained of my umbilical cord, and from vida itself.

It was a long way down, and my legs were tired. My face was scratched up from scuffling down the hillside. I needed to be closer, though, to tell this story with the veracity it deserved.

When I got to the line of sal roja, I stood just at the edge of it. If I took one step closer, the sal roja might devour me. Even so, the sal crept toward me. I wasn't moving, yet the space between us was decreasing by the second.

I took another step back.

Suddenly there was a whirring sound. I didn't move fast

enough, and something pinched my ear. An arrow had struck the ground in front of me. My heart stopped. I searched around me, hoping the next shot wasn't meant to strike me somewhere lethal, even with all the sal negra in my pocket.

"Salvación, we should go!" Alejandro shouted. Apparently, he'd followed as well. I was surprised, but also relieved that at least one person seemed to be in this with Víctor and me.

We twisted back, but not in time. An Indigenous man, round faced, shirtless, and warm skinned, on the most magnificent mare I had ever seen, was riding toward us. Were we trespassing?

"Don't get closer to the line." The rider ignored Alejandro and Víctor and seemed to be speaking only to me. "It's dangerous here. You should go home. This isn't a place for kids."

"I'm not a kid," I said, standing up straighter. "And we were leaving."

He looked like he was about to argue, but just took a deep breath and sighed, as if he didn't want to deal with any of this today. He blinked a lot, as if he were tired and barely staying awake. I didn't blame him, considering what we were standing in front of.

"Please give us a few minutes. I just need to see this."

"What do you know of what's happened here?" He got off his horse in a flawless swoop and approached me.

Víctor moved to partially block me.

I stood my ground, as I didn't think the stranger was going to attack me. "We're not responsible for it."

"Not all of us anyway," Víctor mumbled.

The man snorted, as if asking what that was supposed to mean.

"Don't pay him any attention," Alejandro said. "We're here because we want to help and stop what's happened. How can we help?"

I understood then that although sal negra and sal roja were new to me and my family, they weren't new to those who had lived in this area long before us, just like they hadn't been new to señor Hernández. Of course, the people of this land *knew* the land—and everything it might have to hide.

He didn't look like he was going to answer us. After all, why should he help?

"There is a mark, much, much smaller than this, but still close enough to our people that it won't be longer until it reaches the town. If you know how to stop this, please, help us."

He seemed to examine me, looked me up and down. "Why do you wear a mask?" he asked.

I didn't know what to say, not really. I turned to Alejandro, who seemed like he wanted to know the answer to this too. "I'm not who people expect," I replied.

He seemed to understand what I was trying to say. He got back on his horse. "I won't ask you again to leave these lands. But I will say, you need to dig. We've marked this land. Soon my people will arrive and we'll dig a trench around the infected area, three people deep, and seal it off until the mineral disappears."

Of course, I didn't know why that never occurred to me. If there was no land for the sal roja to spread to, it wouldn't be able to grow at all. It was genius.

"How long will it take to disappear from the infected soil?"

"Sometimes it takes months. Sometimes it takes years. Sometimes it never does. We've never been able to understand it fully." He examined us further then. "There is an artifact that was taken from us, stolen by the man we think did this."

So the amulet belonged to the Indigenous man and his people. Señor Hernández stole it from them. Now I felt even guiltier for failing to retrieve the amulet.

"The man you speak of is taking over our home too—talking about starting another war. We know he has the amulet. Perhaps we could help each other." It was a hopeful request, perhaps too thoughtless, though, since the man only laughed. His horse neighed as if laughing with him.

"We have our own battles to fight," he said. "This is just another war fought on our land—except we don't want ancient evils unleashed. We'll put a stop to the spread, but the rest is up to you."

"How do we stop him? If he has the amulet, how do we stop him?"

"You kill him." He grinned at me. My face must have faltered, since he asked, "Don't like the answer?"

"It's not that I think he deserves to live. I'm just not a killer."

"I know you're not. I can see it in your eyes." He pointed at Alejandro. "But he is. I can see that in his eyes too. He's taken many lives. Perhaps he's looking to atone for what he did, but it doesn't change who he was."

Alejandro only stared, and now I was the one who couldn't look away. Víctor had crossed his arms. I guessed I shouldn't have expected help. I really didn't; I only wished that everything about sal roja wasn't so cryptic.

I thought of everyone's history, the path that led to this moment for all of us. I always thought that it was destiny for Mamá to arrive in Coloma. But her calling brought us all to this place. Were my destiny and Víctor's to battle something of such magnitude?

I felt sick to my stomach. How were we going to win? I'd been Salvación for a few months, and so I felt like I could fight a man and win, run him out of town. But how did you run something out of town that would devour you if you touched it?

It was worse. The Indigenous man and his people were having to clean up the mess someone else made. They shouldn't have had to do that. It, too, began to feel like my responsibility. I had made a promise to protect Coloma. But I felt a duty to protect everything and everyone—and it broke my heart that I couldn't.

In my confusion, fear, I also found anger, and in that anger, I found strength, resolve, focus. I wasn't sure that Hernández deserved to live.

There was no justice that would be strong enough. There was nothing left here—only bad, only wrong, only regret now.

How do you stop a killer when you're not one?

You learn to become one.

I didn't know what Víctor wanted to do or anything about Alejandro, really—only that he had a strange kind of love for a monster and therefore had become a monster himself.

But there was no unseeing this, no way to avoid confrontation. We needed to get the amulet. Even if it meant dying in the process.

To the man on his horse, I said, "Thank you," handing him my pouch of sal negra. "We'll do what we can to stop this."

He opened the pouch, stared inside, then looked up, examining me more closely, as if seeing the real me for the first time. "Where did you get this?"

"We're miners." I pointed to the way we had come. "We have a lot of it where we live. Past the mountain, about a day's hike out, to the bottom of the meadow."

He chuckled. "You mean you're taking it from the land? Have you ever heard of the balance of life?"

I tentatively replied, "Yes," though I wasn't sure the way I knew it was the way the man meant. I waited for him to explain. At my side, Víctor and Alejandro continued to stay silent . . . and watchful. Neither of them—nor I, for that matter—was prepared for a fight. We were too tired, too drained by all we were seeing, as if being this close to the sal roja harmed us the same way being close to sal negra seemed to heal.

"Then you're aware that for every evil, there was something good created. We can't control either mineral, so it's best to keep both hidden. We've done a great job of it, too, until you and your people and all the other strangers showed up."

I opened my mouth to respond, but I had nothing to say. He was right. He was absolutely right. But what was I supposed to make of it?

"What if we leave?" Víctor asked.

He couldn't quite put that offer on the table, though—at least I didn't think so. That didn't mean it wasn't the right thing to offer. We all knew it was. But leaving this place also meant leaving magia behind, forgotten.

"You would give up the black salt?" the man asked Víctor. "You would leave without going to war?"

"We would try," Víctor said.

The man laughed. "Try? Trying won't save your people. Trying won't stop the man who started all this."

"No. We will," I said. I read the man's eyes. When this

conversation started, he'd looked at me with contempt. Now he seemed to understand that there was more to me. "We'll make everything all right again."

"Having the spirit of a warrior," the man said, "doesn't make you one."

I didn't think I was a warrior. But I did know that Salvación could be a hero.

CHAPTER 14

On our way back home, I thought of the village and of the destruction sal roja had caused. There were so few true precious things in this world, and the land that gave us a home, a real home, was the most essential.

I thought of the Indigenous man and how he had talked about balance. I thought of my brother and Mamá, and of Papá siding with señor Hernández. I thought of Alejandro and how I fit into the story.

If I couldn't trust Alejandro to stop his surrogate father, how good an ally was he?

As we came out of the forest, we were met with a surprise: Panchito was there; Alejandro's horse, Prisa, was as well. They'd waited for us here instead of going back to Coloma.

Alejandro hugged and kissed his horse. Víctor did the same, a smile on his face, the first real one I'd seen on him in days. Whatever had compelled the horses to stay, it meant that we would get home faster.

My throat burned as I remembered Carisma, but I managed to stay on the brink of tears the way back across the mountain.

"What do you think we'll find when we go back?" Alejandro asked as we trotted.

Part of me foolishly hoped that the rain had somehow managed to make the sal roja stop advancing. Something in my gut told me that the scorch in Coloma wouldn't work that way. The man said the only way was to dig. If we created a trench around the affected area, it might mean that there was no way for the sal roja to spread, move forward.

"Let's just get home and help, and then figure things out from there."

"Sounds good to me," Víctor replied, yawning. "I can sleep for a thousand years."

"We need to stop the advancing sal roja first," I said to Víctor, even when my head felt heavy, pain spreading at its center.

He stared at me as if he wanted to shove me off Panchito. Still, he didn't argue, didn't disagree. We both knew what needed to be done. So we agreed to stop at the scorch first before heading to town.

It wasn't hard to spot the right place. The sal roja had spread farther since the last time I'd seen it. It had started the size of my fist; now it was probably big enough to swallow a calf.

"It's growing so fast," Víctor murmured.

The three of us didn't say a word for several minutes. I couldn't say what Víctor or Alejandro were thinking. As for me, I felt like Víctor, like I could sleep a thousand years. After all this was done, I planned to do just that.

"This is where we depart," I told Alejandro after I'd given

him enough time. I hoped that knowing what was at stake, he wouldn't betray us. I hoped that my heart was right about him instead of my gut. "I think it's time for you to go home. Hernández is surely wondering where you've been."

"I'm not sure I have a home. I can't stand another day of seeing him and having to pretend that he isn't everything I despise in the world."

"You don't have a choice," Víctor said matter-of-factly. We all had a part to play in fixing this, in making amends, Alejandro most of all.

It was like the fiesta all over again, though. Víctor and Alejandro stared at each other like they were enemies. This time, it occurred to me that I was the thread that would hold the three of us together.

I could distrust Alejandro all I wanted. Víctor could too. But Alejandro was the only one here to help us, the only one on our side. We needed him, and I needed to bring the two together, fast.

"It's his choice," I said to Víctor. Then to Alejandro, I added, "But we hope that you'll make the right choice. We have to stop him, and we need your help to do it. You're the only one who can get the amulet for us. You have to try or we might not be around any longer. We need you to spy on him, report back what you find out. Can we trust you?"

Víctor waited for his answer. If my brother was anything, it was honorable.

"If he catches me—" I knew exactly what would happen: one speck of sal roja and I'd never see anything of Alejandro again. But it was a risk we had to take, no matter how much it made my stomach churn.

"He won't," I said, trying to assure him of something I wasn't in control of. "If what you've told us is true, he thinks of you as his son. We can use that. We need to try to use that. You're smarter than he—"

"You don't know anything about me." His reply made me flinch; its impact must have been obvious because Alejandro quickly added, "I mean, I'm not smart. If I were, I would have let you use sal roja on his bed the night at the inn."

"Well, even if you're not, la familia Peña will help you, won't they?"

I watched Víctor and waited for his reply. He pursed his lips, but he finally said, "Yeah. We will. You can trust us . . . if we can trust you."

Alejandro rubbed at his eyes. It wasn't always easy to do the right thing. He, too, finally turned to Víctor. "Do you think you can convince your papá to rise against him? Damián wanted to get your father on our side specifically because he knew that it would mean having everyone do whatever he wanted. He doesn't intend to give señor de La Peña anything he wants."

I exchanged a glance with Víctor. Papá was acting a fool, and he didn't understand that he was being lied to. As angry as I was with my father, I didn't want to see him hurt.

"I don't think so," Víctor replied.

"Maybe your sister can," Alejandro said.

I fought with all my might not to tell Alejandro that *I* was Lola de La Peña.

Víctor laughed—a throaty, honest sound that made me want to slap his arm. I somehow refrained.

Alejandro frowned but nodded. "I guess I should get back,

then." He mounted his horse, then said to us, "I still can't figure you two out. How do you know each other?" He pointed between my brother and me.

We hadn't ever talked about what we would say if we were found together. What could we say? I waited for Víctor to reply, but he didn't speak up right away, which made Alejandro tilt his head, questioning us.

I shrugged. "It just happened," I said. "The La Peña familia has done a lot of good. They've done a lot for the people of Coloma, as I have."

Alejandro cast his gaze downward. "And we just came to ruin it all," he said, and looked to Víctor. "I'm sorry, for what it's worth. I can't go back in time as much as I'd want to, but I can say that I am so sorry about all this."

Víctor crossed his arms. "I believe you might owe my sister an apology too. She might have mentioned some strange looks from you."

I blanched when he said this. I couldn't believe him sometimes. Did he want to completely embarrass me?

Alejandro half grinned. I thought of yesterday morning, our horseback riding.

"Your sister is something," Alejandro said. "I'll be sure to apologize." And with that, he rode off.

I didn't want him to leave. I was too afraid this was the last time I'd ever see him.

Víctor and I had work to do, which dampened the feeling of watching Alejandro go. Once Alejandro was out of sight, once we made sure no one else was around, I finally took off my Salvación mask.

I rubbed at my face. The places where the mask had touched my skin were itchy. Víctor passed me a jug of water. I uncapped it and poured some on my eyelids and cheeks.

"How are you?" he asked when I was me again.

I shrugged, evading his question. "Vamos, let's get this over with," I said.

Everything had turned upside down in only a few days. We weren't just fighting for our lives or the lives of the people in Coloma anymore; we were fighting to restore the balance that the world needed in order to be at rest. "I want to get back home to see if Carisma made her way back and to make sure the storm didn't do too much damage."

"Well, let's get digging, then," Víctor said.

I rolled up my sleeves, put up my hair, and readied myself for another tiring day.

Víctor and I spent hours digging out a trench around the sal roja, the way the Indigenous man had said to do. I trusted him that it would be enough to hold back the sal roja. In a way, it almost felt like sal roja was the land taking itself back from people, from us. Its way of saying that we didn't belong on it.

But if we didn't belong, where could we go?

"You haven't said a word for hours," Victor said.

I threw him a water jug, which he drank from vigorously. "What am I supposed to say?" I wondered, digging with my shovel. I didn't want to stop. I couldn't until the job was finished. At least Víctor seemed to either feel the same way or understand that we needed to do this today; we couldn't fail here the way I'd failed to get the amulet.

"That everything is going to be okay."

"You saw the sal roja spreading to us from the other town.

You saw how it's eating up the entire world. That's what señor Hernández wants. He wants to kill us all so he can be the last one standing. I don't know if everything is going to be okay."

Víctor let out a heavy sigh, straightened his back, and kept digging. "I don't think he understands what he wants. Men like him never do. He might not even know that the sal roja is hurting the soil."

I laughed. For as much as my brother and I had grown close, sometimes there was still this tendency left in him. Sometimes he was still the same unthoughtful Víctor as he'd been in Sonora. I supposed I was the same Loli at times too.

"Men like him know exactly what they're doing, Víctor. They just want everyone else to think they don't," I corrected.

They tricked you into dropping your guard. Señor Hernández might be evil, but he was also very, very smart. But even a foolish man would know he was doing something that wasn't proper, wasn't natural.

He knew. He didn't care. The only thing he didn't count on was meeting his match in Coloma.

I'd taken a long enough break. I kept digging. Every single inch I gained that helped us secure Coloma's safety was itself a victory. As long as Coloma was standing, as long as Mamá's dream and the sanctity of life withstood it all, we were okay.

When we had finished, Víctor and I stood side by side, looking at our work.

"We left your dress on the hillside. Do you want to go get it?" Víctor asked.

I shook my head. "No, I think those days are over. I don't want to be like Hernández. I might not be able to come clean about being Salvación, but I can at least show everyone who

I really am. I can't be in a dress when danger strikes. You can barely breathe in them."

Víctor grinned. "I'm glad you're not dressing up anymore. You're a charro through and through—don't let anyone else ever fool you into pretending you aren't."

I grinned back, looked at my pants. They felt *so* good. I hiked in them. I rode in them. I dug a trench in them. My legs didn't chafe. I never wanted to take them off and wear something else, not ever again. I'd burn all my dresses if it came to that. I'd slice up all my bodices. If Mamá got angry at me, I'd move out of the house, make a name for myself like doña Luisa.

We mounted Panchito and got on our way.

It was one of those strange days where you're waiting for something to happen, and there's this odd feeling in your tummy, but you're not exactly sure what might creep out of the shadows toward you.

I needed Hernández to drop his guard. I only hoped that Alejandro really could pull this off. If he could get the amulet for us, we'd have the upper hand.

When we arrived home, Carisma was still nowhere to be seen. My heart dropped. But at least the house hadn't been damaged by the storm.

"She'll come home, I know it," Víctor said. But I could see from his downcast eyes that he was stating a hope and dream more than anything else.

Víctor made to go inside, but I wasn't ready yet. I needed to clear my mind. I needed to get clean. "I'll meet you at the house," I said. "I'm going to go for a swim." It was what Papá always did when he needed to think.

Víctor nodded. "I'll bathe after you. Be careful," he said, then went inside.

I sneaked into my room from the window so Mamá and Papá wouldn't hear me, quickly changed out of my too-dirty clothes, slipped on the loosest dress I owned that I figured would be good enough to swim in, then went to the riverbanks nearest our home. This far out into Coloma, people rarely ventured to our property. They knew Papá didn't like unannounced visitors and preferred his family be left in peace.

I fully dived into the water, not caring that it was cold. My skin was hot. My skin was always hot lately, and it wasn't just the summer lingering; it was as if all my rage made my body temperature rise and I was a fire that couldn't be put out.

I lay on my back, the water cold against my cheeks. My hair flowed wild in the river. Fish swam past my hands, brushing my palms. The sound of the river was a lullaby, and I didn't close my eyes and risk falling asleep. The skies above were an endless blue, and I wondered why the sky was that color.

"Did you lose something up there?"

His voice startled me. It was Alejandro; I'd seen him only a couple of hours ago, but here he was again. I wasn't sure I wanted to see him.

Did he have the amulet? That was all I really wanted to know. Perhaps he had. But then I remembered that Víctor had said that he needed to apologize to me.

He was clean now. He looked like his usual self, except lighter in spirit, as if he'd found a will to survive and move forward and right all his wrongs.

"Wondering what makes the sky so blue," I said.

He grinned like he was about to say something but seemed to think better of it.

"What?" I said. "Did you come just to stare at me? Or are you looking for my brother or something? I missed your grand fistfight."

He laughed. "I didn't really hit him very hard," he said. "I think we're kind of friends now, anyway."

I nodded. "That's Víctor for you."

"You know," he continued, swallowing hard before saying, "mi mamá, when she was still alive, when I was little, she used to have these wild stories about everything. She said that when we cried, our tears would evaporate and get stuck in the skies. She said the sky was blue because of our tears."

I laughed. "That's silly, but there's a reason for everything. Who knows—she might have been right. What was she like, your mamá?"

"She was the most beautiful person in the world." He seemed lost in thought. I'd always thought that Alejandro was born into a bad situation and had never gotten over it. I never realized he'd been happy once, before señor Hernández came along, that he'd had a real family.

"What happened to her?"

He bit his lip now, his smile fading, and I regretted asking, but I still wanted to know. I wanted him to trust me enough to want to tell me.

"She was sick with something the doctors had no name for. One day she was okay and then days later she wasn't. It took her fast. Then it took mi papá and my siblings, one by one by one. Until I was the only one left. The doctors, they said that sometimes there are people a sickness can't touch."

"I'm sorry," I said. "Sal negra is changing that for a lot of people."

"It won't be enough. There will be many others who lose people they love. But I don't know . . . Sometimes I guess I think that's what it should be like. Maybe sal negra isn't natural."

"I don't know either," I said. "Did you know that mi mamá heard a calling and that's what brought us here? Something magical led her to Coloma, and it makes me think that maybe that magical thing wanted us at this place at this time—or maybe it doesn't want us to stay. Maybe we're supposed to take the sal negra and go help people with it, out there in the world."

"Perhaps," he said, biting the side of his lip, his eyebrows scrunched as if he wanted to figure out exactly what he wanted to say before speaking. "Sounds like something nice. I don't know that this world is nice, though." He shook his head, his eyes doubting.

"People do mean things, but there are also kind people, people who just want to love the land and do right by their families." I used to think Papá was one of those people.

We stared at each other.

"But to answer your question," he finally said, "I'm here because I owe you an apology."

I raised my eyebrows. "For what?"

There were plenty of reasons I could think of, but I wanted to watch him squirm. I wanted him to list all of them.

"I misjudged you," he said.

"Nope! Try again!" I shouted, making him take a step backward. I didn't think he was prepared for a confrontation. But I wasn't going to forgive him so easily. He wasn't my brother, mi familia—he was some stranger, and he needed to know I didn't require his approval or anyone else's.

"I was wrong," he said, correcting himself.

"You *were* wrong, weren't you? But just so you know, Alejandro, whether I'm wearing a dress or I'm wearing pants, whether I'm cooking food in the kitchen with mi mamá or I'm out racing against you or my brother, I'm never any lesser. I can do all of that and still be amazing."

He nodded. "I see that now. I have a lot to learn about the world." He looked off back toward town, to where I supposed señor Hernández was expecting him home by nightfall.

"Come in?" I splashed water his way.

He laughed again. And I liked it. I enjoyed making him smile, more than I cared to admit. He seemed to hesitate.

"Come on," I called out again. "The fish don't bite . . . much."

He finally got down from his horse, took off his boots and his shirt, and got in the water with one quick dive. He didn't complain about how cold it was. And I liked that about him. He met me in the middle of the river.

"Tilt back and float."

He did what I said, and together we watched the sky.

"Tears . . ." I said, recalling what his mamá had told him. "So, rain would be the sky releasing all the tears from above back onto us?"

"Yeah," he replied, moving his arms so he stayed centered in the current with me. His fingertips touched mine and made my stomach flutter, skip a beat like stones skipping over water. One, two, three.

"I accept, by the way."

"Hmm?" he asked.

"Your apology."

He nodded, grinned. For several minutes longer, he and I were in the water staring up at the sky, and it felt so right.

CHAPTER 15

The river hadn't given me any clarity as to how I could convince Papá to listen to us and take our side. Still, I thought of what Alejandro had asked Salvación and Víctor. I might be the only one who could convince Papá to see that he was doing wrong.

Dripping water, I found Víctor arguing with Papá in the kitchen. I assumed that Víctor had already told Mamá and Papá where we'd been.

"Loli, you're soaking wet!" Mamá said. Her demeanor had changed from the other day. She was no longer fragile, no longer crying. She had found some kind of resolve and there was anger in Mamá's eyes, as if she had made up her mind to take all her pain and take it out on me.

"I needed to think, so I went swimming in the river."

"And what have you figured out?" Papá asked, his voice harsh. "We've heard a lot already from your brother on what you two were doing during the storm. You realize you both could have been killed? You realize that we thought you *were* killed?"

"If Víctor has told you what we were doing, then you already know about the scorch, and how we need to act. And we weren't killed. We're fine."

Papá's face contorted into a scowl. "Oh, I know, all right. I know everything I need to make sure both of you don't go anywhere outside this house ever again. From now until para siempre, you are not allowed to leave this property. Víctor will no longer be mining for sal with me. Don't think I didn't notice that there is a large bulk of sal negra missing. And you, Loli, you will act the part that you were always meant to act. This is the end to whatever game you're playing. Éste es el final."

I waited for Mamá to say something, to defend us. I didn't know why I always looked to her, expecting something. I had been prepared to be disappointed once more when . . .

"The kids are right," she said, concern on her face. "This *is* enough. If your familia tells you that you are in the wrong, I believe it's time for you to listen. I've let this go on for too long."

I didn't think I heard Mamá right. I looked from Víctor to her to Víctor again, and finally to Papá. He wore a scowl, was unmoving, didn't say anything, as if he never thought he'd see the day that Mamá disagreed with him. In that moment, I realized that Mamá had said no to him only rarely. Sure, she'd asked him things that he could have said no to, like leaving Sonora and coming to Coloma; but since then, everything that he'd asked of her, she'd done without question.

Mamá physically moved her body toward me, as if together we might be able to face Papá. Víctor instinctively did the same. It made me feel unstoppable. The only thing that would make the moment feel better was if Papá acknowledged that he had been wrong and helped us stop señor Hernández. Which was why when he said, "Miriam, you can't be serious. They are trying to do something wrong," my heart broke. But it wasn't just any regular heartache. It was the feeling of losing one of your parents. I wasn't sure we could ever go back from this moment; I didn't think I could. Perhaps Víctor had always seen Papá for who he was. But not me; my father was my hero. Now he was the man who stood against us. My heart thumped so fast, fear creeping in my bones that Papá truly wouldn't take our side.

"People aren't coming to us to be healed anymore," Mamá said. And that expression she'd had when I saw her before the storm, when she had been crying in front of our claim when there was no line waiting for her, resurfaced. "I saw him today telling people that he'd heal them if they signed up for the war. They are signing up to die, nothing more. We have always said that we would heal those who need our help for free."

"You don't understand. Sal roja, it—"

"—is death," I finished. "You have to understand. Did Víctor tell you about the scorch?" There were tears burning hot in my eyes, my voice catching raw in my throat. It was like speaking past coals trying to get Papá to move on from the false hope señor Hernández had promised.

"Papá said he didn't believe me," Víctor replied, his tone flat, his arms crossed. At least, if anything, Víctor was taller than Papá. It was a strange thing, though, to be scared of Papá. I'd relied on him so much and so often it didn't quite make sense. But the fear was real.

"Edgar, amor, you have to see that this isn't what's right for

SALVACIÓN · 243

your family. We all think this is wrong. And if we do, that's because it is," Mamá said.

I didn't think Mamá would ever stand up against anything Papá said—not when she loved him so much, or when I knew she felt like she owed him for following her to Coloma—but here she was, standing by my side, not his. Maybe because she could also stand by Víctor, she found it easier to do and say this—or maybe it was really me.

Most likely it was that Mamá had always sought to do right, and it was right for us to try to stop Hernández instead of trying to help him like Papá was doing.

"So, you are all against me on this now? I'm trying to save this family from what's coming, because what's coming is something so evil that you all have no idea. And this is the thanks I get." He laughed. He didn't sound like himself when he did. Papá had never been cruel.

What had happened to him? Was it really just fear of the threats he was talking about?

"You're right, you're in the middle of it," Víctor said. "You have a choice, Papá: you can stand by us or you can stand against us, but if you're against us, I think it's time that you go to Hernández and stay there. The claim you're talking about that I can't go work at anymore isn't yours. It's never been yours. It's Mamá's."

It'd always been Mamá's money.

Papá scoffed, nodded. "By the end of this, I hope you three will see what's right." He walked away, slamming the door, the sound of which made Mamá jump beside me. She clutched her chest after he left. It was as if everything was too much for her, and I worried that she might take ill.

I reached out to touch her, but I withdrew my hands, uncertain. When Víctor walked up to her and hugged her, I wish I had in fact reached out. Mamá wept in his arms, her chest heaving. I almost felt like we'd done something wrong if it had made Mamá so sad.

The three of us stood together, unsure of what to say. We'd endured a whole lot of hurt on our way from Sonora to Coloma, but we'd always endured it together. Papá leaving us hanging felt like losing a part of our very being. We counted on him. We wanted him to be our rock. We wanted him with us on this.

But I knew we were also more than capable of standing up on our own if we had to. And it seemed like we'd have to.

"Mamá," I said. "I'm sorry." I rested my hand on her shoulder.

To my surprise, she took it and kissed it. "It's your papá who should be sorry, Loli. Standing up for what's right takes courage. That takes a type of bravery that not even grown hombres like your papá have all the time. We'll be okay."

I nodded. Mamá never talked to me like that. It had taken Mamá feeling down, losing everything I thought she truly loved, to be this person, and I didn't want to lose her.

"Mamá," I said.

She moved away from Víctor and focused on me. "¿Sí, Loli?"

"Whatever happens, I'm not sure that I'll come out of this alive. Or that Víctor will. Whatever happens, you need to promise us that you'll survive. If it comes to it, make up with Papá, tell him you were wrong."

She grinned. "Oh, Loli. There are many things that you'll need to worry about in this life. So much pain and hurt that will come flying at your face from every angle. But you do not have to worry about me. I am more than capable of standing up to your father and doing it in a way that keeps me safe. I am more than capable of protecting my family on my own."

I wished that could be enough, but it was not. "I know, Mamá. Still, I want you to promise you'll be careful."

"I promise," she agreed. There was something in her eyes, though, that made me suspicious.

CHAPTER 16

I expected Papá to return home. Every day that passed, I waited and searched for him out the window near the door. I listened for the sound of Tornado galloping home. Every night I went to sleep disappointed.

But it wasn't only Papá I worried about.

Ever since floating together at the river, I hadn't seen Alejandro. He'd left Víctor and me with a promise that he'd spy on Hernández, steal the amulet if he could, or at least let us know how we could take it. But there hadn't been a word from him either.

As for Víctor and me, well, we spent most of the day with Mamá. Not at home but at our mine. We needed to collect as much sal negra as we could and be ready to act. Mamá, like me, had never stepped foot inside her own claim. It was something else, seeing her enter the cavern.

She touched the walls of sal negra as if they spoke directly to her. I felt a hum as she did it, as if the sal negra really was alive, and it was almost like Mamá's touch made it more so. "Es magia," she said, pressing her palm against the walls of the mine. When she lifted her hand, the sal negra glowed a light green hue. Despite the stress of the fight we had in mind, I had a grin on my face. Seeing Mamá in her element, surrounded by something she loved so much, was special. Sal negra wasn't the only magia in the world. Mamá herself was magic—and I would do anything and everything to protect her magia, as much as I would for Coloma's.

"I can't believe I've never been in here before," she said.

"What does it feel like?" Víctor asked.

"Like life," she replied softly. "It feels like the moment that you and your sister made your escape from me and into the world. That relief of having life come out of you. It feels like that."

He nodded, looked away, put his own hand on the sal negra.

"It's okay that you don't feel it," I said.

"But you do, don't you?" he asked.

I could do a lot of things, but lying to my brother had never been one of them. I nodded. "It doesn't mean anything."

Still, he seemed strange the rest of the day. He cheered up that evening, when the sun went down and the people of Coloma seemed to be going to sleep—when we heard a familiar neighing.

It wasn't Carisma, though. She hadn't come back. I thought I had made peace with the fact that she likely wouldn't, but I obviously held out the last bit of hope. I was almost disappointed that it was Alejandro. As quickly as the feeling came, it left me. I couldn't believe it. It was him—finally and thankfully so. Had he done it? Did he have the amulet?

I jumped out of my chair and went to my room, shortly returning dressed as Salvación and hurrying out the back door to round my way through to the forest.

Víctor beat me to him. "Did you do it?" Víctor asked, wildly happy.

Alejandro shook his head. "Not yet," he said, almost out of breath, though he didn't seem flustered. He was calm and I could tell he had a plan. "He's been keeping it too close. Plus, your father has been around him all the time. What I do have is information—and maybe a plan?" He said the last part like a question, like he wasn't really sure whether he had a plan or just mush. At least he seemed more at ease since we'd gone on our trip, despite what we saw out there. It was as if he realized that he wasn't too far gone from redemption and we were giving him a shot at setting things right. He aimed to take it. And it made me feel something more for him when he did.

I stepped out of the forest as if I'd been waiting there all along, and definitely hadn't been in the house only a few minutes ago. He glanced over at me, and I swore I saw him blush.

"Well, get on with it," Víctor said when Alejandro went still.

"It's three days till the full moon," Alejandro started. "On the first night of the luna roja, the amulet will show him the path to the sal roja. We need to act soon, act fast."

"What do you suggest?" I asked, waiting for him to get to the good part.

"We bring him exactly what he wants."

"The world on a platter?" Víctor asked with a scoff.

I shook my head, my heart plummeting. "No." I knew what

Alejandro was going to say and Víctor wasn't going to like it. So I said it first. "He wants Salvación."

Víctor's face contorted. "Well, that's not happening. It's too big a risk. He could kill you in an instant." There was a stone tied to my back, weighing me down to the ground.

"He won't," Alejandro said.

"You can't be sure," Víctor replied. Whatever truce they seemed to have had, it was gone now. Víctor looked at Alejandro as if he were the enemy. Perhaps he still was.

But something in my gut, however heavy it felt, told me that this was also the best plan, the course of action we should be following.

"I'll do it," I replied.

Víctor took my arm, pulled me away from Alejandro, glaring at him along the way.

"You can't," my brother said when we were out of earshot.

I pulled out of his grip and rubbed at where his hand had been. "First, ouch. Second, I can do whatever I want."

"No, you can't," he said. "You're still my sister and you're Mamá and Papá's daughter. You can't do whatever you want."

That only managed to make me angrier. Back in Sonora, back in society, perhaps things had worked that way. As the older brother, he should be able to tell me what to do and give me orders that I'd be obliged to follow. But we'd left that behind when we came to Coloma. Here, I was headstrong enough to know I wanted equal rights in my family. And that meant I was able to make my own choices.

This was a choice I was willing to make.

"He'll find out it's you, Loli," Víctor whispered.

That was likely true. I couldn't imagine that señor Hernández wouldn't want to unmask Salvación, but if he did, it'd work in our favor.

"Do you think Papá will let him hurt me if that happens?"

Víctor's expression gave me an answer I didn't like. "No," he said. "I guess he won't let anything bad happen to you, but what if it does?"

I thought for a moment. Alejandro looked upon me with hope. Salvación had always offered hope to the people of Coloma: hope they could live a peaceful life without any external threats to their lives, hope they could someday find a real home here, hope they would find a family of people they could trust not to do them wrong.

I'd hidden in the shadows for way too long, thinking that I'd never have to come into the light. If I didn't stand against evil, though, maybe no one ever would.

"I'm standing my ground, and I won't back down," I said to Alejandro, approaching him anew and leaving Víctor glaring at the back of my masked head.

Alejandro grinned. "This idea will work," he said. "I promise."

"Well, what is the idea, anyway?" Víctor asked.

"I'm going to take Salvación to Hernández, exactly when we are set to leave. He won't have any choice but to take her with us. It's happened before, something like this. Víctor, you'll be waiting for us ahead in the forest and mountains, and you'll be ready with the kill shot. Hernández will have the amulet on his body. When he falls, when he dies, Salvación and I will take the amulet before the others even notice. They might still be looking for a fight, but we'll be well ahead of them. Even-

SALVACIÓN · 251

tually, they'll give up the search. None of Hernández's men are leaders. Without their leader, I believe they'll disband. Especially if they have no idea where the amulet went."

"And what do you intend to do with the amulet?" Víctor asked.

It was a good question, one I already had the answer to.

Alejandro scowled, but it wasn't a scowl directed at my brother. "I don't intend to do anything with it. Destroy it, maybe—"

"We're not destroying it. It isn't ours to destroy," I replied. "But we can return it."

Both Víctor and Alejandro looked at me, staring. "We need to give it back to the people Hernández stole it from. We need to right this wrong and make sure that those who know this place are the ones who hold this power."

"I agree," Víctor said.

"Same here," Alejandro added.

I grinned. "So, it sounds like we have a plan."

"How will we know when it's time?" I asked. "How will I know to be here?"

"In three nights' time, when the northern star is visible and high in the skies, I'll be here for you."

"I'll come back then," I said, nodding.

"Until then, rest. It'll be a hard day," he said. And with that, Alejandro tilted his hat and took his leave.

I spent the time I had with Mamá and Víctor, unsure if the three days until the full moon would be my very last on earth. I was willing to risk death if that was what it took to save the world. I'd wanted to be a hero for a long time, I'd even truly been one for a while, but this—this mission would be my legacy.

It was a warm evening, and we'd just had dinner.

Mamá was braiding my long hair. I had my eyes closed. Víctor was playing the guitar and singing. It was nice, hearing him play the guitar. Even though we were angry and upset, I still had a deep love for Papá. It was the same that I'd always felt for Mamá, even when I didn't think she loved me back.

Sitting here with her after she'd stood up to Papá for us, though, made me feel like she did love me and I'd been wrong all along. I didn't want to withdraw from this moment, but the moon would be full the next day, and we'd be leaving Mamá without telling her anything. She would do everything within her power to stop us if she knew our plans. If she knew that she might lose both Víctor and me tomorrow night, not just Papá, it would break her.

So we stayed quiet. We enjoyed each other's company.

Mamá hummed to the melody that Víctor was playing on the guitar. "You play better than your papá," Mamá said, eyes closed, swaying to the rhythm. Her compliment made Víctor beam.

It was the best thing in the world, to see my family happy. And I hoped that everything we'd planned went smoothly, so we could have evenings like this again.

In the distance, we could hear the bustling town. I wondered what was going on. But we'd finally drawn a line: we stayed at home, venturing into town only for simple things. In turn, everyone in town stayed away from us.

For now, I didn't think about it. For now, I closed my eyes again, ignoring the people in Coloma who were so in love with the ideas Hernández championed that they willingly gave up their souls—like Papá.

At night, when Mamá went to sleep, Víctor knocked on my door.

I opened it slowly and we sneaked out my bedroom window. We grabbed Panchito and waited for Alejandro at the edge of the forest. I searched for any sign of Carisma, something that said she'd somehow survived the storm. I'd never stop looking for my horse, nor did I think that my grief at losing her would ever pass. Between Carisma and Papá, my entire body felt burdened by the heartache. It made me slower than usual. I was distracted often, looking out into the wilderness, waiting for one of them to arrive.

"Loli?" Víctor was staring at me as if he'd been talking and I hadn't been listening.

"Sorry, what was it?" I asked, my cheeks flushing.

"I was asking if you're ready for tomorrow. I think we need to come up with an alternate plan in case something goes wrong."

"Like what?" I asked, genuinely curious. Alejandro's plan wasn't bad. If I hadn't believed there was a chance it would work, I wouldn't have agreed to it. I hadn't come up with anything better.

"I think you should run if something happens. If things start to go bad, as you know they so often can, take Alejandro and keep running until you get home, and get Mamá and run to the ends of the earth if you have to get away from Hernández and from sal roja."

Running wasn't the same as galloping. One was freeing; the other wasn't anything I wanted any part of.

"I'm tired of running, Víctor. I'll either win or die, and that's okay." I was surprised how true the words were. When this all started, with the man who had taken a shot to the torso and used his heirloom revolver to fight his way to the front of the line, I'd been afraid of dying. Today I was only afraid of failing.

Disgruntled, Víctor shook his head but didn't argue with me. At any rate, he hadn't exactly talked about himself in this scenario. If something happened to Víctor—it couldn't—it just couldn't, or I'd die right behind him.

We reached our huge stash of sal negra. There were lots of buckets filled to the brim, small blue flores growing around them all. We couldn't carry the sal negra with us like this. So we had to figure out what to do with it. We were mixing a salve to cover the clothing we'd wear tomorrow.

Tonight, we were also planning what weapons we would take.

"They'll probably take yours away," Víctor said, "but you might be able to hide another gun somewhere, and your knife. Definitely make sure you have a knife with you."

I nodded. "What about you? Is your rifle ready?"

"As ready as it's ever going to be." He'd been preparing ammunition since we came back from seeing Isabela's village. He *was* ready. I could see it in his eyes, in his focus.

He was Salvación as much as I was.

Our last day came and went, all while Víctor and I readied ourselves the best we could to possibly say goodbye to our entire world. I wasn't sure that I was ready. In fact, I knew I wasn't, but I guess you're never ready for the big things in life.

Even if I wasn't ready, at least I wasn't alone. And in some strange way, that was enough to steady my heartbeat, enough to make me hold to my word.

Alejandro's plan had to work. And we would see it through.

After Mamá kissed us both good night and she went to sleep, Víctor and I readied ourselves for the long night ahead. I put on clothing that we'd drenched in agua de sal negra for days and then dried. The moment I did so, the material infused with the sal negra made my skin feel amazing. My whole body felt abuzz with something like electricity. Maybe that was all life was, a lightning storm powering us up instead of our bodies. It was invigorating to know that even if I was walking to my death, I'd feel amazing doing it.

I made sure my entire set of clothing was ready, including making sure that my mask fit me snugly so it wouldn't fall off even in a scuffle. I also readied myself for the idea that after today, everyone might know I was the woman behind Salvación. The mask was mine, the identity mine. How would people take it when they found out? What would señor Hernández say? What would he think if he knew that the daughter of the man he was enamored with was the one fighting to bring him to justice?

Would he hurt Papá? Or like we hoped, would he realize that he couldn't hurt the daughter of the ally he needed? It made my heart clench, thinking that perhaps he wouldn't be moved, that his anger would be enough for him to simply hurt us all.

But I supposed, as we'd seen on the road from Sonora, loneliness was the worst of everything. There had been men and women who, upon finding themselves alone, simply gave up. Perhaps that was why we had made it through the entire journey to Coloma together.

I would have Víctor and Alejandro with me the entire time. I had to trust the boy wouldn't let anything happen to me. I hesitated at the front door. This was it: the moment I had to make the right choice. I could still go back or run away. But then I remembered Isabela's face when she realized that the hero she had made me out to be was only a girl.

Víctor and I left a note for Mamá. It was the cowardly thing to do, but when it came to Mamá, she'd made us both the bravest we had ever been and the weakest. I couldn't stand the thought of saying goodbye. So I didn't, praying that we would see each other again.

She must have been used to it by now—from us, anyway, considering that for a long time, both our parents had known our identity as Salvación. But one thing adults didn't always realize was that we were worried about them too. They were the ones who were likely closer to death than we were. And sometimes we needed to protect them, instead of the other way around.

Víctor and I, we could take care of ourselves. We packed as much food as we could carry without being weighed down by it. We fed Panchito, but even as I settled onto his back, I still searched for Carisma.

I didn't glance back a single time as we headed into the forest, where we would meet Alejandro. I couldn't take a last look at our casita, or else I might not be able to leave.

Alejandro met us by the edge of the forest; he seemed nervous at our approach until he identified us. His shoulders retreated into their sockets, and he sighed with relief.

"What now?" I asked him, checking behind me. We'd spent so many nights sneaking around that it didn't make any sense to be fearful, yet here I was, making sure that no one was lurking, that no one was spying on us.

"Now we take our leave," Alejandro said, offering up his hand, which held rope for binding my hands.

It made my skin cold, knowing that Víctor and I would be separating in a moment.

He must have felt the same way because he reached out for my hand, intertwined his fingers with mine. "Are you sure about this?" he whispered. He wore the same expression as on that day he'd saved me from the river while fearing for my life. I guess there was a lot to fear.

"It's the only way we save everyone and get Papá back."

"And what if we can't convince Papá to come back?"

"We will. I will. I promise."

I nodded once at Alejandro.

Víctor stopped to speak to him before leaving us. "If anything happens to Salvación, it'll be you I come after," he said.

"I wouldn't expect anything less. I'll take care of her."

"Even die for her?"

"Even die for her."

Hearing those words made my heart flutter. Just knowing that someone who wasn't a member of my family would be willing to risk their life for me meant something that I didn't have words for.

Alejandro's eyes had glowed as he made that promise to my

brother. We locked eyes, but I looked away quickly. There seemed to be a sort of confession happening—only I realized that Alejandro was confessing feelings not for *me* but for Salvación. As far as I knew, he still thought Lola de La Peña and Salvación were two different people. A chill ran through me again and my heart plummeted. Soon he'd find out the girl he had been disdainful of and the woman for whom he seemed to have feelings were one and the same. What would he think then?

For now, it didn't matter. None of it mattered except stopping Hernández and saving Papá from himself. That must be the focus—so I focused.

I held out my hands to Alejandro. Binding me had been his idea, but he still hesitated, stared at my arms as if the weight of what he was about to do was only now becoming clear to him. He nodded, more to himself than to us it seemed, and proceeded to tie my wrists together, tethering them in the middle and connecting a cord so he could feign pulling me.

"You look like you are doing this willingly," Víctor said to me, frowning. "We need to mess you up."

"Well, there's mud and sand and twigs under our feet. Get on with it," I told them.

Together they worked to make me look like I'd been in a scuffle. Alejandro even went as far as to make a cut on his leg, wiping his blood in spots on my face and clothing, as though we'd been in a real fight.

Víctor looked on and then said to Alejandro, "We'll have to do the same to you." And then they worked on him too.

When they were done, it was time for goodbye, un adiós I didn't want to say—one I couldn't say.

So just as with Mamá, I didn't say anything at all. I nodded to Víctor, tears in my eyes, blurring my vision. I didn't need to see him to feel the warmth of his brotherly embrace as he pulled me in for a hug. I didn't care what Alejandro thought or if he grew jealous, not understanding that Víctor and I were siblings. I needed to say a proper farewell to Víctor in case anything should happen to either of us.

I didn't even want to think of anything horrible befalling my brother.

When we let go and I looked back, Alejandro's jaw was set tight.

The night finished settling in and we parted ways. The stars were all visible, twinkling up above, and I wondered if anyone had ever seen a star up close, and if we ever would. I wondered what was out there in the vastness of the sky. Perhaps there really was a god up there, peering down at us, following our every move, lingering over every failure.

Víctor walked into the trees. As I watched my brother depart, I saw his hands going to his face as if drying his eyes or shaking off tears. When we lived in Sonora, I'd never once imagined that Víctor might weep for me someday. I wanted to hold on to the relationship we had built through hardship and with a newfound trust.

I wanted to hold on to Salvación even though I was certain that by morning, everyone would know the face behind my mask. The streets were eerily quiet as Alejandro led me to where Hernández's men were gathered. They were quiet at first, but as people looked out their windows, a murmuring began and then got louder.

"Salvación," they said.

"What is going on?" someone shouted.

"Let her go!" another voice cried out. This one I recognized as Luisa's. She was the first person to emerge from her house, joined by others. I grinned to myself. In all our planning, I'd never anticipated that perhaps the people of Coloma wouldn't take kindly to Salvación being caught, to their ángel being unmasked.

Or perhaps this had been part of Alejandro's plan all along. Alejandro didn't stop or answer anyone. He held his head high, his posture rigid and ready for anything.

I was Coloma's angel. Now it felt like I was being presented to el Diablo. And this is exactly what we'd been waiting for . . . for everyone to see Hernández and his men as the villains they were.

Alejandro took me to the inn occupied by one man, though it could house a hundred. We were followed by the townspeople, who pleaded with Alejandro to let me go and to give them some answers.

A group of people was already standing in front of the inn, where Hernández was on the stoop, giving a speech to his men. I recognized several faces among them—faces that had once belonged to the people of Coloma. They were his men now. They were enemies of the world.

"You've come at an opportune time," Hernández said, eyeing Alejandro and me, a slight smirk on his lips that made my stomach flip. "The way to where sal roja lives will be shown to us tonight." He wasn't upset. He almost looked like he was getting exactly what he wanted. And seeing his face so full of life and happiness made me wish that I'd never let Víctor leave my side. Where was my brother now? He wasn't going to be near us. He was going to be hiding in the forest, tracking and following us wherever we went.

It felt like forever until I would see him again. *If* I ever saw him again.

I was made to sit before Hernández. The moment my butt landed on the ground, I searched his men for the only one who interested me—but Papá was nowhere to be seen. I hoped he'd come to his senses and gone home to Mamá, where he belonged.

I might have been afraid if it not for Alejandro, who was still with me, if not for the townspeople still asking them to let me go.

Alejandro placed his hand on my shoulder, pretending to keep me down.

"How nice of you to join us, Salvación," said señor Hernández. He was dressed all in white, as if he were nothingness coming to eat me whole. I gulped as I took in his expression. It was frightening how happy he was to see me.

"What's going on?" asked someone in the crowd.

I was wondering the very same thing. Alejandro didn't meet my gaze. I was still staring at him when Hernández said, "And to you, mi hijo, muy bien. I'm proud of you."

"I just did what you asked," Alejandro replied. He still didn't look at me. I wasn't sure what to make of the exchange. Had he been tricking me the entire time?

I tried to stand, but Alejandro tightened his grip on my collar, hurting me. I wanted to scream, thrash, and learn whether this was all still part of his plan or not.

"Dearest people of Coloma, Salvación is not who they seem!" Hernández said, and all I could do was look on. "They are no angel."

CHAPTER 17

Pandemonium ruled the crowd. From where I sat, Alejandro beside me, I searched for a sign that trusting him was not a mistake. I got nothing. My only solace was that the people of Coloma wanted—no, demanded—that the newcomers answer for this.

Luisa stepped to the front. She approached me but stopped when Alejandro gave her a glare. Why was he suddenly so cold? Was *that* an act?

"You don't need angels in Coloma," Hernández said. "Especially not one who has been sent by the enemy to spy on you."

"Lies!" Luisa said, speaking up.

I wanted her to stop before there was nothing left of her but the remnants of a speck of a sal roja. My body shook as I considered how Hernández might visit wrath upon her, whether now or later. I didn't dare blink.

"Doña Luisa, I am too old and have seen too much to lie,"

SALVACIÓN · 263

Hernández said in a flat tone of voice that made me *almost* believe him.

His soldiers moved as if shielding him from and protecting him against an old woman. Their maneuvers were ominous and alarming.

A glaze of fear passed over Luisa's eyes as she gauged her situation. She retreated into the crowd. It was a relief and a moment of reckoning.

"Do not fear this, mi familia." Hernández called the people of Coloma his family, but they weren't. I wasn't sure that he saw them as anything more than cattle. I wasn't sure if he saw anyone as anything—except maybe for Alejandro.

I watched the boy again. His eyes were glued to Hernández. I feared that there might be a sparkle in his eye as he looked at his father. That fear was unsettling and grew in my chest. I nudged him with my foot.

When he looked to me, I mouthed, "Let me go." He didn't act, just pretended he hadn't heard me. I didn't say anything further to avoid drawing more attention to myself.

Hernández kept going: "This is a special night, señoras y señores. On this night, the moon will turn red, and it will show us the way to the sal roja that will save Alta California from those who aim to destroy it."

So Alejandro had been telling the truth about that. Perhaps he was ignoring me because it was important he seem absolutely in character.

The moon was full and bright, still white.

Many townspeople had shown up for the speech. Others who at first hadn't taken notice of the scene were now staring at Hernández as if they finally saw him in a new light, as if they were suddenly recognizing the danger they were in, the danger that threatened us all.

"When it becomes red, I hope you will all understand that I am a god." The last word was met with another round of whispers. There was only one God for many of us, the God who had brought us sal negra. Hernández's men took another step forward—looming, menacing. "That I am to be followed, listened to, regarded."

Beto walked up through the crowd. "And what if we refuse to follow?" he asked, his hand on the revolver at his hip.

If Beto was here, Papá couldn't be far away. I pleaded for him to show up.

Señor Hernández grinned. If I didn't know any better, I would have sworn he had fangs. "Then there is no more need for you."

It happened so quickly, I barely had time to move. He pulled out a bottle, opened it, and blew sal roja toward Beto. It hit him in the chest.

I wasn't sure what to do, but even with my hands bound, I tried to move toward him. Alejandro, however, kept me down.

Beto's face contorted. Papá had to be here somewhere. I wanted to shout to him, to call him for help. But if he had been there, I knew that despite everything, he would have helped Beto. *Where was he?*

Alejandro kept me in my place.

"Let me go!" I shouted.

His body moved steadily to his breathing, and his perfect expression fell. Alejandro's eyes were afraid. His eyes told me that if I didn't do exactly what he said, I might be the next one to share in Beto's fate.

Luisa did move toward Beto, dropping to his side as he screamed and twitched, writhing on the ground just like the man in the forest. Other neighbors stepped farther back, terrified as they witnessed Beto's body eating itself.

Beto was practically part of our family. He was Papá's best friend. Why was this happening, and why had I thought that I could help anyone at all?

In a mere moment, Beto was no more, and everyone whispered in horror. Many tried to run away, only to be stopped by Hernández's men.

"Now that you have witnessed the true power of the sal roja, will you bow to your rey, to your god? Or will you become absolutely nothing?"

Luisa, my beloved friend Luisa, was the first to kneel, bow her head. I stared at her, unbelieving and yet understanding.

One by one, the people bowed—my people, the people of Coloma whom I fought to protect from everything that I could. I felt a deep heartache, and I flinched away from Alejandro, even when his eyes were asking me to trust him, and not to forget or turn back.

Beto! He wasn't gone, not really. The dead never truly leave. I felt his energy, the soul he had been, becoming a flame. That made me angrier. It refocused me.

As I made up my mind for the thirtieth time, the world around us dimmed. The moon slowly went from white to red. And in the red light of the moon, a path erupted from the direction of the mountain.

It was as he had said: the red moon was going to show us the way to sal roja, and all I could think about was whether Papá was already dead.

All I could think about was how to fix what had gone so terribly wrong.

All I could think about was seeing Hernández meet defeat at my hands.

We had a plan, and it was time for it to succeed.

CHAPTER 18

La luz roja led us through la oscuridad of the forest, pulling us along like a string, a tether that Hernández followed without hesitation. It was almost as if the light leading us was emanating from another plane entirely.

When he reached into the pocket of his white shirt, I thought el Demonio was going to pull out the amulet, but he only drew a hanky to wipe the sweat from his brow. I had yet to spot the amulet, but I assumed Hernández kept it close.

The ropes chafed my wrists, so painful it was hard to think straight. I kept trying to spot Víctor in the shadows through the trees. Surely, he had seen the light shining red from the path. That glow would make it easier for him to follow until we arrived in the perfect place for us to act. But before that could happen, where was the amulet?

Alejandro pulled me along, tugging gently every once in a while, such as when I slowed too much to keep pace. I'd slip, but he always helped me to my feet again. He was gentler now that Hernández's direct gaze wasn't on us, but he still hadn't said a word to me, he still avoided my gaze. That broke my heart. The thousand splinters in my chest dug into my very soul. I refused to cry, but the tears were right there, threatening to spill over.

The forest was for the most part familiar after sneaking around for months with Víctor and then traveling with Isabela during the storm. When we first arrived in Coloma, I had been afraid of the world, of everything I didn't know. But I'd changed so much since then. I was still changing. And perhaps that was what life was, just a line of days when you had the chance to evolve and become someone else, someone better. Apparently, Hernández hadn't understood that meaning of life and seemed to become eviler.

El Demonio looked hungry for power. Men surrounded him as though he had enemies on all sides, not just behind him. Was he afraid of me, of a girl—of Salvación? Did he know that there was more to the vigilante than me, that the other half of Salvación was hiding, waiting to attack?

I hoped Víctor was safe and that he would remain so. And I hoped that Mamá was too. She hadn't been in la plaza. But I wouldn't be surprised if the men Hernández had left in Coloma had rounded everyone up. A part of me still hoped that Papá had gone home too. That my parents were together.

I needed to figure out a way to get to the amulet, especially before we found anything dangerous.

By the look of the light, though, the sal roja was still miles away. At least I hope that was the case. The farther we were from town when we found it, the better.

A way into the forest, past a ridge, I spotted Víctor in the brush. Barely visible. If you hadn't been looking for him, you probably wouldn't have seen him. We locked eyes; he gave a small nod.

I gave Alejandro the signal we'd agreed on—a pull of my ear—and held my breath. It was now or never.

All the shooting practice with Papá, all the training with a sword, every single time I wasn't who I was expected to be, I was learning to be who I would one day need to be. I took another deep breath, hoped that Alejandro would stick to the plan. The moment Víctor fired, he'd need to cut me loose; otherwise, my brother and I would be killed in minutes.

The first shot rang through the air, and I watched as one of Víctor's bullets hit a man in the shoulder. Víctor was aiming not to kill but to slow, to stop.

In one movement, Alejandro pulled out his knife and sliced through my bindings. He took my now-free hand and pulled me toward Hernández.

We didn't move away from the bullets that Víctor let ring but advanced toward Hernández in hopes of retrieving the amulet from his person. We didn't hesitate, acting in unison. We made a good team.

One of Hernández's men came running out from the side when we neared our target. Alejandro slammed into him, giving me room to reach Hernández. But I didn't get to him in time. Someone yanked at my clothes, tore at them. I reached for my pistol, took it out of my belt, and didn't hesitate to shoot whoever it was. Alejandro pulled the man off me, blood smearing on my face as he did, and pulled me to my feet.

It all happened so quickly, and yet happened in slow motion. It was three against three dozen. If I thought about it logically, we had no chance at victory, yet I believed we could pull this off. All we needed was to get to the amulet and take it, stop Hernández from executing his plan of action.

I couldn't give up. I needed to win.

I went after the retreating men, unafraid of them. Unafraid, I realized for the first time, truly, of dying. I knew I was doing the right thing, and doing what was right was worth more than my mortal life.

Víctor came out of where he was hiding, shooting as he went. His aim had always been superb. Papá had been taking my brother hunting since he could hold a rifle up against his weight, and tonight it showed.

When I went forward, I felt a hand wrap around my torso, pulling me back, back, back. "We need to leave! Or we'll die!" Alejandro said.

I couldn't believe it: our chance for the amulet, fading away.

I kicked Alejandro and he dropped me. I succeeded in squirming away and followed Hernández past the brush and higher up the mountainside, sliding past the men who tried to stop me. At least the first few. Suddenly they were all around and they caught me. They held me, two men, each taking one arm, even as I struggled against them.

And Hernández reappeared when they did.

"It's time we find out who you really are, Salvación," he said. His fingers found my mask.

"Leave her alone!" Víctor said, moving toward me, but he was too far away.

Before I could say something, the mask was gone and off my face and my identity had been revealed. I didn't look toward

Hernández. I didn't care what he thought. I turned to face Alejandro, who was at Víctor's side.

Alejandro stood stock-still for one moment. "Lola?" It was a relief not to hear disdain in his voice. He didn't seem angry. There was confusion there, yes, but I saw in his face that everything was clicking together, why Víctor and I were so close if we weren't in love: we were siblings. Then he grinned at me, nodded, and everything felt okay. It felt okay to be Lola de La Peña and Salvación in a way that I hadn't felt before with anyone outside of Víctor; not with Mamá and Papá, certainly. Alejandro accepted me for all of who I was.

And as fast as everything clicked for him, it clicked for me. I felt the outline of my knife in the pocket of my pants. I pulled out the knife Víctor had given me, swiping it open as I did, and stuck it in Hernández's leg. He yelled. It might have been wrong, but his was a scream I welcomed with a smile on my face. He let me go and gave me room to move. The men panicked, many approaching to try to help their boss only to be met with a fury of colorful cursing.

At closer range, Víctor now had the musket that doña Luisa had given him. One of the shells from it struck the man nearest to me. It made the others realize that their boss wasn't their priority if they wanted to leave unscathed. They fled their boss's side, looking for my brother. Papá had taught Víctor to move like a shadow in the trees, fast and cunning as a fox. And his maneuvers were keeping Hernández's men busy.

Suddenly, I found that I had Hernández at knifepoint. I might have been Lola de La Peña, but that didn't take away from the fact that I was also Salvación.

"Give me the amulet or I will end your life." I had never meant the words until this moment. I *would* kill this man—for what he did to Isabela's people, for what he did to the man in the forest, for what he did to Beto, and for everything he was doing to the land and the people indigenous to it.

He smiled, then laughed, which made my whole being boil with rage. I hated the man. I had never hated anything in my life. But how could one not feel anger toward someone who was el Diablo himself? There was nothing to be gained by pretending that all people should have a second chance. Alejandro deserved it, the way Papá had always believed, but not this man who cared for nothing but power.

"I don't have the amulet, niña tonta." He called me a dumb girl, and I had to agree with him: If he didn't have it, then who did?

I didn't get the chance to ask. I recognized Víctor's voice, and he was yelling. Hernández knocked the blade from my hand. We both scrambled after it. He was faster than I was. He grabbed it first and didn't hesitate to slash at my leg. I barely moved out of the way in time, helped only by the fact that I'd already been in motion.

Now he was the one with the upper hand.

Hernández did not attack. "I don't have time for you," he said, turning to the red light, which had started to fade. There was a time limit, I realized—a very short one.

"We need to go!" Víctor said, finding me suddenly and helping me off the ground, where I was putting pressure on my leg wound. He grabbed Alejandro and yanked him along, too, surprising me. I would have thought Víctor would leave him behind.

SALVACIÓN · 273

We ran toward the light, a few men giving chase. Víctor shot behind us into the crowd but didn't seem to hit anyone. Alejandro suddenly took hold of my hand and wasn't letting go, no matter how much I hobbled. I used my free hand to pull sal negra from the pouch at my hip and rub on my leg to help it heal. But all I succeeded in doing was spilling a handful of sal, dozens of small flores azules sprouting where it landed.

We slid suddenly, all three of us, down a slope, and I found myself yelling until we came to a stop. Everything hurt. I hadn't felt pain in so long thanks to the sal negra, but now everything was raw and aching and I didn't want to move.

I opened my eyes and lay there, unflinching, unmoving. How do you keep going when you've reached your limit?

Everyone knew who I was now. Alejandro knew. Hernández knew.

I knew I had to get moving. The light was right there, a clear path ahead of us. In mere minutes, it would be no more. It would leave and we would never figure out where the sal roja was. Without the amulet, we needed the light more than ever.

"La luz," I said, but still couldn't stand up. I reached my hand down to my pouch. I took sal negra on my fingertips, still wet from the soil, the fall, blood, whatever. I brought my hand to my mouth, licked at my fingers, not caring if the taste of sal was mixed with earth and copper and it didn't taste good at all.

It helped. I blinked. My body stopped aching. I blinked again. I felt like I could get to my feet. Everything was healed.

I sat up and looked about me, feeling renewed.

To my right, Víctor was lying facedown, his leg askew. His head was bleeding. I didn't have time to panic. I had sal negra.

As long as he was still alive, Víctor would be okay. I was too afraid to check for a pulse, so I applied the sal negra to his head injury first.

He gasped, then sighed. Then screamed. "My leg!" he said. "My leg!"

Alejandro came up to us, not a scratch on him. His tattered clothing made it obvious that he'd already used some sal negra on himself. Together we healed Víctor. Alejandro gave him a spoonful of sal negra, and in mere minutes, Víctor was standing once more, though memories of the pain would probably linger. Indeed, although his leg was straight now, he kept staring down at it, running his hand over the limb.

"Are you okay?" I asked.

"Yeah, la magia is incredible."

I grinned and said, "¡Vamos!" I moved, only to feel pain in my leg where I'd spread the sal negra. I fell to my knees, trying to see straight once more. The blade, the movement: I was trying to recall Hernández's actions, but I didn't remember him ever pulling out any sal roja. Yet something strange was definitely happening to my body. I could sense it. I could feel something odd inside my bones, spreading underneath my flesh.

Alejandro and Víctor had no clue what shape I was in, so I used all the remaining sal negra on my leg. For now, there was relief that allowed me to follow the others. I ran, trying to shake off the sal roja I was sure coursed through my veins. But I couldn't shake it off; it was there. I could feel it. I could feel it eating into me. I could feel the sal negra fighting back too.

I fell, convulsed, my body struggling to keep itself together.

Víctor didn't waste a second. He picked me up and carried

me like a sleeping child, cradled in his arms. I couldn't hear their voices anymore, and I wasn't entirely sure what I could do for myself.

In Sonora, I had people to do everything for me. I never wanted to be that person again. Sometimes when you changed, you became someone you could be proud of. There was so much that I couldn't feel proud of right now. I should have fought harder and made Papá listen. If I wasn't going to make it out of this alive, I didn't want to have regrets.

Cool grainy hands suddenly caressed my neck, even as I watched the light we were chasing continue to fade. Then a jolt of energy rushed through me. I opened my eyes wide and made eye contact with Alejandro. His hands on the sides of my neck. All I could do was stare at him. He never looked at me this way when I was Lola de La Peña. I examined his face, froze, and breathed in the relief sal negra brought as it touched my skin and fought the sal roja that I'd thought was sure to win.

He stroked my forehead, rubbing the sal negra against my head with his palms, then against the skin at my collarbone, then my stomach. I wasn't sure which felt better, his touch or the sal negra.

The pain eased. Soon enough, I was ready to stand again.

"We have to hurry," I said, grinning. Alejandro smiled at me, and all I wanted to do was kiss him.

That would have to wait. We stood. We kept running. I tried to hide the lingering pain way down deep that told me this wasn't over, that the sal roja was still fighting to win, to destroy my body, to eat me alive.

Still, there were even greater things to worry about: the light had led us to a cliff.

"There's nothing here," I said. Nothing but a giant drop, and that was where the light went. As far as the eye could see, there was nothing but pitch-black.

"Shit," Víctor said.

"I don't get it," I said. "Is this a dead end?"

Then I remembered what Papá had said about sal roja and sal negra coming from the earth itself. There was no way it would be easy to reach. Sal roja was hidden for a reason.

Alejandro licked at his lips. "We need to jump," he said.

"What? Are you thinking straight? Look at that drop? We'll be dead just from the fall," Víctor replied, backing away.

"This is how it works," Alejandro said, eyes on the drop. "I've never seen a drop like this, but it's always like this: somewhere dangerous that's hard to reach. The light wouldn't be taking us along this route if it wasn't a route we could survive."

Víctor gestured to the canyon. "Well, then after you."

They kept bickering.

Magia came from somewhere, and that somewhere seemed to be a giant leap of faith. I looked to Víctor. Then to Alejandro. They both meshed into one figure as my eyesight went blurry. I felt the sal roja in my stomach. I felt the sal negra losing.

A gunshot sounded behind us. Hernández was coming. Men with guns who could easily shoot us as we stood right here on the ledge.

I made a choice. I wasn't going back to my old life. And I wasn't going to die here, not by being shot at—and not by being eaten alive by the sal roja.

I ran—not back, not to the side, but straight. I leapt into the air, following the light.

And then I was falling into oblivion, taking the leap of faith.

CHAPTER 19

Where did magia come from?

I knew where life came from: the wombs of people who carried children; the love that two people could have between them, or sometimes not. Life came from nothing and from everything all at once.

Not long ago I didn't need to know where magia came from. There was magic in the world. It healed. It seemed like a miracle. That was enough for me. It came from the earth. This amazing world gave it to us.

Magia had chosen Mamá to wield it, and she led us from Sonora to Coloma on nothing more than a whim. When we arrived, there it was, the thing she had convinced us of, waiting for us. It was as if la magia was meant *for us*.

How could Papá's concept of it change so much in such a short time? How was it that one man had changed him so much? A man he didn't even know, who wasn't his blood, who didn't share the trials and tribulations that had assailed us from

Sonora to Alta California. How could he trust that man over his own family?

It made me so angry. It made my heart hurt.

Sometimes, I guess, what you want to happen, what you want to protect, it doesn't let you see straight. Sometimes, I guess, people have bad inside them that's waiting to be let out.

And sometimes you're fighting for something so pure that nothing can stamp you out.

I landed in water. The current of el río was so strong that I didn't get the chance to look up to see if Víctor and Alejandro were following me. The current pushed me under the water, which entered my mouth . . . and tasted of sal. I didn't have to fight to reach the surface. There was so much sal in the water that it stung my eyes and kept me afloat. Still, up on the surface, the current was ferocious and it slammed me this way and that and into the rocks.

I heard my name every time the sal made me rise and I came up for air. I heard Víctor calling me. He was alive.

I wondered if by the time this was all over, Alejandro would be there too. Had he followed me to the ends of the earth? Or perhaps I had only brought us to our death and the end.

The current finally slowed—I went down one last swell and a small waterfall and was met with still water and a shore. I coughed up salt water, used my hands and knees to crawl farther up the bank.

I lay on my back, needing to breathe, and hoped I hadn't made a stupid mistake. The sting in my eyes died down as I slowly came back to my senses. Whatever we had jumped into, it wasn't necessarily a river. I mean, it was, of course, on a basic level, but the water was filled with sal negra.

We were at the bottom of a strange canyon, with steep mountains bursting with trees on all sides.

It would be impossible to climb back up the ridge we'd jumped from. If there even was a way out of here. It seemed we'd leapt into an entirely different world.

Víctor's voice swelled. "Loli!"

I sat up quickly and looked for my brother, who was making his way over to me. I met him halfway and launched into an open embrace.

"Thank you for following me," I said, holding on tightly.

"I wouldn't have let you jump alone. Of course I wouldn't have."

When we let go, I noticed Alejandro about thirty feet behind him.

"¿Estás bien?" Víctor asked.

And then I realized that the pain—the pain from the sal roja—was completely gone. In fact, I had never felt this good my entire life.

"The sal negra in the river, I think it might have healed me." I smiled, laughed, rejoiced to be free of pain. I wasn't going to die. And the light, the light was right there still, guiding us where we needed to go.

Alejandro sat nearby, his eyes toward the cliffside. "That was wild."

"The river is filled with sal negra. Have you ever experienced anything like it?" my brother asked Alejandro.

Alejandro shook his head.

After we had caught our breath, Víctor said, "I'll go scope everything out, follow the light a bit farther to see what's there. I'm assuming we'll have a while before Hernández and his men muster up the courage to jump."

I nodded to Víctor, not even thinking of being fearful that he'd find the sal roja and somehow get some on himself. Instead of offering a warning, I sat down with Alejandro and said, "Sounds good."

Alejandro and I sat silently afterward, our knees pointed at the river. I avoided looking at him.

"I can't believe you're Salvación," he said. "This whole time?"

I wasn't surprised he'd brought it up. He needed answers. He deserved answers after everything we'd been through together. I wasn't necessarily ready to offer all of them up, but it was time—I didn't want to hide anymore. I wanted to be both Lola and Salvación. And who better to start down this road with than Alejandro?

"Víctor and I, we're both Salvación," I explained. "When we first arrived in Coloma, sometimes bad things happened that we wanted to do something about. Our parents wouldn't—they were too afraid, too focused on just having nobody bother our family to care about the others in town who didn't have Papá's strength and fighting skills to protect them. No one in town would take care of it, so we created Salvación. You see, Papá trained us since we were very little, just a couple of kids in huaraches running around in Sonora, to fight. We knew how to shoot guns. We knew how to use swords. We knew people and how to confront them. It only made sense for us to try to keep everyone in town safe. Ultimately, we did it to protect our mamá."

He stood, held out his hand at me.

"I understand," he said. "We can do this. We can make things right."

"The light goes on for a while longer," Víctor said to our left, at the trailhead leading into forest.

We followed the light. The whole place was untouched, with high brush and wild vines all around. Nature had never fully scared me. I always understood that there was a force that you couldn't fight, and you just needed to let it do its thing. Nature wasn't necessarily evil even when it did bad things like bring a storm. I wanted to understand it more, but what I did understand was that there were parts of nature people weren't meant to see. This might have been one of those places.

We followed the light until we arrived in an open area with a black mountain at its center. There were massive trees and pinecones, as if this area of the world had never been explored. Perhaps it hadn't been and that was why sal roja remained where it belonged, hidden away from the world.

The first indication that we were getting close was the familiar sound of a pickaxe hitting rock. Víctor and I eyed each other; I saw fear in his eyes that I knew was reflected in mine. Recognizing the sound, we ran, Alejandro following.

When we got to the sal roja, I fell to my knees once again.

There in front of us, digging into the rock and about to unleash sal roja, was Papá.

CHAPTER 20

apá! Stop!" Víctor and I shouted together.

Papá was sweating, shirtless, and he wore that expression on his face that said he was going to get what he wanted, even if it killed him. I'd seen that look only when he was fighting to get us to Coloma from Sonora alive, when he was at his most serious, when you knew that you needed to do what he said and how he said it and when he said it in order to survive.

I saw the amulet on the ground by his side, red light emanating from its center. It seemed to be calling to me. At the end of it all, I had to be the one with the amulet. We had a promise to keep to the Indigenous man. We would return what was rightfully theirs and was stolen by Hernández. We would start to right the wrongs we had wrought on the land of the people who truly cared for it.

"What are you kids doing here? You jumped?" Papá didn't seem angry. He was surprised, genuinely excited to see us.

SALVACIÓN · 283

Víctor stepped up in front of me, as if to shield me against our father. "Of course we jumped. We'd do anything to stop Hernández, we just didn't think we'd find you here."

Papá scoffed, the smile evaporating from his face. Ever since Hernández arrived and filled his head with thoughts of another war, a war easily won with sal roja, Papá had had this mean look on his face. I thought of Mamá and how worn out she seemed. How she needed sal negra and magia to continue. Papá was like that now—only he didn't want sal negra. He wanted the sal that would get him killed.

But then Papá took in Alejandro by our side and his face fell.

He hadn't expected Hernández's right hand to be with us. Did it cast doubt in his mind?

"Hernández has deceived you, Papá. He doesn't plan to use the sal roja to help us or the people of Coloma. He wants to take over the world, and he'll kill anyone he has to in order to make it happen."

"It's true," Alejandro started, stepping forward. "He's not who you think. He's a terrible man who has done terrible things. What you're uncovering now, he doesn't plan to use it to save Alta California; he plans to use it to *take* Alta California, and the rest of the known world, for himself. If you keep digging, you'll only succeed in killing yourself. The first to break through always unleashes the sal roja on themselves. The man sent you to die, señor de La Peña."

Papá glared at the pickaxe in his hands. "I don't believe you," he said matter-of-factly.

"I saw Hernández kill a man with the same sal roja that

you're going to unleash on yourself right now. I saw him kill Beto with it," I said, my blood boiling. My hands shook. I wished things had been different. Not too long ago, we were dancing in our home. Not too long ago, I thought that Papá would protect us from anything and everything.

Now he paused for only a moment, didn't even seem sad that his best friend was gone. "No," he said, lifting the axe once more and bringing it down.

We took a uniform step back—Víctor, Alejandro, and I. When a hand reached out to take mine, I was surprised that it wasn't Víctor's but Alejandro's. His grip was firm, comforting.

"I understand that you don't want to see another war. The last one was hard. It was hard on me too. I lived through it. But there are things that you don't understand. The moment we give up, the moment we truly let all those who want to take this land for themselves but don't want to respect the land win, is the moment that this whole place will perish and change. The Yankees are coming, and they'll kill everyone."

The passion in Papá's words brought me to tears, because they were likely bathed in truth: things were changing and not for the better. And things would continue to change as long as the news of magia spread, dangerous things.

"He's not going to stop, we need to be out of here when he breaks ground," Alejandro whispered beside me.

I pulled my hand free of his. I would never leave Papá. I thought of all that he had taught me. Even though I now realized he taught me to fight, likely to fight in another war, he still taught me to defend myself when many others thought girls didn't need to know how. I thought of all the times we'd danced in the living room, all the times he had made me feel that it was okay to be who I wanted to be, okay to wear pants if I wanted to, okay not to want what society said I should want.

I couldn't leave him.

Víctor approached our papá, his hand outstretched. "Papá, you need to stop! You'll die!"

At his words, Papá froze. He regarded Víctor, and I could see the answer in his eyes.

He had known this entire time that he would be a sacrifice.

"No!" I shouted as he brought the axe down once more. The pulsing red rocks beneath him were about to crack.

I went to jump forward, but Alejandro grabbed hold of my midsection and pulled me back as I flailed in his grasp. I didn't want to be protected. I wanted Papá to come to his senses. I wanted him back in my life.

I headbutted Alejandro. "You have got to stop doing that!" he yelped as he let go of me. I didn't turn to see what damage I'd done. The sal negra he was carrying would fix it, or he'd go back into the salt river and come out healed.

I knelt at Papá's feet, clutching his shins. "Please! Please come home with us!" I begged. "Mamá, think of Mamá. She needs you! You can't leave her."

I was a fool. I was a daughter. And if Papá died right now, I would never forgive myself.

"Take her," Papá said to Alejandro, who was right behind me. There was blood coming out of his nose, but he didn't care. The boy took me in his arms and threw me over his shoulder. Víctor didn't do anything.

I wasn't angry at my brother so much as I felt utter disappointment rip through my bones. Víctor and Papá had never been close, and now Víctor was indifferent.

My eyes were wide as Papá kept digging, as Alejandro and Víctor ran.

I shouted at him to stop.

I shouted at him to come with us.

I shouted that I loved him.

And then Papá broke through.

CHAPTER 21

aybe he's fine," I mumbled, rocking back and forth, unblinking, while we sat once more at the shoreline. Neither Alejandro nor Víctor said anything.

Then after what felt like a million hours, Víctor said, "Maybe he was right."

I scrunched my nose in my brother's direction. I couldn't believe he had just said that. "What?"

"What will happen without sal roja?"

"Sal roja is death. You want to unleash death on the world?"

"I want to unleash death on those who do the world harm. There's a difference. Isn't that what we've always fought for with Salvación? A way to stop all those who are not good people."

I shook my head. "What would Mamá think of what you're saying? You are not God, Víctor. You don't get to choose who lives or dies."

"Then maybe we shouldn't heal people. Isn't it the same thing?"

He had me there. I didn't have a great reply. I knew only that sometimes we did things that benefited us and others, and that was okay. It was okay to help people survive horrible things. It was not okay to unleash the horrible things that got people hurt in the first place, to be those horrible things.

"How long will we have to wait?" I asked Alejandro.

"Until tomorrow," Alejandro replied.

We'd have to wait the rest of the day and night to see if somehow Papá had survived.

"I'm hungry," I said, yearning for a distraction. "We should try to find some food, then figure out what we're going to do to stop Hernández."

"I think we know what we have to do," Alejandro said. "Sal roja is the only way out of this for us. We use it one last time and then never again."

I feared he was right. Still, we wouldn't get far on empty stomachs, and there was still a lot for us to figure out and accomplish before the final battle.

Alejandro proved that he was an expert fisherman. He made a net using vines he quickly weaved from trees. Víctor had always been great at building a fire, so while he did that, I searched the forest for mushrooms and berries.

I didn't find any mushrooms, but I did find bushels of the largest blackberries I'd ever seen. They were sweet as honey and I ate about a dozen before I decided I'd better stop and take some to my brother and Alejandro. It was as if this entire part of the world was giant, and I wondered what made it so.

I ate more berries as I peered into the forest. There wasn't anything like being surrounded by nature. There had been nights when Víctor and I sat on the mountainside, watching the trees sway overhead, listening to the whooshing sounds they made.

I realized that this was what Papá was terrified of losing. There was no doubt that the world was changing. The arrival of Yankees into what was once México showed that things were evolving, that life would never be what it was before. Papá's fear was that the evolution wasn't anything good. It was going to be hurtful. It might even mean we would perish. It might mean that the Coloma we knew would cease to exist.

I knew I wasn't on Hernández's side, but should I have been on Papá's? Was he right to fear what he did? Was there even any way to stop what was happening to the world without losing our humanity?

I wasn't sure about a lot of things. Although I felt stronger than ever since coming to Coloma, since putting on the mask, I understood I still had a lot to learn. The past few days had taught me that much. Seeing the scorch. Talking to the Indigenous man.

I knew one thing: I didn't understand this land as much as I found it beautiful. The Indigenous man, he understood this country. He and his people knew sal roja. They knew sal negra. Which meant they knew the earth and the land and respected them in ways that Hernández, and to some degree even my family, never had.

We ate silently. My brother didn't speak comforting words. I didn't speak any to him either. I wasn't sure about Víctor, but regret filled my bones. We were both in shock.

The day grew cold and soon I was shivering, my clothing

still wet from el río. I'd always gone out as Salvación but returned home to warm sheets and a cozy bed and the safety of the walls of our home, the safety of knowing my family would protect me should anything come for us at night.

That protection was gone.

Víctor had started the fire and kept it going with firewood I collected, but no matter how tall it got, it never seemed to warm me enough. Perhaps it wasn't my body that had gone cold.

I wasn't sure what was going on with my brother. He hadn't cried for Papá. He seemed angry: angry at me, angry at our parents, angry at the world. Since the night with the Yankee who stole our sal negra, he had seemed different, almost curling into his former self, the boy who didn't want anything to do with me back in Coloma. Even when he took my side, he'd been different.

For the first time in a very long time, I felt alone.

I might not have been the only one. Alejandro sat next to me, handing me fish on a long stick that served as a skewer. It tasted of sal negra. I nearly gagged on the first bite but chewed it down anyway.

Alejandro was shivering too. Now the three of us were shaking. And here we were, stuck, but yet not ready to move on or even leave the beach.

I shimmied toward Alejandro, my body longing for the kind of warmth that came only from feeling somebody sitting beside you. His leg and arm pressed against mine, offering instant heat. He snuggled closer to me, as if yearning for it as well. Soon enough, I found my head falling toward his shoulder. When my head finally landed there and I snuggled into him, he froze and didn't say a word. After a few minutes, Alejandro laid his head on top of mine.

Víctor sat across from us, on the other side of the fire, something like flames burning in his eyes, a reflection of what blazed in front of him, but also what smoldered within. He *was* fire now, and he seemed ready to torch everyone and everything. I only hoped he wouldn't burn himself.

The sun rose and we had barely slept, which hadn't been the best idea. I doubted any of us was in the mindset to get any rest. Unknown things kept creaking in the dark. We'd ended up, the three of us, leaning our backs against each other, the best way we could ensure no one would sneak up on us. By the time it was daylight, I felt like the dead. My eyes were heavy in their sockets, my head hurting so that every time I moved it, a pulse rang inside my skull. I wanted to sleep. I didn't expect to get any soon.

This would be another painfully long day. All of us were eager, though, to go back to see what had happened to Papá.

"It's time," Víctor said, but he avoided eye contact when he said it. Had I lost my brother too?

We hiked back up the mountain to the spot where we had left Papá. There was no sign of him. Enough time had passed that perhaps he'd simply moved on.

But then I saw it. I gasped, taking a step back instead of going toward it. The amulet was on the ground. Undamaged. If he was okay, would my father have left it behind?

"No puede ser," Víctor said. "This can't be happening." He yelled suddenly, which was more startling than the discovery. Víctor went to the nearest tree and punched it, kept hitting it, yelled some more.

Alejandro looked on but didn't say anything. He signaled to my brother with his chin.

I had to say something, calm my brother. But how did you calm a storm that you yourself were caught up in?

I might not be hitting things. I might not be hurting myself or yelling. But there was an indescribable feeling of utter pain that swelled in my throat and rose to my eyes. I sobbed. I hadn't cried this way since our voyage to Coloma from Sonora, not since the children began dying all around us and we couldn't help them, not since Víctor saved me from the river and I'd barely survived.

The burst of my emotions made Víctor stop.

I wasn't entirely sure what I had ever imagined losing a parent would feel like. I still wasn't sure if Papá *had* died. Or maybe I *was* sure, only I couldn't quite believe that it had all led to this moment.

On his way over to me, Víctor kicked the ground.

I was on my knees then, trying to find Papá's remains in the soil surrounding the amulet. Had his flesh been here? Had it disappeared completely from this earth? Had he crawled like the thief on his hands and knees? Would we have nothing left of him but memories? His guitar? Mamá?

"He's gone, Loli," Víctor said. "He's gone."

I kept scratching at the earth. It was Alejandro who caught my hands in his, who held them up to his chest while I cried.

Víctor hugged me. I pulled away from Alejandro to hug my brother back. I sobbed and he rocked me until I had no more tears left to give.

The sal roja stone was pulsating nearby, too close for comfort. But in our sadness, we didn't notice that we could have touched it had we simply reached for it. Papá had cracked the entire rock in two. And there it was. From where we sat, the fist-sized stone was a beautiful red. Lots of deadly things looked beautiful, though. There were beautiful plants that could kill. There were many beautiful animals that could do the same. It seemed like we sat in front of la muerte itself.

"How do we mine it?" Víctor asked. "I'm tired of hiding; I want to take the fight to Hernández. We mine it, we use it against him, and we make him disappear once and for all and forever."

Alejandro sighed, staring intently at the sal roja. "Very carefully." Then to us, he added, "How much sal negra do you have left?"

I pulled out my pouch. It felt light—there might have been an ounce of sal negra left. Víctor pulled out two sacks the size of mine. Alejandro was the only one who pulled out a full sack. He frowned.

Alejandro blinked hard. If something went wrong, we all knew our sal negra wouldn't be enough. If something went wrong, we'd be dead, gone like Papá in the wind as if we'd never existed.

"Well, shit. That's not enough sal negra, but I'm the only one who has done it before. I should do it now," Alejandro said. "I need to set things right."

He had a point.

Still, I thought of every moment we'd spent together since Alejandro found out I was Salvación. I guessed his impression of me as a girl who was interested only in her looks and status had been replaced by, what? Admiration? Something more? Something that I felt too?

What was the tightness in my stomach? I wasn't entirely sure if it was fear of losing the entire world or of losing Alejandro after just having lost Papá. Unlike Víctor, I found myself, for the first time since starting to dress up as Salvación, wanting to simply walk away, leave, stay safe. In the grand scheme of things, we didn't owe the world anything, did we?

We had owed our family everything, and it had led only to losing Papá.

"You should both go back to the shore in case something goes wrong."

I shook my head. We'd done that once before. "No, we're staying right here, and when we leave, we're leaving together."

"Well, maybe at least let's hide over there." Víctor pointed behind a grove of trees. "Good luck," he added as he took his leave and went behind the trees.

I was slower to hide. I didn't know what to say to Alejandro. I hadn't said goodbye to Papá, I didn't want to make the same mistake.

Here was a boy who had been through so much and had allowed so much pain to happen to others. There was a lot I didn't know about him—who his parents had been, where he came from . . . This was his chance to finally redeem himself.

I wasn't sure that his past mattered in his journey forward.

I knew that he wanted to be a better person.

I knew that I didn't want him to die.

I knew that I couldn't take this away from him.

I tossed my arms over his shoulders and embraced him. He froze, confused by it all, then hugged me back, as if he knew that there was a good chance this was the last time he would ever hold anyone in his life.

"You can do this," I whispered. "You can."

He nodded into my neck. "I'll try."

When we let go, we stared at each other.

"Can I kiss you?" he said.

Despite the gravity of our situation, I was still a girl, and I was smiling. "Yes," I said.

I'd barely let out the word when he was settling one hand on my cheek and kissing me. His lips weren't soft, but they were warm, and he tasted of sal negra. I'd kissed boys before, but they'd never made my stomach swirl like this one had. I was sparkling.

When he stopped, I tried to hand him my sal negra, but he shook his head. "You might need it. And it's not enough to matter anyway. I can do this." He repeated the words and gave me a grin that was meant to set me at ease but succeeded only in making me more fearful for him as I left him.

Víctor and I watched as Alejandro pulled out the little sal negra he had and slathered it all over his hands. He took out a tin container, a small hammer, and a chisel. He sniffed, wiggled his nose, and sniffed again. He took a deep breath in and let one out. And repeated this three times. He shook out his arms and legs and took a final breath. Then he chiseled sal roja into the tin container. The small flecks looked like fire coming off the stone. It was a tedious task, unlike how we normally ground salt rock with a mortar and pestle, and all the while Alejandro had to make sure that the sal roja didn't touch him a single time.

Alejandro swore. A lot. And I wondered how many times he'd had to do this before.

Víctor's eyebrows furrowed and he took my hand in his,

as if he was ready to run should any spark come our way. Or perhaps it was in case he needed to protect me from watching a boy I cared about die from sal roja, as if he understood that Alejandro meant more to me than I would ever admit.

We watched until Alejandro stood up. "You can come out now," he said, silencing the loudness of my heartbeat. "Here we are!" he said, victory in his glowing face.

Before we could celebrate, a voice boomed from behind us and said, "You've done a good job, niño."

CHAPTER 22

It was Hernández—with his fifty men behind him.

But I wasn't looking at him. Víctor had eyes on him. I was still staring at the boy he was talking to.

"Now bring it over," Hernández said, "and I'll keep my word. You'll be free to go."

I opened my mouth, disbelief flooding me. After all of this, I still couldn't fully trust Alejandro. Had he made an agreement with Hernández? Was he still protecting him, the way he'd done at the inn? I'd kissed Alejandro just moments ago. I'd let him kiss me. Rage filled me and I was now all fire like Víctor. Víctor squeezed my hand, grounding me. I knew my brother's mind. Right now, Víctor would find us a way out, an escape route.

"You can't be serious," I said to Alejandro.

"You really thought that my right hand had changed sides?" Hernández asked. This time, I did turn around. "I knew it was you all along, Lola de La Peña," he said. "From the moment in the plaza, I knew it was you, niña tonta. I saw the fire you carry in your eyes. I saw a hate for me that would be unmatched. You couldn't ever hide from me.

"But I underestimated how someone so small and so weak could do so much. Could instill the same fear in grown men that I did with sal roja. It doesn't matter anymore. I have all the manpower, and now that your papá is gone, all while doing my bidding, you only have your brother. Now you really are mine, and you're about to be gone from the world and locked in the dark for a very long time until you shrivel and die."

As Alejandro walked past me, I looked at the deposit of sal roja. It was enormous. There was enough sal roja to bring down the entire valley, to scorch Alta California for all time, to kill every living thing for miles.

The Indigenous man, his people, they might fight. But how could you fight against sal roja? With a single speck of it, Hernández would end their lives. And it wouldn't be fair. It would be evil, cruel, unjust, inhumane—all the words all at once.

The only thing these men didn't count on was that I still had weapons on me. And I'd checked them already to make sure they were dry.

Not too long ago, I'd stopped a blond man. A man as evil as Hernández, I'd thought. The man's heirloom revolver was still with me, the one he'd never come back to claim. It still had three rounds, and so all I had to do was aim true to make this nightmare end.

As Alejandro walked past me, he didn't say a word, he didn't even look at me. His face had changed in a moment. Had it all truly been an act? Had he not changed at all? Was caring about him, maybe even loving him, going to be my downfall?

I remembered the look on his face, though, the anguish when I hid in the forest and he let that man die when he should have intervened. I knew there were things about his life with señor Hernández that haunted him.

Then I saw it, at his back, but I couldn't react fast enough.

With one hand he pretended to pass Hernández the tin of sal roja, only to let it fall to the ground; with the other, he pulled a large blade from where it had been hidden at his back and stabbed the man.

"Arrrggh!" Hernández yelled, trying to pull out the blade. When he couldn't reach it fast enough, Hernández pulled out his gun and didn't hesitate to shoot Alejandro. The bullet hit him in the chest. An eye for an eye.

I yelled, reached out when I wasn't anywhere near close enough to catch Alejandro as he fell back.

There was something about not seeing Papá die that made it all not seem real. Alejandro being shot in front of me, though, that was real. That was the now. And it hurt like hell.

I pulled out the heirloom revolver, I cocked it, and I fired. My first shot hit Hernández on the shoulder. He reeled with another yell, falling onto his back, but someone in his company dragged him away immediately. They would surely have sal negra on them. They would surely heal Hernández before he hitched his last breath.

I could go after him or I could help Alejandro.

I knew what I *should* do. But I ignored everything that told me to go after Hernández and end it all.

I tried to get to Alejandro, but Hernández's men shot at me. I jumped and dodged, one round scraping me in the arm, another across my leg. But none of them stopped me for very long. I kept approaching, fighting to reach Alejandro, who was murmuring that he was hit.

There's something about facing your death that makes you do strange things. I was willing to die to reach him. Víctor was nowhere in sight. He didn't have any weapons anyway, I didn't think. And I hoped that he'd gone running. I managed to make it to Alejandro and dragged him back in an instant, moving him this way and that, but he was heavy, and growing heavier by the second as he lost consciousness.

"Please don't die!" I screamed, like my words could heal anything. "Please."

Hernández was injured too. If we were lucky, the man would perish, and that would be the end of this.

We weren't fast enough. I slowed down, unable to will my arms to move Alejandro any longer. My legs ached. I was so tired and my head hurt so much that I wanted to curl myself into a ball and fall asleep forever. Perhaps this was it, and I'd have my wish soon enough.

Hernández was soon on his feet and coming after us, his men at his back.

He stared down at me. I held Alejandro and hugged him. He'd gone quiet, but I didn't want his body pried from mine. I felt like a fallen angel facing down el Diablo. I closed my eyes, accepting my fate. This was it. This was death. It wasn't sal roja. It wasn't the storm. It wasn't the voyage to Coloma. It wasn't the terrible heartache of watching the people I loved die or be injured. It was this, silent and terrible, and by the hand of a man undeserving of life. I held on tighter to Alejandro. I pressed above his heart. It still moved slightly. Up and down. And then it didn't.

CHAPTER 23

Funny thing about life is that it likes to be the one that decides when it's through with you.

Today, it wasn't done with me.

A shot rang. But this time it came from behind Hernández's men.

A man appeared from the brush, then another. I recognized them. They weren't Hernández's men. They were from Coloma. They were *my* people, Salvación's people.

And then there she was. The real Ángel of Coloma, sunlight framing her and making her ethereal.

Mamá.

She was a miracle come to my rescue.

She'd always been the miracle we had to protect.

Hernández had been so very wrong. We weren't alone. I didn't just have Víctor.

Mamá had come to help us. And she had brought, it seemed, all the people of fighting age in Coloma.

A battle ensued and then as quickly as I spotted her, I lost Mamá to the crowd.

Shots were fired on all sides. The sound of swords and other hand weapons colliding rang in the air. The forest trees swayed and swished, and the sound of crunching leaves and twigs echoed.

I laughed, I cried. I held on to Alejandro and whispered, "Todo estará bien," even when I felt him stop.

I took the time to continue dragging Alejandro away from it all, aiming to find a moment to apply the sal negra I still had and heal him.

The only problem was that Hernández only had eyes for us, and he had the sal roja tin in his grasp. He yelled my name, voice harsh and thundering, his eyes fuming as he locked on to where we were. "Salvación! You are mine!"

I stopped dragging Alejandro long enough to shoot the heirloom revolver once more. I missed and hit a tree.

Hernández smiled, pointed his gun at me, moved to fire. Once more I found myself shutting my eyes tight, holding my breath, expecting the world to go silent, expecting to find out exactly what happens when you die.

I opened my eyes again when nothing happened.

Hernández's arm had gone up. Víctor appeared, bringing the man to the ground. With Víctor by my side as Salvación, I'd always felt stronger. Together, we could do anything. And it was about time Víctor stopped hiding in the mountains. It was about time Víctor showed his real strength.

Hernández had thought that he took away the strongest member of our family. He hadn't realized that everything Papá was, Víctor was too. In a lot of ways, as I watched my brother fight, I realized that Papá would always live on through my brother. Their movements were the same. Where Papá had chosen to practice with me more, Víctor had always been watching from the sidelines, learning anyway.

My brother took out a sword that he must have gotten from someone.

Hernández laughed as they began their dance, both with swords in hand now.

I left Alejandro and went to help Víctor, standing to try to get a good shot. I had only one last bullet in the revolver. If I missed this time, there wouldn't be another chance.

And then Alejandro was up, too, out of nowhere. He rammed Hernández. The man fell to the ground, again, but Alejandro was too injured. Hernández took ahold of him, putting his hands around his throat and lifting him off the ground. "You betrayed me! You were like my son and you chose them!"

Alejandro couldn't respond. But I still couldn't get a good enough shot.

I didn't have the time. I fired. I watched in horror as I missed again.

My face fell. Hernández must have understood my somber expression because he grinned evilly at me.

"Let him go!" Víctor said, the rage in his voice and the concern surprising me. Had my brother grown to like Alejandro as I did?

"Or what? You have no edge. You are dos niños tontos and you're the first ones I'm going to destroy with sal roja."

Víctor gaze was downcast as if to say, *I tried, Loli, I really tried*. "I'm sorry," he mouthed to me. Then he threw something at Hernández.

"No!" I yelled, dropping the revolver and dashing forward.

I knew what he had. The sal roja tin. He hurled it straight at Hernández and Alejandro.

All the sal roja that Alejandro had mined was in the bottle that hit Hernández in the face, spilling open.

Hernández immediately let go of Alejandro. I grabbed Alejandro's arm, and together with Víctor, we pulled him toward us.

Hernández writhed just like the man in the forest had. Just like Beto had. It seemed ironic for him to die in this same way, also in a forest, instead of at the seat of a throne he so desperately wanted. He was fading. He was melting into the sal roja. He would be nothing soon, only a bad memory.

But if we didn't act fast, so would Alejandro, who was screaming now too. His body went rigid. He didn't move as much as tense up.

As Hernández's body was melted away by the sal roja, Víctor and I had our full attention on Alejandro.

"¡Loli, tu sal!"

I quickly got the last sal negra I had out. It wouldn't be enough. Nowhere near enough if any sal roja had gotten on Alejandro.

The firing had stopped all around us, and it occurred to me that we had won. That Coloma would endure.

Mamá appeared then.

I had tears in my eyes. "Please, Mamá. Ayúdame."

Mamá pulled out more sal negra. She mixed it with water she carried on her, and together we tried to get Alejandro to drink the concoction. But the agua de sal negra simply slid down the side of his face. I sobbed, feeling the full weight of everything that had happened the past week. I'd have to tell Mamá, eventually, what had happened to Papá as well.

"El río," I managed through my tears, remembering that the river had healed me of sal roja. If it could do that, perhaps it could make another miracle happen. Mamá nodded to me. The three of us carried Alejandro down the mountain to the edge of the water, even as he screamed and writhed in our grasp. I put him in and sat with him while his body floated.

I wasn't sure if he was worthy of being given a second chance. I hadn't thought the man who stole the sal negra, whose heirloom revolver I'd used, had been. And he hadn't done half of what Alejandro had done, I didn't think. But I remembered Papá. The way he had been before Hernández came to town. He had always said that people deserved second chances. I only wished that Alejandro would be around long enough to live his second chance through.

I also remembered Isabela. It had taken her days to wake up. Perhaps all we had to do was wait it out and he'd be okay. He *had* to be okay.

It'd been at least two hours since we'd been sitting in the water, and although Mamá, Víctor, and everyone else had left us to go dig a trench around the sal in the forest, I wasn't prepared to let Alejandro go yet. My eyes were closed, as I didn't want to see him fading.

The more I sat in the water, the better I felt myself. I noticed that the scratches on my hand were disappearing. That my headache faded and I felt a new energy course through me. The energy of sal negra was unmatched. And as heavy as my heart was, my bones, my flesh, my hands, and my legs felt strong.

I saw it then. The black stone in the water. Shimmering on the floor of the clear river. There was sal negra at the bottom of the river. It made sense then, how the water would wear the stone down and be filled with sal negra. This river was a miracle.

I laughed out loud; I'd seen so many miracles by now, so many beautiful things, that this served as a reminder that no matter how ugly things got, no matter how sad life made me, the world could still be beautiful. There was magia all around us.

"Your laugh is my favorite thing in the world," a voice said softly. Alejandro took in a deep breath and sighed lightly.

"You're okay?" I said to him, staring down. My tears ran down my cheeks and landed on his face. He nodded, wiped at my tears as he gently moaned, seemingly trying to stand up.

I kissed his forehead, resting mine on his.

"Just rest," I said. "Let the water keep healing you."

He nodded. "Thanks for saving me," he said after a moment.

"Thanks for betraying Hernández."

He chuckled. "Is he?"

"Gone? Yeah."

Despite everything, Alejandro's body seemed to still at the news. It was a heavy thing to learn, that the man whom you considered a father had passed away. But it was all for the best, I wanted to tell him. It was all for the best.

Instead, I said, "You're free now."

Everyone bathed in the river. Everyone healed. Everyone prepared themselves for the idea that we might not find a way out of the canyon.

It took us days of trekking to do so.

We followed the river, went around in circles, got lost on several occasions, but eventually, we looked to the stars and found a way back to Coloma.

Hernández's men were all either dead, gone, or still in the valley, perhaps lost, perhaps making a place for themselves by the river that healed. Some had joined us like Alejandro.

"We don't have to worry about them," Alejandro said. "Many of them were as stuck as I was. And the ones who weren't are likely gone by now." I nodded fast and was thankful that everything seemed to be settling down without my having to offer too many apologies.

There was a lot to celebrate.

Mamá for starters, who I learned had single-handedly freed the people of Coloma from Hernández's men. It seemed that Víctor hadn't been the only one paying attention to the lessons that Papá taught me. She was a hero. She'd always been one, but now she was just as great a hero as Salvación was.

We'd had an enormous victory in which we'd all played a part.

I didn't know what to think, but I knew that this was only the beginning.

We cleaned up the town, then fixed the broken windows, the damaged inn, part of which had been burned down. Luisa's entire store had been destroyed, but she had plenty of help to build it up again and was smiling when I saw her.

Even then, sometimes I needed time away from everything. In those moments, Víctor and I sat in our usual spot in the mountains, looking out at the entrance to Coloma, scared that perhaps Hernández's men might act after all. Find their way back here.

"I almost can't believe we won," Víctor said.

"I never doubted us," I replied, with a grin. It wasn't true. There was plenty of doubt. Plenty of fear. But the thing about doubt and fear is they're always there and never lingering. We'd been lucky. We had.

We also lost something more valuable than sal negra along the way.

Víctor nudged me with his elbow. "You remember the day we saw the first miracle, what Papá told us?"

I nodded. "He said that we were the only miracles he ever needed. I'm not entirely sure that Mamá would have appreciated him saying that to us."

"We never told her."

"I think there was a lot that Papá did and felt that we never told each other."

Víctor looked away. I'd gotten my brother wrong this entire time. He hadn't always been vying for Papá's approval; he'd just been scared that I was under Papá's constant spell. And I had been.

"I need to show you something," I said, reaching into the pocket of my pants. I was determined that I'd never be caught wearing a dress ever again. After all, though Mamá had made up her mind already to go home to Sonora, I wasn't going to be following her. I didn't think I could stand the voyage. I didn't think I could stand to be part of a society that didn't understand me.

I just hadn't told Víctor that yet.

I showed him the amulet, which I had kept hidden from everyone after the fight in the forest. I didn't think that it was anyone's right to decide what to do with it.

"That's—"

"I know." I watched as the sal roja inside the amulet all moved to one side, as if it were a compass and hourglass in one. I wasn't sure how it worked. I hadn't asked Alejandro. I didn't care to know because I didn't want it. Who knew when the next time the red moon would appear and show the way to more sal roja? I hoped the day would never come again.

"I plan to give it back to the Indigenous man."

"That's wise," Víctor said. Then he seemed to take me in. "You've changed a lot since Sonora, you know? Remember when all you cared about were dresses and boys?"

"I seemed to recall all you cared about were swords and your next kiss," I said.

"Fair enough," my brother replied. "We've both changed, then."

"I'm glad about it. You're a much better brother now." I paused. It was time. "Which is why it's hard to tell you that I won't be going back to Sonora with you and Mamá. I don't belong back there. I don't want to be forced to be una señorita. I want to make my own path. I like my pants and riding a horse and shooting and feeling the wind in my hair on a stormy day. I'm staying here, with Alejandro." I was rambling, but it was only because Víctor's face had frozen. I wasn't entirely sure what he would say. If he asked me to go with them, if he begged me to reconsider, I would. But I might be unhappy till the day I died if I did.

"I actually told Mamá this morning that I wasn't going back to Sonora," he confessed.

I laughed, hugged him. "I can't believe it. Does that mean—"

"I knew you weren't going to go. Mamá does too. She wanted to stay, but I think everyone in Coloma understands now that there is a place for them, but it's not a place that belongs to them. It's better for sal negra to be forgotten. Better for sal roja to be a part of a history no one talks about."

I nodded. Smiled.

"I couldn't do this without you," I said. And I meant it. Víctor and I, we were both Salvación.

"¡Mira!" Víctor said, pointing. There was a horse approaching. It didn't seem to have a rider. It—was familiar.

I turned to Víctor with giddy excitement.

"Go!" he said.

I kissed him on the cheek and ran down the mountainside, meeting Carisma, who stood still as she saw me.

She approached slowly, almost as if to confirm that it was really me; I touched my head against hers. I kissed her mane. I hugged her and I didn't let go for a very long time. I wasn't sure where she'd gone, what things she had seen while away. I had so many stories to tell her. So much to catch her up on. For now, I looked her over. She was a little dirty, perhaps hadn't been eating the best, but she was alive and another one of the miracles that I had the blessing to be a part of.

I needed to take Carisma home before I stopped at the fiesta that was planned for the night and met Alejandro where I said I would. Only, I also needed to have a conversation with Mamá. I took Carisma home, at least where home would be for a little while longer.

I gave Carisma plenty of water and food, and she seemed happy to be back in a place she recognized. She lay down to rest, fell asleep while I sang to her about the moon and the stars, songs that I'd learned from Papá and which would be another part of his legacy.

When I had my fill of being around Carisma again, I went inside and found Mamá in her room with a box on her lap.

"Mamá?" She'd been crying. She still was. But she was also smiling.

"I'm proud of you. All the amazing things you've achieved. How you've managed to grow into a bright and fearless woman," she said. "But I also miss him."

I approached the bed. I sat on the floor and hugged her legs, resting my head against her knees, kissing each one lightly.

This was the closest I'd ever felt to Mamá. It was sometimes hard to see love when love was in front of you, I guess. Never glaring, always present.

"I know this is really hard for you, to leave sal negra."

Her eyes shone as she shook her head. Tears sprang from her eyes the way flowers sprang from sal negra touching soil.

"It was hard for me, for a long time, before all that happened, before I lost your father and almost lost you and Víctor. But I also see what I'd been blind to accepting."

"What's that?" I asked, starting to get teary-eyed myself. I sniffled, cleared my throat, and fought back against all I felt, missing Papá, almost dying so many times the past few days.

"I got a calling to Coloma, I found sal negra, but just because I thought it was meant for me doesn't mean it was. I see that clearly now, after everything you've told me." She shrugged. I could sense the heaviness in her heart, the way her shoulders sank low, her back hunched more than ever.

I let out a laugh. It was strange to see something I'd never thought would happen take place right before my eyes. It felt like another miracle, Mamá realizing that not all those who have magia within their very souls needed to take it from someone else. Mamá was magia enough.

"I'm really happy that you realized this," I said.

She flicked off her tears, straightened. "I already spoke with Víctor," she said, handing me the box. Inside were Papá's pistols. "You should have these. Papá would have wanted you to."

I held the box close to my chest, squeezed it tightly.

"There are times," she continued, looking out toward the small window in her bedroom, back toward the way we came from the riverfront, "that I feel him."

I looked up at her. Could he still be out there? Perhaps he had simply left the amulet for us to find. Perhaps he had only gone into hiding.

"Where before I felt the pull of sal negra, now I feel *him* pulling me. I spoke with some of the others—Luisa, strong men who shoot well and can protect us, who have agreed to travel with me and follow this pull."

I opened my mouth slowly, confused, but also understood that Mamá had a path to follow as well. One that also wasn't going to take her back home to Sonora. And her path might lead her back to the love of her life. It was worth trying. I would have tried for Alejandro.

"I haven't told Víctor. He'd probably say it was way too dangerous and Papá deserved what happened to him. I'll tell him before I leave. But I also need you two to understand that this might be our goodbye. You, me, and him, even so, will always be connected by an invisible tether, a thing that I don't have a word for—"

"Amor," I said, cutting in. "Love will connect us. And you don't have to explain, Mamá. I love Papá still too. I'm so sorry that I couldn't bring him home. I couldn't convince him. If there is a chance that he's still alive and you can find him, I truly hope you do."

I gave the box with Papá's pistols back to Mamá, who took them with a nod and a grin. I had a feeling she'd need them more than I would. She set the box down, then went to hug me. She ran her fingers through my hair the way she did when I was a little girl and kissed my forehead.

I didn't tell her about the amulet. I didn't want anyone to know about it. It had to be my secret until I handed it back to the Indigenous rider.

We stayed in the room for a while longer, and she gave me a few other items that she wasn't planning on taking with her.

It was strange, to think that we would be leaving the house here with a few things remaining in it, but empty. I wondered if people would find it one day and what they'd think of our belongings. What they'd see in them. Who they would think we were.

Mamá gave me photographs of her and Papá. She gave me a few pieces of jewelry she said to keep close, never part with—or in desperate times, trade or sell. She gave me some of her blouses, since I had few that suited my new attire. She gave me her blessing. She gave me her love.

She had given us all a miracle.

She was el milagro.

I kissed her cheek and said, "Te quiero, Mamá."

I finally arrived at the fiesta, which was sure to go into the morning.

There was music.

And food.

And laughter.

And everything that Víctor and I had fought so hard to protect for the people of Coloma.

"Loli, amor," Luisa said, coming up to me. She handed me a pouch. "Some herbs, some strong cheese, and a few other things you might need on your journey, mi Salvación."

I paused. Had Luisa known it was me the entire time? It didn't matter. I hugged her tightly and took the items, then said, "I heard you're traveling with Mamá."

"That woman has helped so many people, it's time someone helps her find her peace."

I nodded. It was so true. I wanted nothing more than for Mamá to find her peace. She'd earned it.

"Gracias, Luisa," I said. "Please take care of yourself too." I handed something to her as well. A small container that I'd kept hidden along with the amulet.

She stared up at me, confused as to why I was hiding it from sight.

"It's sal roja," I whispered. It was another one of our secrets. The fact Víctor had gone back for sal roja. "I'd planned to keep it for myself, but I think that you and Mamá might need it more. Should anything happen, use it on those that might aim to do you harm. Please keep it hidden. Please keep it protected."

She bowed her head. "Thank you, Salvación. Thank you, Loli." She put it in her pocket and took her leave.

I looked back out at the party. Maybe we'd all come from different parts of the world, maybe we'd come here hoping that we would strike it rich, that we would heal the sick, that we would do something right.

Now it was time to let go of what belonged only to the land, no matter what Abuelo had wanted. Though part of me thought he'd done all this only for Mamá.

Alejandro was playing the guitar. I didn't know he could. I watched him until he noticed me and handed it off.

"Hi," he said.

"Hi," I replied, shy around him for the first time ever. With Hernández gone, with the threat of the end of the world gone, there was a new light that surrounded Alejandro. He might not have fully redeemed himself for all the bad things he'd let happen, but he was off to a good start.

"I'm packed," he added, hopeful, perhaps a little fearful as well that I'd changed my mind. "Ready to leave in the morning if you're still sure."

"I am," I said, patting my side where I had my usual pouch of sal negra. I wasn't sure what awaited us out there in Alta California, but I was thrilled at the idea of learning more about the land, of figuring out where we fit in it all. Of learning to understand what other magical things we might find.

There was magia.

What more was there?

It's strange how sometimes you lose being a kid so fast. A lot happened on the way from Sonora to Alta California that made me into Salvación. A lot happened here in Coloma that made me lose sight of what being a kid was and what responsibilities were. But for a while, after we delivered the amulet to the Indigenous man, I thought there would be a lot of time for fun. And I knew that both Alejandro and I were ready for it.

"What's the first thing you want to do out there?" I asked.

He didn't even have to ponder it, as if he already had a mental list of all he wanted to see. "I want to float in a river and stare up at the blue sky with you," he said.

"Hmmm," I responded, remembering the last time we did that. "That sounds like a dream," I sighed.

"Dance with me," he said.

I nodded, realizing that I'd thought I would never get to dance again if it wasn't with Papá. I wondered if Mamá was right; if he was out there somewhere, still alive, perhaps back in the forest where the sal roja lives. I didn't tell Alejandro what Mamá had said. It seemed like trouble asking for the past to become the future. I wasn't ready for that yet. We would have plenty of time on our journey to talk about the things that still slept in our minds. If he was alive, I didn't doubt that Mamá would find him. Would Víctor and I ever see our parents again? I hoped that we would, but I also knew that we were ready to be out on our own even if we never did. And that we were leaving Mamá on good terms.

Alejandro spun me around, tilted me back to the sound of the music, kissed me again. Our steps were sloppy, I'd never been the best at dancing, but it didn't matter. His were too. But this was fun, living, joy.

This wasn't how I'd thought this story would end, but I guessed that sometimes life surprised you in the most fascinating ways.

This also felt like a beginning instead of el fin.

Would I ever dress as Salvación again? I wasn't sure. But I did know that I was preparing for an even bigger fight that might be right around the corner.

EPILOGUE

Before we went too far, we visited the scorch outside of Coloma to ensure that it wasn't spreading. It had worked, the advice from the Indigenous man. The sal roja was dormant. I wondered what would become of the scorch in the future. And what would become of Alta California.

How would sal negra shape it if it was found again? We'd closed down all the mines after having taken our fill of the sal negra. Blown them up, hidden then, obstructed them so that they couldn't be found so easily.

Still, one day they might be found, if more people came, if more Yankees arrived, and they were never going to stop coming. The war had ended, the treaty signed. There was no going back as Papá had died believing.

I wasn't sure of the answers. Part of me feared them and the consequences of finding out that magia was real. There were more señor Hernándezes out there. There were worse people, I was sure. Even though it seemed unfathomable. What a horror it would be if there were.

I hoped that in our travels we would meet good people who knew that there was a right way of life and a wrong one—those who weren't afraid to defy the crowd and fight for what was right, despite losing valuable things—and find a place among them.

Víctor was still at home, saying his goodbyes to Mamá. I hadn't wanted to be there for it. It felt too hard to see them together for the last time. As if I was the one tearing them apart. But the reality was, I needed my brother with me. I couldn't stand the thought of his leaving me to fend for myself. I needed a part of home in my journey or I might not make it.

Alejandro rode up to me. His horse, Prisa, was weighed down with all the gear we'd need during our travels.

I was on Carisma, who had once more settled into her usual way of life at my side. "Can I ask you something?" I said.

"You can ask me anything," he replied, grinning. He'd been grinning a lot since señor Hernández died in the canyon, like a weight had been lifted off his shoulders, as if he didn't need to fear any longer.

I wasn't sure that was fully true. But I welcomed the quiet before an oncoming storm. I welcomed breathing and not having my head spin with doubt.

"Kiss me," I said.

I didn't need to ask twice. He rode forward to my side and pulled my chin gently to him.

"Yuck," Víctor said, appearing from out of nowhere. "You both don't plan on doing that the whole time we're out there, do you? Because if you are, I welcome you to shoot me dead now."

I laughed. Winked at Víctor. "Oh, hermano, don't you worry, we'll find you love outside of Coloma. I just know it."

The three of us talked a little more. And we laughed. And we joked. And we fell into the rhythm or something of that sort so quickly. It was what I dreamt of when I envisioned my future, my life as I wanted it to be now.

We stood at the edge of town and took it in with satisfaction. The trees swayed in the breeze, their leaves starting to change for autumn and rustling left and right and everywhere between. It was as if they were saying goodbye to us, too, as if they were seeing us off.

We weren't the only ones leaving today. There were others who had packed, who really were heading back home, sal negra filling their pockets or wagons. I wished them farewell and good wishes on their journey.

Many stopped by us on the way out; some tipped their hats. It was strange to think that some things never changed.

When all three of us were ready, when we'd said our own silent goodbyes to Coloma, we rode off into the wilderness, toward a horizon where the sun had already begun to set. We'd need to stop to make a fire and find shelter before the bugs came out to prey on us.

"¿Carisma, lista?" I kissed her mane. She let out a loud neigh and took a few steps back. I beckoned her forward. At first she seemed like she wasn't going to go, and then she was off, racing toward our future.

We stopped at what was once Isabela's town, which Hernández had destroyed.

The land would be altered for who knew how long. But for now, there was a ditch dug up around it as well, which Nisenan people guarded. I hoped that the rains would help heal this land.

We hadn't been sure he would be there, but we found the Indigenous man we'd met before. He rode up to us, something like surprise on his face. "No mask?" he said, grinning. There was no judgment in his gaze, seeing that Salvación was a young girl.

I shook my head. "Just me," I replied, handing over the amulet that had allowed Hernández to find the sal roja. I still didn't know where it had come from, who had made it. But I was guessing that the man I handed the amulet to did.

"You surprise me," he said. "You saved Cullumah."

"I had a lot of help," I said, glancing to where Alejandro and Víctor traded for clothes and other goods. "Colo—Cullumah—will be empty soon. We've hidden the sal negra deposits to help keep the world safe a little while longer. I left one open for you to decide what to do with it. It's located at the eastern rim of the town, to the right of the long house there that once belonged to my family."

"It seems I underestimated you. I see that the evil man who took this from us did as well. Where will you go?"

"I don't know, honestly. I think we'll travel for a while, learn about the land, its animals. Simply be."

"It's dangerous in this world—our world. You'll need more direction than that." He reached into his pocket. I took the small token he offered me.

It was a piedra de sal, grande y azul. Blue salt. It took me aback, feeling the sal azul in my palm.

"What does it do?" I asked, eager to know more.

"Let's just say it's for your protection," he replied. "Keep it with you, keep it safe. It's more valuable than all the red salt in the world."

I nodded, confusion settling on my expression. Still, if he didn't want to tell me, he didn't have to. I happily took the sal azul. "I'm prepared to face any dangers."

He nodded, laughed. "I'm sure you are. Be safe," he said.

"You too," I said, my heart heavy. There were so many dangers out there—Papá had been right about that. Still, there was nothing else to do but keep living.

I joined my brother and Alejandro. We rode once more with el viento at our side and el sol setting before us. The scorch was at our backs. Sal negra filled our pockets, and its magia lingered in our hearts.

I wasn't sure where we were going or if the places we went to would have magia. All I knew was that while I still breathed life, I would stand up against all those who did wrong.

I was Salvación, whether I wore the mask or not.

ACKNOWLEDGMENTS

How do you find the words to thank everyone who has made the magic of your book possible?

The only right place to begin is by thanking my incredible family: Joe, Río, Mami, the Chernuykhins (Sebby, Catarina, Sis, Dennis, and Alex), the Santoses (Dad and Robby), and all the Proudmans and Bays (especially Anden, Carmen, Brantley, Dylan, Lucy, Jayden, Jordan, and Clay, but also Joseph, Jenn, Larry, Chris, Mandi, and Jacob). I am nothing but the culmination of so many people who have shaped me into the writer and person I am today. I love you all. To Linda and Natasha, I miss you dearly and know you both would have been so proud of me for this novel.

Thank you so much to my team at Wednesday Books who made this book possible. To my editor, Mara Delgado Sánchez, who has been a fierce advocate (and who allowed me to keep all my favorites scenes!)—I am eternally grateful to you for championing this story. As a young Mexican

324 · ACKNOWLEDGMENTS

girl who grew up loving books but never even knew how they could possibly be made (perhaps I thought they appeared out of thin air?!), you have literally made my dream come true like a fairy godmother. Thank you also to the wonderful Vanessa Aguirre for helping bring *Salvación* to life, and proving that fairy godmothers sometimes come in pairs. To Brant Janeway for marketing, Zoe Miller for publicity, Melanie Sanders and Merilee Croft for production, Michelle McMillian for design, Kerri Resnick for art, Eliani Torres for copyedits, Nancy Inglis for proofreading, Esther de Araujo for audiobook production, Victoria Villarreal for audiobook narration, and Roxie Vizcarra for illustrating the glorious cover for *Salvación,* thank you all from the bottom of my heart for your time and work.

I'd also like to thank my wonderful agent, Kate Testerman of KT Literary, who is always an email or phone call away, for all your help, wisdom, and support. I truly appreciate all you do for me. As well as my first agent, the incredible Hannah Fergesen, who always encouraged me to write what I love—this book is that!—and taught me the meaning of revising with purpose, which I think helped me considerably on this project.

I want to throw a huge shout-out of gratitude to the team at Gallt & Zacker Literary Agency. Marietta, Nancy, Ellen, Linda, Beth, Erin, Saribel, and Ashlee, it became my second dream to become a literary agent, and I am honored to be able to do this among you. To all my clients, you make me a better author every time I'm lucky enough to read your words. Amanda, Brandi, Cassandra, Cornelius, Erin, Hayley, Janni, Jarrard, Jide, Léa, Malak, Melanie, Melissa, Nevien, René, Sable, Shannon, Ying-Hwa, and all those to come, you're amazing. To Lauren Spieller,

ACKNOWLEDGMENTS · 325

Paige Terlip, and Thao Le, thank you for your mentorship and kindness. I will never forget it.

To all the people who I know I can always reach out to: Shannon A. Thompson, Alex Brown, A. J. Sass, Angela Montoya, and Torrey Maldonado. To Stephanie Cohen and Meghan Maria McCullough, my amazing editors for *Relit*. To Amparo, Angela, Raquel, and Yamile, thank you all for the amazing blurbs. To my #LatinxPitch and Las Musas family, thank you for always making me feel like I have a home in the Latinx community.

To my #KidLit4Ceasefire and Story Sunbirds family, thank you all for helping me continue to believe in a better world for our young readers. They deserve it. To Mariam and Ahmed, my dear friends in Gaza whose safety I pray for every day: the more I worked on this book, the more it reminded me of the Palestinian plight, and to you, I will continue to say *Free Palestine, from the River to the Sea*. This book is about finding peace, and I hope you do.

And to my readers: authors, publishers, and books in general are nothing without you. I thank you from the bottom of my heart for picking up *Salvación*, and I hope you love it as much as I've loved writing it.

ABOUT THE AUTHOR

SANDRA PROUDMAN (she/her/ella) is the editor of the young adult Latinx science fiction and fantasy anthology *Relit: 16 Latinx Remixes of Classic Stories* and a contributor to the young adult horror anthology *The House Where Death Lives*, both out now. *Salvación* is her first full-length novel. She is also a literary agent passionate about bringing underrepresented voices to the forefront. When she isn't busily immersed in all things publishing, you can find her spending time with her amazing husband and adorable toddler gathering roly-polys and going on adventures, catching up on all her shows, or trying to get the perfect tortilla puff.

Connect with her on X, Instagram,
and TikTok: @SandraProudman
Visit her website: www.sandraproudman.com